The Blind Angel
New Old Chassidic Tales

Rabbi Tovia Halberstam

The Blind Angel

NEW OLD CHASSIDIC TALES

Translated and Retold by
Joshua Halberstam

The Toby Press

The Blind Angel
New Old Chassidic Tales

The Toby Press, 2015

The Toby Press LLC
POB 8531, New Milford, CT 06776–8531, USA
& POB 2455, London W1A 5WY, England
www.tobypress.com

Cover art: © Yoram Raanan
Cover design: Tani Bayer

ISBN 978-1-59264-359-2

A CIP catalogue record for this title is
available from the British Library

Printed and bound in the United States

For my father ע״ה

רמון מצא תוכו אכל קליפתו זרק

חגיגה טו ע״ב

Contents

Translator's Foreword

True, a story can put you to sleep, but it can also wake you up.

RABBI NACHMAN OF BRESLOV

Several years ago, my then 87-year-old mother, may she live to 120, moved from her house in Borough Park, Brooklyn that had been her family home since 1951. My sisters and I helped sort through the household possessions that had amassed over these many decades. In the process, I came upon two boxes tucked away in a corner of a closet. One contained my father's writings: journals from his youth in Rzezhov, Poland; clippings of articles he'd written in America for publications in Warsaw; essays, stories and a weekly humor column for a Yiddish newspaper in the United States (often under a pen name – my favorite being Tovia Derligner, Tovia the Liar). The other box contained about 250 Chassidic stories in Yiddish. These were the stories he had told on the radio over a span of two decades.

Radio station WEVD was established by the American Socialist Party in 1927 and named in honor of its then recently deceased leader, Eugene Victor Debs. Five years later, the station was bought by the *Forverts* (later renamed *The Forward*), the country's leading Yiddish newspaper, which shared the socialist leanings and general secularism of the station's former owner. For the two million Jewish immigrants who had flocked to the United States at the turn of the twentieth century and during the decades that followed, WEVD served as a guide of sorts, offering a smorgasbord of programs to help them navigate their way through the new country. The "station that speaks your language" as it billed itself, broadcast, of course, in Yiddish.

Today, people have forgotten that prior to World War II, Yiddish was the lingua franca of eleven million people, with more native speakers than, say, Greek, Hungarian, Swedish, Dutch or Czech. For many years, WEVD was not only the most popular Yiddish station in the US, it was also the most popular ethnic radio station in the country. But the steady process of assimilation into mainstream American culture meant a dwindling number of listeners interested in – or dependent on – Yiddish radio. And the devastation of the Shoah ensured that an influx of Yiddish speakers would not make it to these shores to replenish its audience.

Among the survivors who did find their way to the United States were Chassidic Jews, immigrants who, unlike nearly all others, were determined to continue using Yiddish as their mother tongue. WEVD began catering to these new listeners, offering discussions of Talmud and religious music in addition to the folk tunes and theater songs of previous years. In the late 1940s, my father began to broadcast his program *Chassidim Dertzaylin* (literally, "Chassidim Retell"). Thousands tuned in each week to hear the next installment of a particular story or segment. The allusions, tropes and mood of these tales resonated deeply with his audience. They lived according to the same ritual calendar, shared the same sense of humor and tragedy, and were nourished by familiar communal experiences as they embarked on rebuilding their traditions in a new country. Their eagerness to listen anew to these classic legends underscored the vital place of storytelling in the life of Chassidism.

Indeed, storytelling has always been integral to Chassidism, the mystical movement that began in the early eighteenth century and swept across Eastern European Jewish communities over the following two centuries. In his comprehensive overview of Chassidic stories, *The Hasidic Tale*, Gedalyah Nigal notes, "No social or religious movement in the entire course of Jewish history has engaged so intensively in storytelling as Hasidism; nor have stories occupied such a central and important place in any other intellectual movement within Judaism."

From its inception, telling stories about Chassidic masters and relating their insights was a pivotal means by which the movement gained followers. The founder of Chassidism, Rabbi Eliezer ben Israel (1698–1760), the Ba'al Shem Tov (literally, "master of the good name," also referred to by his acronym "the Besht"), was known for regaling otherwise alienated Jews – the unlearned, women, children, and suspicious scholars, too – with his captivating tales. His disciples would do likewise. These stories, which focused on tzaddikim, the Chassidic masters, or simple men and women, emphasized serving God through joy rather than asceticism, the connection to the supernatural, the vitality of community and the majesty of music. Typically, the stories dealt with the quotidian demands of everyday life: poverty and livelihood, matchmaking and divorce, illness and recovery, along with the spiritual concerns of sin and repentance, and reward and punishment in the afterlife. Implicitly or explicitly, many of the tales sought to counter the criticism of Chassidism's opponents, the misnagdim, as well as the contempt of the contemporaneous Haskalah movement, which urged Jews to embrace the values of secular, modern Europe.

In some stories, the Chassidic tzaddik resolves a problem through his mystical prowess; in others, he finds a solution through his discerning judgment and psychological intuition. Some tales illustrate the workings of "practical Kabbalah," in particular, the Chassidic insistence on eliciting the sparks of "divine holiness" that permeate the universe. As one tzaddik put it: "Kabbalah aims to bring the earth up to heaven; Chassidism aims to bring heaven down to earth."

But the role of the story in Chassidism goes beyond pedagogy. For Chassidim, storytelling is itself a sacred performance. The tale, properly told, is akin to prayer for both the teller and the listener. The basic structure of the Chassidic story has endured for hundreds of years – rare for any literary genre, especially a Jewish one – but so, too, has the vital religious role of storytelling wherever Chassidim gather.

My father, Rabbi Tovia Halberstam, of blessed memory, born and raised in Poland, came with his father to the United States as a young man. A scion of Chassidic leaders on both his maternal and paternal sides, he traced his unbroken lineage of rabbis back to the sixteenth century.

His father was the first Chassidic rebbe in Borough Park. While my father, too, was ordained as a rabbi and commanded a wide and deep mastery of traditional Jewish learning (and regularly taught Talmud classes in his father-in-law's Chassidic shul) he chose not to wear the mantle of a Chassidic rebbe. His reasons for this decision were surely complex, a confluence of circumstance, inclination and conviction.

In any event, his interests, particularly his literary affections, were certainly atypical of his upbringing. He read not only the classical Yiddish and Hebrew writers but also broadly across Western literature, possessed by an abiding curiosity about the mores of alien cultures. I came upon a journal from his youth in which he translated Aesop's fables into modern Hebrew (though I'm not sure from what source language) and another in which he translated Yiddish words and phrases to Esperanto. He also produced copious creative work of his own, both nonfiction and fiction. And he brought this extensive background and creativity to the Chassidic folktales he published in newspapers and told on the radio.

The basic storyline of many of these tales is familiar to anyone raised in the Chassidic tradition. In a few cases, adaptations have been previously published – while Chassidic stories were told in Yiddish, they were generally written in Hebrew, the "holy language" of the Torah – but many stories live on only in oral transmission. Some exist in a multitude of versions, and a number are attributed to different Chassidic rebbes. But these tales remain largely unknown to English speakers and the Western world in general.

To be sure, Chassidic stories have become increasingly popular in recent years. The Kabbalistically-imbued allegories of Rebbe Nachman of Breslov, a great-grandson of the Ba'al Shem Tov (told in Yiddish and transcribed into Hebrew by his amanuensis, Nathan Sternharz), are recognized for their significant impact on later Jewish literature. More familiar still, are the depictions of Chassidic masters by Martin Buber and other modern writers such as S. Y. Agnon and Elie Wiesel. But these accounts tend to be elongated anecdotes, parables and didactic vignettes. Missing are the complex narratives, replete with robust and disparate personalities that more fully characterize many traditional Chassidic stories. In my father's retelling, these tales are enriched by the dramatic arc of the literary short story and told in a more nuanced, descriptive

Yiddish than those familiar with "Chassidic tales" might expect. At the same time, they manage to preserve the religious sensitivity and folkloric qualities of the venerable Chassidic legend.

Translating these stories into contemporary English was a formidable challenge, even allowing for the fact that textual fidelity matters less when it comes to folktales than literary works. After all, my father could assume an intimacy with the customs, cadences and general social context of Eastern European Jewry that I cannot. Because these stories are embedded in a vanished world, the task of translation involved more than finding linguistic equivalencies – of simply substituting an appropriate English word or phrase for a Yiddish one. As Irving Howe and Eliezer Greenberg write in the introduction to their *Treasury of Yiddish Stories*:

> Here it is surely correct to say that translating from the Yiddish is more difficult than from, say, the French…. In translating from French, a certain community between French and English culture can safely be assumed, while in translating from Yiddish it is necessary not only to present a rough facsimile of a verbal sequence, but somehow to summon a world that exists beneath the words. Inevitably, though at great risk, the translator becomes a tacit social historian.

What is true of Yiddish in general is especially true of the distinctive lifestyle and sensibilities of Chassidim. And yet, the charm of these tales is universal. Like all legends that withstand the test of generations, they engage the reader's heart and bespeak enduring insights.

Today, Chassidism is the fastest growing segment of Jewry the world over. This development is truly astounding. Not surprisingly, therefore, the history of Chassidism, its social structure, religious perspective, intra- and inter-communal relations, are now the subject of countless books, studies and courses, aimed at both the general reader as well as the professional scholar. Nonetheless, the Chassidic tale still remains the best entry into the world of Chassidism. For me, these "retellings" also provide an opportunity to bring my father's love of the Chassidic story to a new, inquisitive audience. I believe it's an undertaking he'd much appreciate.

NOTE TO THE READER

The names of Eastern European towns and shtetls, and the rebbes that lived in them, are transliterated and, therefore, there are alternate spellings for these names. The "kh" is now the accepted transliteration for the Hebrew and Yiddish letters *het* and *khaf*, the phonetic "throat-clearing" equivalent of Loch in Scottish, and is used here unless the older "ch" spelling is widely known, as in chutzpah, Chanukah or the name Chaim. As is true of many folktales, many of the stories included here did not originally have titles. The titles given to these stories are sometimes my own and not my father's. Finally, these tales are close retellings, not literal translations of the stories told and written by my father. Any errors are mine, not his.

Joshua Halberstam
Winter 5775/2015

Heavenly Matters

People are accustomed to look at the heavens and to wonder what happens there. It would be better if they would look within themselves, to see what happens there.

REB MENACHEM MENDEL OF KOTSK

The Blind Angel

Rivka Parnes had recently returned to Brody from Vienna, where she had taken her daughter to be examined by the most prestigious cardiologist in all of Europe.

"There is nothing we can do," the doctor had said. "She hasn't much time."

His words echoed in Rivka's ears like the death sentence they were.

Half a mile away, in the rear of a hardware store on busy Lemberger Street, a young man named Yekhiel Tsurif was so absorbed in his silversmith's craft he didn't notice his friend enter the room.

Had he heard the news?

"The Tzaddik of Sassov is coming to Brody for Chanukah," his friend said, bouncing on his toes. "He'll be with us to light the first candle tomorrow evening. All the rebbe would say was that he was coming here to redeem a soul."

Within an hour of the tzaddik's arrival, long lines formed for men and women eager for a moment of his time. Waiting impatiently were Torah scholars and the scarcely literate, landowners with fur-lined coats and beggars wearing patches upon patches, venerable Chassidim who'd been to the rebbe a dozen times before and hopeful first-timers, unwavering devotees and curious skeptics – all seeking a word of advice, a message of reassurance, a blessing, or simply the chance to tell their grandchildren they'd visited the Rebbe of Sassov. Among them was Rivka Parnes, wearing a black kerchief pulled down to her reddened eyes.

When her turn finally came, Rivka stood silently while the rebbe finished reading the petition she'd handed him. "As the tzaddik can see from my note, my daughter Bluma is deathly ill. The doctors say there is no hope."

"There is always hope," the rebbe said.

"Yes, of course. And if the rebbe would please pray for my daughter's health, then surely this wish will be realized."

The Sassover Tzaddik raised his palm and shook his head. "God hears your entreaties, Rivka. I assure you, your Bluma will live and thrive and marry and, God willing, you will enjoy many years together with your many grandchildren."

Rivka Parnes smiled for the first time in months, the weight lifted from her heart. She thanked the rebbe and prepared to leave when the tzaddik called her back.

"Oh yes, there is one thing. Just one thing. Your menorah."

"My menorah?" Rivka was startled. She owned several.

"The silver menorah, the one you inherited from your father," the rebbe said. Could she please bring it right away?

A few hours later, the shul was crowded with Chassidim thrilled to be with their rebbe on the first night of Chanukah. They also gathered around to admire the famed Parnes menorah, which stood on the table next to the rebbe.

"Yekhiel Tsurif!" the Sassover Rebbe called out. "Come here. You are an artisan. I'd like to hear your professional assessment of this menorah."

Yekhiel slowly picked up the menorah, uneasy with the attention now focused on him. "It's exquisite," he said. He ran his hand over the smooth lines and perfectly shaped knobs, appreciating the fine craftsmanship.

The rebbe's gaze fixed on Yekhiel. "I'm pleased you're fond of this menorah. I'd like for you to be at my side when I light the first candle tonight."

When the rebbe later completed the Chanukah blessings, the Chassidim roared "Amen" and, with one voice, sang the holiday melodies.

When the singing quieted, the rebbe turned to Yekhiel Tsurif, who'd been beside him throughout the ceremony.

"*Nu*, so what do you think of this Chanukah lamp?"

"As I said before, it is a true work of art. May the rebbe enjoy it until he is a hundred-and-twenty and greet the messiah with it in his hand."

"No, no," said the Sassover. "This isn't my menorah. It's yours. I will tell you why. And you will all understand why this is truly a festive Chanukah."

He asked that Rivka Parnes come to the front for she, too, must hear what he had to say. A hush descended as Reb Moshe Leib Sassover began his tale.

Years ago, there lived in Brody a devout Chassid by the name of Yekhiel Tsurif – your grandfather, Yekhiel, as I'm sure you've heard, was an outstanding silversmith admired throughout the region whose artistic skills you inherited along with his name. Well, Yekhiel Tsurif may have been a brilliant craftsman, but he was also a hopeless businessman and barely eked out a living.

Now, this Reb Yekhiel was a devotee of Reb Zusha and whenever possible would spend the holidays with his rebbe. As is the custom of many Chassidic rebbes, Reb Zusha distributed silver coins to his Chassidim when they set out to return to their families, and Yekhiel Tsurif prized these silver mementos above all other possessions.

When Reb Zusha died, Yekhiel Tsurif grew increasingly anxious about his treasured collection of coins. What if it were lost or stolen or inadvertently used to make an ordinary purchase? Yekhiel alighted on an inspired solution. He would melt the coins and use the silver to cast a menorah. As you can imagine, this became a labor of great love, fusing his artistic talent with his Chassidic devotion. The striking result stands before us on this table.

Affluent Jews beset Yekhiel Tsurif with generous offers to purchase his menorah. The most adamant of all was Nuchim Parnes, the richest Jew in Brody, who offered three times the highest bid. But Yekhiel rejected all tenders. The lamp was priceless, he said, and not for sale.

Years passed, and Yekhiel Tsurif's daughter reached the age of betrothal. An excellent match was arranged with a young man renowned for his piety and scholarship. There was, however, one hitch: money for a dowry. Yekhiel would have to support the young man in full-time Torah studies for several years, a cost Yekhiel Tsurif could certainly not afford. The poor man sought loans from friends and acquaintances, but the funds were insufficient to secure the marriage. Bearing the awesome responsibility for his daughter's future, Yekhiel Tsurif grew increasingly desperate, until one night he knocked on the door of Nuchim Parnes.

He explained his situation. He needed a loan to pay for a wedding and to subsidize his potential son-in-law in his Torah studies.

"A loan? A loan he wants." Reb Nuchim suppressed a chuckle. "And what do you intend to provide for security? The chickpeas in your kitchen cabinet? Your estate...your hovel? Let's forget this loan business. Whom are we kidding?"

Yekhiel Tsurif wanted to flee then and there but understood that walking out empty-handed meant no marriage for his daughter. "Reb Nuchim, please. Without your help..."

"You want my help?" Nuchim Parnes said. "Okay, so let's talk business. You want something I have. Money. You have something I want."

Yekhiel Tsurif's temples throbbed, his chest constricted. He dreaded what surely would follow.

"Yes, your silver menorah. You're well aware I've been eyeing it for years."

Yekhiel Tsurif blanched.

"Why not be realistic for once?" Nuchim Parnes continued. "It's your good fortune I have such a craving for your menorah. In exchange for it, I am prepared to pay the entire cost of your child's wedding. So, do we have a deal?"

Yekhiel bit his lip. The menorah was his link to his beloved rebbe. It was the light of his home.

Nuchim Parnes pressed on. "I appreciate what this menorah means to you. And I also want to partake in the great mitzvah of helping a young Jewish woman celebrate a wedding and build a home. So I'll add to the bargain. Not only will I pay for the entire wedding, I'll finance the first two years of your future son-in-law's studies. All for a menorah."

He stretched out his hand to consummate the arrangement.

An hour later, a heartbroken Yekhiel Tsurif returned holding a box in his hands. He loved his menorah, but he loved his daughter more.

Nuchim Parnes kept his end of the agreement. The wedding was a glittering celebration – a wealthy banker could do no better – and the dowry, too, arrived as promised.

The Sassover paused and sipped from a glass of water, but the Chassidim did not stir. "Yes, there is more to the story," the rebbe said.

A few years after the wedding, Nuchim Parnes died, and his soul arrived at the heavenly tribunal. The lawyers for the defense presented his history of good deeds, his meticulous care in fulfilling the commandments, his record of philanthropy for the needy. But the prosecution presented a catalog no less compelling, filled with questionable business dealings and arrogant outbursts toward his employees. Back and forth the trial swung, tilting one way, then the other. When the arguments were closed, the scale tipped decidedly – against Nuchim Parnes. His soul would be sent to the region of the infernal.

But just as his sentence was to be pronounced, a commotion erupted in the rear of the heavenly courtroom. A blind angel stumbled into the room, shouting for a halt to the proceedings.

"I am the angel Nuchim Parnes created when he provided for Yekhiel Tsurif's daughter's wedding!"

The angel staggered to the front of the tribunal. "Place the weighty mitzvah of aiding a needy bride on the scale, and let's see where matters stand."

The scale was now tipped in the other direction. The soul of Nuchim Parnes was directed to enter Paradise.

Alas, this would not be the end of his trials. According to Kabbalah, each time we perform a mitzvah, we create an angel who will be our advocate, and with our most important mitzvah we create the angel who will escort us into the Next World. But the actions we commit in this world are rarely wholly good or evil. And when we perform a good deed with flawed motivation, the corresponding angel is corrupted as well.

Nuchim Parnes performed the wonderful mitzvah of providing for a wedding, but his mitzvah was compromised. By demanding the menorah in exchange for his charity, he banished the light from Yekhiel Tsurif's home. And so the angel he created was also bereft of light; the angel was blind.

And all these years since the verdict, Nuchim Parnes and his blind angel have been seeking the entrance to Paradise. Two lost companions, they roam from place to place, hostages of the dark.

The Sassover picked up the menorah and handed it to Yekhiel. "Take this. It is your patrimony. Redeem the soul of Nuchim Parnes. Now that the mitzvah is made whole, sight will be restored to the blind angel, and he will be able to find the gate of heaven."

Yekhiel's hands trembled as he accepted the menorah, but the Sassover Tzaddik laughed as he clapped his hands. "Ah, to free a soul from captivity!" Rising to his feet, he called his Chassidim to join him in a dance.

Trading for Paradise

We're all familiar with the truism that success in business depends not only on skill, but also on luck. We also know that luck comes and goes. As a young man, Efrayim had luck on his side, along with a penchant for business, and quickly became a well-to-do merchant. But then luck waved farewell, leaving Efrayim with nothing. He accepted his fate without complaint. Such is life, he'd be the first to tell you.

Well, such stoicism is fine and good for oneself, but Efrayim had a family to support and the impending reality of having to marry off a daughter. Marriages were expensive propositions; there was no way he could afford the necessary expenditures. At a loss, he traveled to his rebbe, the Rebbe of Apt, to seek his advice.

"How much does one need to make a wedding?" the rebbe asked.

"At least a thousand rubles," said Efrayim.

"I see. And how much money do you have?"

"I earn a pittance, rebbe. My total savings I have right here in my pocket. A single ruble. That is all."

"*Nu*, Reb Efrayim, you are a merchant, are you not? So, with the help of God, go do business with the single ruble you have in your pocket."

"Rebbe, what sort of business could I do with one ruble?"

"Here's my suggestion," the rebbe replied. "Whatever someone is willing to sell you for a ruble, buy it. It doesn't matter what it is. Let's hope that the Almighty helps with the rest."

Efrayim left the rebbe puzzled but hopeful; after all, the rebbe implied that his single ruble would multiply a thousand-fold. What more did a Chassid need to hear?

Upon leaving the rebbe, Efrayim's first stop was an inn where local businessmen regularly gathered. On this particular day, a group of diamond merchants were exhibiting their wares. Packets of brilliant gems were displayed on the table and prices were named: five hundred rubles, a thousand rubles, five thousand rubles, twenty thousand rubles. Reb Efrayim stood silently to the side and fingered the single ruble in his pocket.

Reb Hershel, one of the wealthiest merchants in the group, produced a particularly brilliant stone, which he was proudly showing off to all assembled. A sparkling diamond, the largest Efrayim had ever seen, shimmered against Reb Hershel's palm. Noticing Efrayim's ogling, Reb Hershel could hardly contain his contempt.

"Impressive, eh? Perhaps you are interested in making a purchase?" Reb Hershel laughed.

Efrayim half nodded. "If the situation arises."

"And you have money?"

"Yes, I do." Efrayim clutched the coin in his hand.

"You do? Nice. And how much, if I may ask?"

"I have a ruble."

In unison, the merchants burst out laughing. "I have a ruble!" they repeated. "He has a ruble!"

Reb Hershel, of unusually good temper that day, took hold of Efrayim's lapel, and with feigned seriousness said, "You know what? Let's do some business. Obviously, with a lonely ruble you aren't buying a diamond, but I'll sell you something worth a bit less. How's this: For a ruble, I'll sell you my place in Paradise."

Efrayim, committed to fulfilling his rebbe's advice, agreed.

"It's a deal," he said. "Your Paradise for my ruble." Then, noticing the smirks all around him, he quickly added, "On the condition that we make this a legal, binding sale."

"What do you mean?" Reb Hershel asked.

"I mean a legitimate transfer. I want the contract in writing, signed and witnessed."

"That's fine with me," Reb Hershel said, unable to hide his amusement.

Paper and ink were quickly procured, the terms recorded, and the deal completed: For the price of one ruble, Efrayim now owned Reb Hershel's share in the afterlife.

While Efrayim retired to a corner of the lodge to read a book, Reb Hershel used the ruble to buy a round of drinks for his fellow merchants who were still snickering at the stupidity of this foolish Chassid.

Not long afterward, Reb Hershel's wife entered the lodge and quickly learned the cause of all the good humor.

"You fool!" she shouted at her husband. "You utter fool. Maybe, just maybe, at some point in your life, you managed to earn a tiny slice of heaven. And now you've gone ahead and sold it? What are you? A nothing in this life, and now, not even a possibility of anything in the afterlife. I've had it with you."

Reb Hershel knew better than to interrupt her.

"A nothing. That's what you are. I want a divorce."

Reb Hershel urged his wife to compose herself, but she would not be calmed. Instead, she repeated her demand for a divorce.

"All right, all right," her husband relented. "Since you're so insistent, I'll give that fool back his money and get back my share in heaven. So relax, will you?"

Reb Hershel walked over to Efrayim and with all the nonchalance he could muster, asked to undo their transaction. "Enough joking around. Here's your ruble, now give me back that contract."

Efrayim shook his head. "Sorry, but for me this was no joke. A deal is a deal."

"A deal? You can't be serious."

"Absolutely, I am."

Seeing the Chassid was entirely earnest, Reb Hershel replied with matching seriousness, "All right then. We're doing business. Give me back the contract, and I'll throw in a profit for you."

Efrayim nodded his head in agreement. "That's fair. A profit makes sense in a business exchange. I'll take a thousand rubles. That's how much I need for my daughter's wedding."

Reb Hershel exploded. "Are you crazy? A thousand rubles for what? For nothing. Well, then, you get nothing. A thousand rubles. Such chutzpah!"

But Reb Hershel's wife, who'd been listening to the entire exchange, went over and whispered to her husband. "Listen, just get this deal done. Offer the man a hundred rubles and let's be—"

"Forget it," Efrayim interrupted. "I'm not negotiating. My rebbe, the holy Apter Rebbe, instructed me to use my single ruble to purchase the first offer extended to me and suggested this would get me the thousand rubles I need. I won't settle for anything less."

Reb Hershel's wife called her seething husband aside. "Let's be realistic. This fellow isn't going to budge. Give him the thousand rubles, get back the contract and let's be done with this."

Reb Hershel realized he had no alternative, not if he wanted to remain married. He handed Efrayim a thousand ruble coin and bought back his contract.

His wife then approached Efrayim. "Who is this remarkable rebbe of yours? He must be unusual indeed. Can I meet him?"

Efrayim promised to arrange for her to visit the Apter Rebbe.

When the day of the meeting arrived, the woman told the Apter Rebbe with uncharacteristic humility how pleased she was to help make possible a wedding for the poor man's daughter.

"But I'm truly curious," she said. "May I ask the rebbe a question that's been gnawing at me for the past several days?"

"Please," said the rebbe.

"Tell me, was my husband's lot in heaven worth a thousand rubles?"

The Apter Rebbe broke into a wide smile. "You know, both Efrayim and your husband were fooled. And both did well with this exchange. You see, when Efrayim gave your husband a ruble for his share in Paradise, he was wasting his money because at the time your husband's share was not even worth that much. But now that he has performed the great mitzvah of providing for a wedding, your husband's share in heaven is worth much more."

Charity Redeems
From Death

There are specialists even in the realm of the sacred. To be sure, the saintly Chassidic rebbes were scrupulous about fulfilling all the mitzvot with fervor, yet some were known for the distinctive attention they paid to particular religious deeds. One was renowned for raising funds for the poor, another for redeeming captive Jews, still others for their devotion to song, or prayer, or storytelling.

At one time, the town of Ostrov had the honor of being home to two of the Ba'al Shem Tov's most illustrious students, Rabbi Yaakov Yosef of Polnoia and Reb Pinchas of Koretz. And each had his specialty. Rabbi Yaakov Yosef of Polnoia was famous across the Jewish world for his prodigious scholarship. After he joined the nascent Chassidic movement, he added a mastery of Kabbalah and the mystical tradition to his vast command of Talmud and Jewish law. Among the many virtues for which Reb Pinchas of Koretz was celebrated, particularly noteworthy was his devotion to *halvoes ha'mes*, the imperative to honor the dead by escorting them to their interment. The Koretzer Rebbe made sure to participate in the burial rites of all his townspeople, irrespective of whether the departed was pious or a sinner.

It was the custom in Ostrov, as elsewhere throughout Eastern Europe, that when a member of the community passed away, the synagogue assistant, the beadle, would make his way across town carrying a charity box as he called out, "Charity redeems us from death, charity redeems us from death." In this way, the townspeople were alerted a funeral would soon be taking place.

One late afternoon, Mordecai the tailor died. Not that any of the Jews of Ostrov cared. Mordecai had no relatives in the vicinity, nor any Jewish friends. His clientele were local gentiles and his social circle consisted entirely of non-Jewish acquaintances with whom he'd share inebriated evenings, replete with ham sandwiches and vodka. Not that Mordecai the tailor cared a fig that the Jews considered him an outcast. And why should he? As far as he was concerned, he wasn't one of them, anyway.

But Jewish law mandates *all* Jews receive proper burial rites, regardless of the deceased's personal habits. So when the Angel of Death came to retrieve the sinful soul of Mordecai the tailor, a Jewish funeral was dutifully prepared, and the beadle began his trek through the streets proclaiming in his practiced drone, "Charity redeems us from death, charity redeems us from death."

Who would bother to attend this funeral? Why make time for a reprobate who wanted nothing to do with his own people? At best, they'd manage to gather the bare minimum for a minyan, the quorum of ten men who'd recite the Kaddish prayer, hurry through the rites and be on their way.

Surely, the Rebbe of Koretz need not be among them. True, the rebbe regularly attended the funerals of simple Jews, but Mordecai the tailor was no simple Jew. He was a contemptible boor who disdained his own heritage and was surely undeserving of the rebbe's time. When the beadle arrived at the rebbe's street, he hastened his pace and lowered his voice; better the rebbe should remain unaware of this particular funeral.

The Rebbe of Koretz, however, happened to standing at his window precisely at the moment the beadle passed his home. Seeing the charity box in the man's hand, the rebbe inquired who had died.

"Trust me," the beadle answered. "This is one funeral the rebbe can skip."

"Who passed away?" the rebbe persisted.

"As I say, a coarse blasphemer." The beadle struck his lips with his hand – one should not speak ill of the dead.

"But who?"

"Mordecai the tailor."

"Mordecai the tailor," the rebbe repeated, his voice heavy. "Well, well."

The beadle turned to continue his rounds when the rebbe called to him. "Please be certain to inform me when the funeral will take place. It's imperative I be there."

Soon, the stunned beadle was reporting to anyone who crossed his path how the Rebbe of Koretz was insisting on attending the funeral of Mordecai the tailor. But why? That was the question everyone asked and the beadle could not answer.

That, too, was the question Rabbi Yaakov Yosef of Polnoia asked himself when he was told of his illustrious colleague's interest in the deceased. Surely, something unusual was afoot. The Rebbe of Koretz must know more about this Mordecai the tailor than he was letting on.

"Well, then," Reb Yaakov Yosef decided, "if Reb Pinchas is so adamant about attending the funeral, so will I."

Curiosity spread across Ostrov like an untamed blaze. "Did you hear?" one townsperson asked breathlessly of the other. "Both our Chassidic giants plan to attend the funeral of that good-for-nothing. Perhaps we should attend as well."

Not since Ostrov had become a predominantly Jewish city many years earlier had the funeral hall been as packed as it was that morning. The elderly came. The women came. Even the children came, all with the same perplexed look on their faces.

At the conclusion of the funeral, the Koretzer Rebbe led the procession to the nearby cemetery. The rebbe stood next to the gravesite as the burial was performed, in perfect accordance with Jewish law and custom.

"All right, my friend, I give up," said Reb Yaakov Yosef, placing his hand on the Koretzer's shoulder. "I've been alongside you throughout the funeral and here during the burial, and I still have no clue. So tell me. What is the story with this Mordecai the tailor?"

By then, a crowd had gathered around the two Chassidic masters, eager to learn the explanation for the rebbe's baffling attention to the deceased.

"Was he one of the *lamed vovniks?*" one of the assembled asked, referring to the thirty-six Jews of every generation who, according to tradition, live unnoticed lives of righteousness and whose secret merit upholds the world.

"Hardly," said the Koretzer Rebbe. "No, as far as I know, Mordecai the tailor was as much the sinner in private as he was in public."

"So why do you show him such respect?" asked Rabbi Yaakov Yosef, quieting the crowd.

The Rabbi of Koretz offered a half smile to accompany a long tug at his beard. "Well, you see, I promised him a place in heaven and I wanted to be at his burial to make sure my promise was fulfilled."

Rabbi Yaakov Yosef leaned in toward the Koretzer, not needing to state the obvious question: Why promise a place in heaven to an unrepentant sinner?

The Koretzer settled back on his heels, looked around at the crowd circled around him and then at Reb Yaakov Yosef. "Let me explain," he said.

A few months ago, on a cold, wintry evening, Beril Shuster, Beril the shoemaker, as he's known to some of you, knocked on my door. Beril apologized for his unscheduled visit, but said he had an important request. Would I officiate at his daughter's wedding? His daughter Khaya, admittedly advanced in years, had finally been presented with a decent match. More gratifying, still, was the attitude of the groom, who didn't demand a dowry. This was no small matter to Beril, a man of limited means, who could hardly afford to sustain the young couple for the first years of marriage, as many grooms expect of their fathers-in-law.

When Beril informed me of the date of the wedding, I had to inform him that, alas, I'd already committed to meetings that day involving important communal affairs. Seeing the disappointment on his face, I suggested that if he wanted me to perform the ceremony, the wedding could be held in my house late in the evening after my work was completed. And so it was arranged.

The Koretzer paused, tugged again on his beard and continued.

On the night of the wedding, everything was in place. The families of the bride and groom had all arrived in their festive best. But then, right before the groom was to walk to the wedding canopy, a disturbance was heard in the back of the room. It seemed Beril had promised his future son-in-law a Turkish wool prayer shawl and had failed to deliver. The son-in-law insisted Beril procure the talis then and there. Beril pleaded with the young man, explaining that he hadn't had the money before the wedding to make this significant purchase, but would get it for him the following day.

But the groom was obstinate. He would not stand under the canopy and allow the wedding to proceed unless he was presented with a Turkish talis as promised.

"Please," begged Beril. "Please don't shame your bride. Tomorrow, I'll have the talis for you. My word."

"Your word?" said the groom. "You've deceived me several times since I've been engaged to your daughter, promising gifts that never materialized. And once I'm married, you're even more likely to renege on your pledges. Enough is enough. No talis, no wedding."

The guests stood waiting with increasing frustration. I among them. Finally, I had to speak. "Please," I beseeched the groom, "Let's continue with the ceremony." This young man, however, was exceedingly clever, and proceeded to produce a proof-text from the Torah to justify his behavior.

"The verses in Deuteronomy 22 that speak of a man taking a wife, immediately follow the passage enjoining a man to wear a talis. Thus, it is only right I receive a talis before I marry."

The groom, clearly, would not budge. In the meantime, at stake was the mitzvah of *hachnosas kallah*, facilitating a marriage and ensuring a bride's joy. It was imperative the wedding take place. So I suggested to the groom that we hold off for an hour. I myself would go into town and try to raise the money for the talis.

The groom agreed, but it was already late. When I stepped out into the street, I was greeted by a dark, moonless night. The lights were already extinguished in all the houses. Nevertheless, I kept walking, hoping to find a home whose inhabitants were still awake. And finally I did.

It was the home of Mordecai the tailor. Finding the door open, I walked in to find the tailor hunched over a cloth, needle in hand. When Mordecai finally looked up, he was, naturally, startled to see me standing in his doorway.

What would bring the rebbe, alone and so late in the evening, to his home, of all places?

I explained the situation and asked Mordecai for his help. He listened to the request with disdain, but finally withdrew a few kopecks from his pocket.

"As you are well aware," the Koretzer noted to the assembled at the gravesite, "a genuine Turkish talis costs more than a few kopeks. So I turned to leave and continue on my mission, one that increasingly seemed hopeless. But as I reached the door, I heard footsteps behind me."

"Rebbe, please wait a moment. Suppose I gave you the money? The entire sum, all you need to purchase the very finest talis."

"That would be wonderful," I began to answer. "The mitzvah of helping—"

"Yes, yes, I know," Mordecai interrupted. "But I want something in exchange. I want you to give me a guarantee."

"Guarantee? For what?"

"That I will be admitted to heaven."

The Chassidim listening to the rebbe's story clucked their tongues when they heard what Mordecai the tailor had asked for.

"How could I secure heaven for this sinner?" the rebbe asked his audience. "How could I pledge eternal reward for a man who transgresses all the commandments? How could I do such a thing?

"Then I recalled the Talmudic discussion that lists the few good deeds that yield rewards in both this world and the next. And even for these few mitzvot, the principal reward is reserved for the World to Come.

"Among this select group," Rabbi Yaakov Yosef suddenly interjected, "is the mitzvah of *hachnosas kallah*, assisting in the wedding of a bride."

"Precisely," said the Koretzer. "And that's what I thought about standing in the foyer considering Mordecai the tailor's request. I looked around and didn't see a single Hebrew book or even a mezuzah on the doorpost. Instead, all I saw was Mordecai's uncovered head and the bottle of non-kosher wine on his table. Then I thought of the distressed bride waiting under the wedding canopy in her gown. So I agreed to the proposal. Mordecai the tailor excused himself and a minute later returned with enough money to purchase a fine Turkish talis.

"When I heard Mordecai the tailor had died, I realized I'd have to attend his burial to remind the angels who'd come for his soul about his charity that saved a marriage. And a good thing too. Because those angels arrived expecting to bring Mordecai to the lower rungs, but now found it impossible to grab hold of his soul. You see, Mordecai the tailor's soul was wrapped in a protective talis, the spiritual talis created for him the moment he performed the mitzvah of *hachnosas kallah*."

"I don't understand," came a voice from the crowd. "A life of constant, blatant sinning, and one good deed gets him into heaven?"

"Indeed," replied the Rebbe of Koretz. "This is the lesson we learn from the life of Mordecai the tailor. No one should assume he or she is precluded from the rewards of the afterlife. For with a single worthwhile deed, one can purchase eternity. But this too: we can never be sure who has made such a purchase."

The Peddler of Tzfat

This tale, retold by Reb Avrohom, the son of the Chassidic master Reb Zusha, takes place in the days of the holy Kabbalists, at a time that predates the rise of Chassidism. And these events occurred not in Eastern Europe, but in the mystical city of Tzfat, the home of the great Kabbalist, the Ari z"l.

In the sixteenth century, a large portion of the Jews living in the Holy Land, then a part of the Ottoman Empire, lived in Tzfat. Their plight was fraught with difficulty, and poverty was rampant. And of the many poor, Zekharia was the poorest.

Zekharia was a carrier, a *pakn treger* as they say in Yiddish, someone who hauled books or anything else that needed to be delivered. He'd lug his packages along the narrow streets of this ancient city, from house to house, from neighborhood to neighborhood, barely finding a free minute to stop off at the *beis medrash* to pray with a minyan.

In truth, for Zekharia, deciphering the Hebrew prayers was no less difficult than ferrying the heavy packages on his shoulders. Concerned that he read so poorly he might miss a word, he prayed slowly, enunciating every syllable. After prayers, he observed the learned Jews, and even the not-so-learned, remain seated at their places at their tables to pore over a page of Talmud or discuss the ideas contained in the newly printed edition of the Zohar, the sacred book of Kabbalah. Soon, the entire room would be filled with the sound of Torah study. It tore at Zekharia's heart to know he could never be among them.

What is the point of all my hard labor, he wondered. Why all these hours of toil for a piece of stale bread but no minutes to recite a few lines of Psalms? He looked at the others and thought: how pointless, how miserable my days and nights.

He went to the Rav of Tzfat, the foremost rabbi of the city, with a question on his lips.

"Tell me the truth, Rav. Am I a good Jew? A truly good Jew? I cannot learn Torah. I barely manage to pray. I cannot even find time to recite the Psalms."

The Rav looked at Zekharia and saw a man in pain.

"That you are unable to learn Torah and hesitate in your prayers is surely not your fault. But are you a good Jew? If you heed the commandments, avoid what is forbidden, and do not deceive others, then you are a good Jew."

"But Rav," Zekharia countered, "you say 'you are a good Jew if you keep the laws,' but I do not know the laws, what is required or forbidden. I don't even know the laws concerning how one must deal with one's customers."

"Don't worry, Zekharia," said the Rav. "I'll teach you. I'll study with you how to behave towards customers. And let me bless you that you have an easier way to make a living, one that will give you time to recite the Psalms."

A few weeks later, the city's water carrier moved away and Zekharia was appointed the official water carrier of Tzfat. Zekharia told the Rav the good news about his new position; the work would surely be easier, but he needed lessons to learn how to deal with a new set of customers.

The Rav studied with Zekharia the relevant Jewish laws, exhorted him never to deceive anyone, and gave him yet another blessing for a still lighter workload.

For the next several years, Zekharia labored as the water carrier of Tzfat. His customers appreciated his diligence and trustworthiness and were happy to employ his services. Over time, Zekharia managed to put aside a bit of money and soon had enough to purchase a donkey that freed him from carrying the heavy jugs on his back. He thought to himself, With God's help and the Rav's blessing, I was able to buy a donkey. Someday, perhaps I can do still better and use the donkey to sell milk instead of water.

Before long, Zekharia's aspiration came to be. And as before, Zekharia consulted with the Rav on how to conduct himself in selling his new commodity, and the Rav once again offered his blessings and cautioned Zekharia to avoid deception and to treat all his customers honestly.

With his donkey at his side, Zekharia trudged through the town selling milk to his patrons, who always greeted him warmly, applauding his punctuality and precision. Soon it occurred to Zekharia that there was no need to slog through Tzfat's streets all day selling milk when he could open a small stand and let the customers come to him. And so he did: Zekharia sold his donkey and opened a small concession in the middle of the city. Before long, Zekharia expanded his product line to include cheese, butter, and other dairy products. Business thrived.

Zekharia added still more items to his inventory, other foodstuffs and wares. And, as always, at every step of his growing business, Zekharia went to the Rav to seek his blessing and counsel.

Zekharia was now considered among the well-to-do in Tzfat, and was honored accordingly. But he never forgot that he was formerly a *paken treger* who could barely articulate his prayers and always attributed his success to the blessings he received from the Rav.

Bitter times soon came to Tzfat. For days, weeks, then months, the heavens closed. Not a drop of rain fell on the parched fields; the wheat and produce were scorched by the sun. The sky burned like sheets of copper. The inhabitants of the city prayed for relief, but none came. As the drought dragged on and the people's hunger intensified, the Rav of Tzfat ordered a communal fast day. He directed the entire community, young and old, to come to the synagogue to pray and do penance, as though it were Yom Kippur.

During a break in the service, a member of the community approached the Rav.

"I dislike reporting on another person," he began, "but I think the Rav should be aware of what I saw. On my way to shul I passed Zekharia's house and was stunned to see him sitting with his family enjoying a full meal, eating and drinking as though it were a holiday."

The rabbi was stunned. "Zekharia? Eating and drinking? Today, on a fast day?"

When the man insisted it was so, the rabbi, his talis still wrapped around his shoulders, immediately set out for Zekharia's home.

When he arrived, he didn't knock, but simply opened the door and let himself in. Indeed, there was Zekharia sitting at the head of his table, eating and drinking, as relaxed as could be.

"How could you?" the rabbi exclaimed, not bothering to hide his anger. "Jews are suffering. They are fasting all day, gathered in the synagogue praying, and you sit here enjoying a festive meal?"

Zekharia looked up, surprised to see the rabbi in his home.

"I don't understand," he said. "Is today the fast of Tisha B'Av? Some other fast day I am unaware of? Why are people fasting today?"

"Did you not hear?" the rabbi asked, more softly now. "That a fast day had been decreed for today?"

Zekharia shook his head, the puzzled look still on his face.

The rabbi could see from the Zekharia's expression that he was unaware of the proclamation, and informed him that the entire Jewish community was at this very moment fasting and praying for an end to the drought.

Zekharia walked to the window and stuck his head out to look up to the heavens.

"Master of the Universe," he cried out. "You know that I am ignorant, worthy of little. When I want to serve You properly, I ask our worthy Rav what to do and then do as he says … even when it's not easy. Why? Because this much I do understand: our Rav is a righteous man, and one must abide by his judgments even when it's difficult to comply. But for You, God Almighty, nothing is difficult. So I have a question. Why aren't You doing as the Rav asks of You? He asks that You give us rain, the rain we so desperately need. So why don't You? What the Rabbi asks of me, I carry out. So I ask You, dear God: Would You be worse than Zekharia the package carrier?"

Even before Zekharia concluded his plea, a small cloud appeared in the sky. It began to rain, at first gently, then harder, until it became a downpour that filled the fields and gardens.

At the end of his story, Reb Avrohom would nod his head and conclude, "Yes, such is the power of a simple, honest prayer."

The Sins of the Old

Yoelish was one of the modern ones. Already in his youth he spouted the "enlightened" ideas of the day, eager to contribute his cosmopolitan perspective to whatever discussion swirled around the table. But don't think for a moment Yoelish was some sort of innovative thinker. Hardly. He was merely one of those who confused the current with the advanced.

Nor should you imagine that Yoelish was some kind of radical. In fact, he was a proper Chassidic Jew, as were most people in his shtetl. He dressed like a Chassid and participated in all the appropriate rituals; on occasion, you might even catch him swaying during prayers with all the fervor of the genuinely pious. But people in town knew better. They heard him talk; they read his expressions. There was no doubting that the fellow had been infected with the virus of heresy.

That was long ago. These days, the elderly Yoelish spent his days in the public park, reading the papers, talking politics and gossiping with his companions.

One day, the Radomsker Rebbe was strolling in the park and, noticing Yoelish sitting on a bench, walked over to wish him a good afternoon.

"So what does a Jew do here all day?" asked the rebbe after exchanging the usual greetings.

"What does one do?" Yoelish answered, turning his palms toward the sky. "We relax, warm ourselves in the sun, read a little of the news, talk foolishness. Pleasant, idle days."

"Pleasant idle days?" said the rebbe. "And this is enough for you? Don't you think you ought to spend your time doing something more meaningful? Now in your later years, isn't it time you gave some thought to repentance?"

"So what's the big sin of sitting on a park bench, enjoying God's world?" Yoelish replied. "What else do you expect me to do?"

"What else?" the rebbe exclaimed. "I can tell you what else. A man like you should be sitting in the *beis medrash*, studying Torah."

"Me, study? No, I'm afraid my mind is no longer up to that. Whatever I learn goes in and right out. So what would be the point? I'm better off sitting here, where at least I get fresh air."

The rebbe smiled and shook his head. "No, it isn't better that you sit here. Your so-called pleasant idling takes away the little employment assigned to the *yetzer horah*, the evil inclination. I'll tell you a brief story that will help you see why."

With nothing else competing for his time, Yoelish leaned back and listened.

As you know, Yoelish, the two holy brothers, Reb Elimelech and Reb Zusha, of blessed memories, traveled around the countryside, spreading the teachings of Chassidism. One day, they entered a kretchma and noted a group of elderly Jews sitting around a table engrossed in a game of cards. You could tell from the dress of these men, their beards and sidelocks, that they were fine, observant Jews. The two brothers wanted to interrupt their game and discuss more important religious matters, but were unable to draw their attention.

"Zusha," Reb Elimelech nudged his brother, "these old Jews are not lifting their eyes from their cards for even a moment. Go talk to them." After some hesitation and more urging from his older brother, Reb Zusha walked over to their table and placed his hand on the deck, preventing the dealer from distributing the cards. "Pardon my interruption, but are you aware that with your card playing, you are ruining the mission of the *yetzer horah*?"

"Just because we're playing some cards?" one of the men asked, grinning.

"Indeed," said Reb Zusha, taking a seat around the table. "Let me tell you why."

One day, the *yetzer horah* was ambling about and found himself in the Garden of Eden. He was shocked to encounter souls he recognized as notorious sinners. He ought to know – after all, he'd worked hard to lead these people to sin. So what were they doing in heaven?

The *yetzer horah* went up to the Heavenly Abode to ask for an explanation.

"They repented at their end of their lives," he was told.

"And that's enough?" stammered the *yetzer horah*. "What about their sins? Their multitude of sins, I might add."

Said the Heavenly Abode, "When these people repented, the transgressions of their youth were disregarded. And so, they were accorded a place in the Garden of Eden."

The Evil Inclination shook his head in disbelief. So much for my inviting temptations and clever manipulations, he thought. How pleased he'd been by his victories! Now, he saw, they were all for naught.

The *yetzer horah* turned to the Heavenly Abode. "With Your kind permission, I'd like to resign from this job. It's a pointless mission. I do what I'm assigned, and do it well, only to learn my work has been in vain. No, thank you. I quit."

The Evil Inclination's request was accepted and a new Evil Inclination was appointed in his stead.

Reb Zusha paused to look at the old men sitting at the table, who urged him to continue.

Some time later, the former *yetzer horah* met his replacement.

"How's business?" he inquired.

"Good. Things are going well."

"Really?"

"Absolutely. Thank God, I'm busy day and night convincing people to do wrong. It's a full-time occupation, as you know."

"But don't you realize what a waste of time this is?" the former Evil Inclination cautioned. "Aren't you aware that when these sinners of yours attain old age and no longer have that youthful desire to transgress, they can repent, and all their sins will be forgiven?"

The new appointee chuckled. "Of course I'm aware. That's precisely the reason I do most of my work, not with the young, but with the old. I make sure that penitence is not on their agenda. I'm no fool."

Reb Zusha now spoke directly to the card players.

"So you see, you gentlemen are making it too easy for the Evil Inclination. He doesn't have to bother with you – sitting here playing cards with not a thought about repentance. He doesn't have to pay you any attention."

The men stroked their gray beards, and ended their game.

The Radomsker Rebbe put his hand gently on Yoelish's shoulder. "I assume you understand the meaning of this tale. If you spent your days in the *beis medrash* engaged in Torah study and prayer, you'd have thoughts of repentance, and thereby provide a formidable contest for the Evil Inclination. But spending your days here on the park bench in pleasant idleness, you leave the Evil Inclination with nothing to do. Why not present him with a little challenge?"

A Litigation Against God

Chassidim believe that when a tzaddik decrees, the heavens comply. But not always. At times, the forces of the "other side" prevent the tzaddik's words from reaching the Seat of Holiness, and on those occasions, the tzaddik must turn to the prayers of another tzaddik. And in circumstances when the tzaddik cannot depend on the powers of another saintly person, he must rely on the supplication of a simple Jew.

In the days of the great Chassidic tzaddik Reb Elimelech of Lizhensk, the government issued a draconian edict requiring every Jew who married off a child to pay a tax of four hundred Rhenish guilders.

This decree caused enormous suffering in Jewish homes. A marriage was an expensive affair, what with the dowry, trousseau and the wedding party itself – an additional four hundred guilder was an exorbitant sum even for the well-to-do. But for the poor, the levy was devastating, condemning Jewish girls of marriageable age to spinsterhood as their fathers could not afford to marry them off.

The Jews petitioned and prayed, but the regime would not be moved. The young women could only curse the government and their fate.

Such was the bitter lot that enveloped the home of Feivel the horse trader. His daughter Feiga was a young woman in the bloom of her youth, engaged to a fine young man, but the steep matrimony tax rendered their marriage impossible.

Feivel would observe his forlorn daughter sitting sadly in her room and his heart would break along with hers. He'd sometimes retire to the barn, where he'd pet the sheep and tend to the geese before taking a seat across from his horse to pour out his heart.

"My dear horse, things are not good. No, they are not good with my daughter Feiga. Such an excellent match for her, that boy. Can you imagine how painful it is to see her like this, so desolate? I tell you, it is simply unfair. But what can I do? I have nowhere near the four hundred guilder the Kaiser demands."

Sharing his pain with his horse sometimes brought Feivel a bit of temporary solace, but it did not change the reality. No matter how hard he worked, he knew he would not be able to raise the necessary funds. As for Feiga, her mood darkened with every passing day.

One day, Feivel raised his hands and looked to the skies and demanded, "How could You allow such an innocent sweet girl to suffer such pain?"

With no answer forthcoming, he decided to travel to the rebbe. Yes, he thought, let the famed Reb Elimelech of Lizhensk deal with his predicament. For was not the rebbe responsible, at least in part, for not compelling the government to revoke its cruel statute? Was the rebbe not an agent of God here on earth?

Feivel entered the rebbe's study ready to vent his charges, but was struck mute by the friendly smile on the rebbe's face

"Good morning," Feivel muttered.

"And a good morning and good year to you," the rebbe replied. "How can I be of assistance?"

"I am here to bring a lawsuit," Feivel said with trembling lips.

"All right," said the rebbe to Feivel's surprise. "We can arrange a tribunal."

Rebbe Elimelech signaled to his assistant. "Ask for two other judges to come at once. Someone wishes to make his case before a court."

Soon, two men entered the rebbe's study and were seated. The rebbe turned to Feivel.

"We are ready to proceed. Tell us against whom you wish to bring charges and we will send for the person."

"You don't have to send for him," Feivel said.

"And why not?"

Feivel lowered his eyes toward the ground. "The defendant is already in the room."

The puzzled judges looked at each other, then at Feivel, who was now pointing his finger toward the ceiling.

"I am calling Him to a legal proceeding."

"Calling whom?" demanded one of the judges with growing impatience. "Speak clearly."

"Him," Feivel stammered. "I wish to bring God to a Din Torah. It is against Him that I will lodge my complaint."

The two judges sprang from their seats. "How dare you! Such nonsense! Wasting our time like this."

"Wait. Return to your seats," Reb Elimelech said to them. He then spoke to Feivel.

"Don't be afraid. The trial will proceed. Let us hear your charges against God and we will reach a judgment."

Feivel took a deep breath and cleared his throat.

"Rebbe, I am a simple, ordinary Jew. A horse trader. I don't know a great deal. But I do know that God gave us 613 commandments and one of those commandments is to marry and reproduce. Well, Rebbe, I have a wonderful daughter who is engaged to a fine young man. My Feiga likes him and he likes her. All would be good, but, alas, I don't have the four hundred guilders the Kaiser demands for a Jewish marriage. If things continue as they are, my Feiga will, God forbid, remain at home, looking at the walls while her hair turns grey. So I ask, if God commanded us to marry, then why does He allow the Kaiser's marriage tax?"

Feivel steadied himself and looked at each of the judges. "Now tell me. Am I justified in my charges or not?"

The judges placed their heavy legal tomes to the side; they knew they weren't going to find a solution to Feivel's case in their codes of law. Instead, they waited for Reb Elimelech to speak. But Reb Elimelech seemed to be elsewhere, his eyes glazed over as he stared into space. He stroked his beard and moved his lips, as if in conversation.

Only after several minutes did the rebbe return his attention to the room, addressing his fellow judges.

"Well, you've heard the plaintiff's charges. What is your decision?"

"A judgment against God?" one of the judges stammered. "I mean, can we really—"

"We certainly can," Rebbe Elimelech said. "Let me remind you of the dictum, *lo bashamayim he*, the Torah does not exist in heaven. It exists here on earth, where we humans are the arbiters of its dictates. We decide how to interpret the Torah's teachings. Do you fear rendering a ruling here? I do not. I think we can, indeed, reach a decision based on an established legal precedent.

"As you know, a free person and an indentured servant are not permitted to marry each other. Suppose, however, that this servant belongs to a partnership and one of the partners frees the servant from his share. This servant is now half free, half enslaved. As a result, he will not be able to marry anyone, neither a free person, nor another servant. But we are all entitled to marry! Therefore, the courts compel the remaining owner to free his servant so that he will be able to marry another free person."

The two judges shook their heads, not comprehending the rebbe's argument.

"What is the relevant legal principle here?" Reb Elimelech asked, anticipating their question. "We learn from this case that a court has the power to coerce an owner to take an action that will assure his servant is able to marry. This means that we too have the legal standing to call on the owner, in this case, the Master of the Universe, to comply with our judgment and have the Kaiser withdraw his tax so that Feivel the horse trader can marry off his daughter."

Rebbe Elimelech leaned back in his chair and looked at the judges. "Do you concur with my ruling?"

"We do," they replied.

The rebbe looked over to Feivel. "It seems your litigation has been successful. I assure you the tax will soon be rescinded. Now go home and prepare for your daughter's wedding."

And so the wedding soon took place.

The Besht Arranges
a Marriage

One day the Ba'al Shem Tov arrived in a village and was approached by a poor woman in tattered clothes, pleading for charity. As the Besht gave her some money, he noticed the skinny child clinging to her hand. He pinched the child's pale cheek and asked his name.

"Chaim," the child answered. "My mother calls me Chaim'l."

"Tell me, Chaim'l, do you know Torah?"

"No, but I do know how to pray and can even recite the Ashrei prayer by heart."

The mother listened proudly.

"A shame," said the Besht to the mother. "A boy of six years should know some Chumash as well."

"Sir, my Chaim'l is, praise God, already eight years old, but as you can see, with the little I can provide, he looks no more than six. As for his not yet knowing any Bible, what do you expect? How can he study when his mother is forever wandering, begging, and where the boy spends his day is not where he spends his night?"

The Besht stood quietly for a moment. "Why don't you give me the child to care for, and I'll teach him Torah."

The woman was aghast. "Give you my Chaim'l? You can't be serious. You could give me the wealth of the entire world, and I wouldn't part with my only child. He is everything to me."

"God forbid that anyone should take your Chaim away from you," the Besht said softly. "I have no such intention. On the contrary, all I am offering is to clothe and feed the child, provide him with shelter and teach him Torah. Of course, you can visit him whenever you please. I hope, with God's help, he will grow into a fine young man from whom you'll draw much joy."

The mother barely heard the Besht's words as she tried to wrench her son away from this stranger. She turned on her heels and was prepared to go on her way when the Besht's assistants took hold of the woman and pulled her to the side. Did she know who was offering to raise her child? Was she aware this was none other than the celebrated Ba'al Shem Tov?

The woman quaked with emotion. She'd had no inkling of this stranger's identity. Her eyes welling with tears, she returned to the Besht.

"Yes, take my dear Chaim'l and raise him to be a decent man, an upstanding Jew."

She kissed Chaim, hugged him tightly, and promised to visit him often.

In the next years, the Besht personally attended to the child's education, teaching him Torah, law and ethics. Chaim proved to be an excellent student, always thirsting to learn more. As he approached the age of bar mitzvah, the Besht procured a special tutor to guide him in his study of the Talmud and Commentaries. As she'd promised, his mother visited him regularly, and listened with pride when others praised her son.

By the time Chaim turned thirteen, he'd already mastered a substantial swath of Torah. And because he was a student of the Besht, he'd also been exposed to Kabbalah and other mystical texts.

Years passed, and Chaim reached a marriageable age. Everyone knew about his pitiful past – that he'd been orphaned as an infant, his father was no one to be proud of, and his mother subsisted on handouts. Nonetheless, even the most esteemed rabbis and the community's wealthiest men wanted Chaim as a son-in-law. After all, hadn't he been raised by the Besht himself? The Ba'al Shem Tov listened to the suitors' proposals, one after the other, but rejected them all.

Then, one day, a matchmaker from Zhitomir visited the Besht to suggest a match for Chaim with a young woman from his town. He described the girl's virtuous character and privileged family background.

"Sorry, but not for my Chaim," the Besht replied. "However, I am interested in your town."

The matchmaker raised his shoulders, indicating he didn't understand the Besht's meaning.

"I'd like you to arrange a marriage for Chaim with someone from Zhitomir. But not to the young woman you had in mind."

"With whom, then?"

"With the daughter of Shloime the son of Yecheskel."

"Who?"

"Shloime the son of Yecheskel," the Besht repeated.

The matchmaker had no idea who that was, but the Besht said he'd provide the matchmaker with a letter of introduction to give to this Shloime. The Besht went to his room and reemerged soon after with a sealed envelope and generous compensation for the matchmaker's efforts.

"Let's hope he agrees."

When the matchmaker arrived in Zhitomir, he announced he was on a mission for the holy Besht: to arrange a marriage for the extraordinary Chaim, the boy raised by the Besht himself, with the daughter of Shloime the son of Yecheskel.

"With whom?" The chief rabbi of Zhitomir furrowed his brow, wondering who in his town deserved this glory. Which scholar went by this name? Who among the well-to-do? He could think of no one.

Nor could anyone else. But the determined matchmaker continued his search, canvassing all the likely men of Zhitomir. When no one by this name was found among the elite, the matchmaker reviewed the names of the other townspeople: the small businessmen, the laborers, even the very poorest residents. No one answered to the name Shloime the son of Yecheskel.

Had the matchmaker gotten the name wrong? He was certain he hadn't. Perhaps he'd come to the wrong town. No, he was positive of this too; he was sent to Zhitomir.

When he approached the men in the study hall to inquire about Shloime the son of Yecheskel, they could only shake their heads, tsk their tongues, and turn their palms upward – until one man clapped his hand against his forehead.

"Who knows?" he said. "Maybe he means him."

"Who?" his friends asked.

"Never mind," the man said. "A stupid idea."

But the matchmaker pressed him.

"Believe me," said the man. "It's a ridiculous notion."

"You must tell me," the matchmaker persisted.

"A silly thought, I tell you. There's this abject fellow who lives around here, a worthless character. To call him an onion trader is putting it kindly. 'Shloime-onioner' they call him. I had this fleeting idea that maybe his actual name is Shloime the son of Yecheskel. Of course, it's nonsense. The Ba'al Shem Tov would not want to marry off his Chaim to the daughter of a man of this sort."

Still, the matchmaker insisted on learning where Shloime-onioner lived. Enlisting two yeshiva students to accompany him, he set out at once.

The matchmaker soon found himself standing in front of a tiny, dilapidated hut on the outskirts of town. A few skinny chickens ran about, chased by several young boys and girls in torn, dirty clothing. A man with a scraggly beard and greasy cap stepped outside just as the visitors approached.

"Shloime?" the matchmaker asked.

The man nodded.

"And your full Hebrew name?"

"Huh? Shloime the son of Yecheskel. What business is this of yours?"

"I have a letter for you. From the holy Ba'al Shem Tov."

Shloime took the envelope, withdrew the letter and held it near his face.

The Jews waited for his reaction.

"I don't know how to read," he said, finally. "And who is this Ba'al Shem Tov you say sent me this letter?"

The matchmaker exhaled a long column of air. "Very well," he said. "I'll read it for you."

> *Greetings to you, Shloime the son of Yecheskel. I, Israel Ba'al Shem Tov, have raised a sterling young man named Chaim. The time has come for him to marry, and as I'm aware you have a daughter of marriageable age, I would like to propose a match between the two. I should add that if you do not have sufficient funds for a wedding, I promise to cover all expenses. In addition, I will assume responsibility for providing for the young couple for the next few years. I pray you will agree to this proposal.*
>
> Israel Ba'al Shem Tov

Shloime-onioner didn't give the request a moment's thought. "If this Israel Ba'al Shem Tov is willing to pay," he said, "why not?"

The splendid affair took place several weeks later. The Besht celebrated as if it were the wedding of his own son. Chaim delivered a learned discourse, engaging the assembled rabbis in intricate discussions of Torah, while Shloime-onioner sat on the dais, his eyes glazed over, not understanding a word.

When most of the celebrants had already gone home, and only a few honored guests remained, several of the Besht's students asked their rebbe to explain the reason for this marriage. Why had he rejected every other proposal in favor of the daughter of this unlearned onion trader?

"I'll explain," said the Besht. "And I'll tell you not only why I arranged this match, but the reason I raised Chaim in the first place."

Many years ago, there were two good friends who married and had children, one a son and the other a daughter. To reinforce the bond between them, the friends agreed that one day their children would marry. But as the years moved on, the fortunes of the two friends diverged. One became wealthy, while the other grew so impoverished he was forced to move away from his town to a distant hamlet.

There, in a place that could not provide even a minimal Jewish education, the poor man raised his son Shloime. Needless to say, the prosperous friend came to "forget" the match he had made with his erstwhile friend so many years before. When his daughter came of age, he married her off to a suitable man.

No doubt as punishment for this breach, the rich man died, and soon thereafter, so did his son-in-law. His widowed daughter and her small child managed to live off the inheritance for a short while, but the funds soon ran out. Alone, and without any means of support, the woman was compelled to beg door-to-door. Meanwhile, Shloime, the son of the humiliated friend, remained in the hamlet, a pauper barely able to provide for his family.

In the other world, the world of the afterlife, the rich friend's soul could find no solace. It wandered about the netherworld, a punishment for reneging on this solemn pact, and humiliating a poor young man.

The Besht looked up at his students gathered around him. It had been a long night of celebrating, and it was time to leave the wedding hall.

"As you, no doubt, can guess by now, Chaim is the grandson of that rich friend. I understood that to make amends, these two families had to be joined, as promised. With the marriage of Chaim to the daughter of Shloime the son of Yecheskel, the broken agreement between the two friends is honored. Their troubled souls can now finally rest in peace."

The Maggid Defeats
the Heavenly Prosecutor

In the Jewish hovels across the shtetl, the Havdalah candles had long been extinguished, signifying the end of Shabbos, and the everyday worries of the coming week were already creeping into the impoverished homes. Only in the small Chassidic shul did the joy of Shabbos still linger.

As they did every Saturday evening at the third meal, the Chassidim hung on to the Day of Rest by sitting around the table exchanging Torah insights, telling stories about the great sages, and singing their beloved Shabbos melodies. When all the songs had been sung and the darkening sky urged them to return to their homes, they'd turn to Reb Yoshe Ber and ask that he regale them with one last Chassidic tale.

This evening, instead of a story, Reb Yoshe Ber offered yet another tune. What was the rush? Why not hold on as long as possible to the Shabbos? Workday pressures could wait.

But then, without warning, right in the midst of his song, Reb Yoshe Ber started to speak. The Chassidim settled into their chairs, ready to hear another tale about the great Chassidic masters of the past.

"Friends," Reb Yoshe Ber began, "we're all aware that the High Holidays will soon be upon us." He looked around the table. "Alas, none of us has any idea what the heavenly prosecutor plans to argue against us in the heavenly court. What will we be charged with this year, and with what evidence? I'm afraid we do not know. But it wasn't always like that. In the old days, the holy tzaddikim knew what was contained in the heavenly prosecutor's brief, and they were ready with a defense. But these days, with our multitude of sins, we are like sheep without a shepherd, and so we must be our own shepherds, mindful of our every step.

"We're familiar with the maxim, 'When the tzaddik decrees, the Almighty complies.' But we know it's not that simple. There are times when the tzaddik's declaration is not enough, when the tzaddik needs to add cleverness to help the cause. For surely, you've also heard the saying, 'Wisdom is stronger than prophecy.' Yes, sometimes the tzaddik must contribute a dash of wisdom, a piece of strategic advice, to help the heavenly defender make his case in the battle with the heavenly prosecutor. And so it once was with the holy Maggid, may his memory be a blessing."

It was the custom of the Maggid to lead prayers on the High Holidays. Every year, he robed himself in his pure white kittel, draped his talis over his head, and slowly walked up to the *beemah* to begin the Kol Nidre service. But this year the tzaddik did not utter a sound. He just stood there on the platform, motionless, silent. The congregation waited.

Five minutes, ten minutes, twenty minutes passed. Still not a sound. What was preventing the Maggid from praying? The congregation remained silent as well, for surely, something was wrong. Perhaps the holy tzaddik was contending with a looming threat to the community. The congregation waited.

Finally, the Maggid turned to face the congregation, removed the talis from his head and let it rest on his shoulders.

"Is there anyone here from the town of Peluv?" he called out.

The room immediately erupted in a cacophony of murmurs. Peluv? Why was the Maggid looking for a person from this town, a place few had even heard of?

From the back wall, a simple Jew began to make his way to the front of the synagogue, as the Chassidim stepped aside to make a path for him. When he approached the *beemah*, a shadow of a smile crossed the Maggid's face. The entire congregation quieted, eager to learn the meaning of the Maggid's strange query.

"Are you from Peluv?" the tzaddik asked.

"No," said the man. "I am not. I'm from a hamlet near Peluv, a shtetl called Ranovitz. But my work takes me to Peluv every day."

"Your work?"

"A milk seller. I sell my milk in Peluv."

The Maggid paused a moment. "By any chance, are you familiar with the poretz's dog that roams around the town's marketplace?"

"The nobleman's dog?"

"Yes, if you know something about it, please tell us. Your account might assist the plight of the Jewish people."

The man shrugged, confounded by the odd request. Now, when we are about to begin the Yom Kippur service, the Maggid asks him to relate the history of a dog! And this will help the Jewish people? He had no dramatic story to tell. Dumbfounded, he just shook his head, speechless.

The Maggid, noting the man's discomfort, urged him on. "Please, tell us what you know. I assure you this is important."

"I don't know the entire story," the man said, "nor can I vouch for its truth, but I can tell you what I've heard. This dog that now wanders about the streets and alleys of the town once had an excellent home. Apparently, when the poretz, the nobleman of our region, was vacationing in Trieste, he encountered this dog and became enamored with it. He was determined to purchase the animal. The dog's owner, seeing how set the poretz was on acquiring the dog, presented an outrageous asking price, a thousand gulden. The poretz didn't flinch, but immediately proffered the sum requested. He brought the animal back with him and ordered that a special hut be built for it. A crew was hired to take full-time care of his cherished pet.

"Well, it seems that on one occasion, the dog didn't comply with the command of the poretz, and the impetuous nobleman abruptly had the dog's hut destroyed and banished the animal from his estate. He wanted nothing more to do with it. Ever since, the dog prowls the town of Peluv, scrawny, always hungry, gnawing on discarded, pitiful bones occasionally thrown his way. That's what I know about this dog."

The Maggid lifted his arms to the heavens. "*Nu*, Angel Michael. Did you hear? Did you hear? Did you hear?"

After a few moments of silence, as though waiting for a reply from the angel, the Maggid placed his talis back on his head and at last began the Kol Nidre service.

At the conclusion of Yom Kippur, the Maggid sat at the table with his followers, his face aglow. Yes, he would answer the obvious question about what had transpired the previous night.

In the town of Makov, a shtetl near Krakow, there lived a Jewish gentleman, well respected for his philanthropy and knowledge of Torah. But, as we know, the wheel of fortune turns on its own accord, and the man lost all his wealth and became utterly destitute.

This Jew managed to subsist on dry pieces of bread; he'd rather go hungry than beg others for sustenance. But he was not alone – he had a family to consider. When his dear daughter, his only child, attained the age of marriage, he knew that pride does not pay for a wedding. Dignity does not provide a dowry. The poor man had no recourse but to travel about the land, asking for alms.

As you might imagine, possessing an aristocratic character is a problem for a beggar. This man was not very good at asking for charity. He'd accept what he was given, never suggesting he be given more. Months went by, and all he'd managed to garner was thirty, forty gulden. A wedding would cost at least five hundred gulden.

Eventually, his wandering took him to the vicinity of Peluv. Exhausted and hungry from his journeys, the man sat down on a stone on the side of the road. As he sat, he confronted his woeful circumstances. Nearly a year had passed since he'd begun this pathetic existence. Other Jews were now preparing for the High Holidays, busying themselves with repentance, prayer and philanthropy, yet he did not even have a place to study Torah, to say nothing of distributing charity to the poor. Considering the limited sum he'd managed to gather thus far, it would take years before he'd have enough to return home. Up until this moment, he'd managed to suppress the reality of his situation, but now it all came rushing at him. His heart beat quickly, and nausea filled his chest. The man convulsed in a bitter wail. Tears ran down his shrunken face, blocking his vision. He was impervious to his surroundings, unaware that his cries had even frightened the birds flying overhead. And then he heard a human voice.

"*Zhyd*, come here."

The Jew raised his head and peered out at the splendid carriage stopped on the road. Inside, the sumptuously dressed poretz was pointing his silver cane in his direction.

"I said, come here, Jew," the poretz bellowed.

Trembling, the frightened man walked to the carriage, prepared for the blow of the cane, or at best, an onslaught of brutal curses. Instead, he was stunned to hear a friendly voice.

"Jew, why are you crying?"

"Dear, gentle poretz," the man answered, his voice attended by audible moans. "Things do not go well with me. I have a daughter to marry off, my only child, and I do not have enough money for the requisite dowry."

"How much do you need for a dowry?" the poretz asked.

"Five hundred. A total of five hundred gulden."

The poretz put his hand into his pocket, removed five hundred gulden, and handed it to the astonished Jew.

"Here you are. A gift from Poretz Shatrinska."

And before the Jew could even thank him, the carriage galloped away. The man immediately returned to his town of Makov, where he did not cease to bless the generosity of the poretz.

"However," and here the Maggid paused, "there were repercussions in the Other World. You see, this brief encounter gave rise to a major litigation against the Jewish community."

The Chassidim did not understand.

"You see," explained the Maggid, "the heavenly prosecutor was now armed with a strong argument. In shtetl after shtetl, the townspeople couldn't manage to help this desperate Jew, one of their own. Yet a stranger, a gentile poretz, heard the man's suffering and provided him with his needs.

"Even the heavenly defender, the angel Michael, was bereft of a successful parry to this charge. And so, before Kol Nidre, I asked that a Jew tell the story of the poretz's dog, thereby providing the angel Michael with his defense.

"For after all, it wasn't compassion that motivated the poretz to give the money to the Jew. No, five hundred gulden was a meaningless sum to him. He was, rather, a capricious man, given to impulsive behavior. Note how quickly he rid himself of his once treasured dog in a moment of anger.

"The defense's argument was successful. The calamitous sentence that awaited the Jewish community was voided, and a year of life and peace followed."

Reb Yoshe Ber leaned back in his seat, signaling the end of his tale. The Chassidim exhaled a collective breath, nodding their heads as though they had personally witnessed the entire proceeding in the heavenly court. The older Chassidim among them sighed as they recalled their youth, a time when the great Chassidic masters could offer advice to the heavenly defender.

But they could not sit around the table forever, listening to stories. The new week was waiting. "*Nu*, friends," Reb Yoshe Ber announced, "it seems the time has come to recite grace."

Life Lessons

If we are not better tomorrow than today, why bother having a tomorrow?

REB NACHMAN OF BRESLOV

Miracles Begin at Home

Hours had passed since Binyomin recited the Havdalah, marking the end of Shabbos and the beginning of the new week. The children were asleep, wrapped in ragged blankets dipped in sugar-water to help ease their thirst. It was Chanukah, and the menorah's burning wicks cast flickering shadows on the bare walls. Raisel, Binyomin's wife, sat huddled in her chair, the shawl that covered her head muffling her moans. All that Binyomin had earned, all they owned, had been pawned long ago, and nothing of value remained even to serve as security for a loan. For this Shabbos, he'd managed to scrape together a few groshen to buy two loaves of stale bread for the Kiddush and Motzeh blessings. But now, once more, they had nothing.

Binyomin looked around the single desolate room that was their home, at his wife and sleeping children, curled together against the chill.

This is it, he thought to himself. I've come to the end.

He'd tried many different jobs over the years, but all had come to naught. He was out of ideas. He thought of the old aphorism, "Change your place, change your luck." Perhaps this was the solution. He'd try his luck elsewhere, move to a larger city…maybe even to Germany, or America. Then again, how could he leave his family? His rebbe? His dear friends? But if not, what was the alternative? He gazed again at his famished children. No, he could not continue this way.

"Raisel," Binyomin called softly. "Raisel, I am going over to the rebbe's *melava malka*. Who knows? Perhaps there I'll come up with a plan for what to do about our circumstance. Maybe I'll hear some useful advice from the rebbe."

Raisel knew how her husband looked forward to this traditional meal that escorted out the Shabbos, and said nothing. Instead, she sighed, as if to say, "You at least have this, a place to go where you'll also find food and warmth, while we remain here hungry and cold."

And indeed, at the rebbe's, there was no shortage of good cheer, no doubt assisted by the shots of vodka swallowed between bites of herring and honey cake. The *melava malka*, the meal of King David as it is known in the tradition, was yet another opportunity for Chassidim to share their camaraderie and hear words of Torah from their beloved rebbe, who sat at the head of the table still cloaked in the holiness of Shabbos. Together they sang and danced, trying to forestall the departure of the extra soul every Jew is given on the Day of Rest.

Binyomin perked up his still half-frozen ears as the rebbe began to speak.

"Chanukah," said the rebbe, "is, at its root, a celebration of trust. The essential message of this holiday is that we must not give up, that we may never conclude all is lost. On the contrary, sometimes precisely when all possibilities seem to have faded away, a miracle awaits you. When all seems hopeless, we discover a sealed jar of oil with which to light the Temple menorah and usher in the holiday of Chanukah, this festival of new beginnings."

Binyomin leaned in closer to the rebbe. Were these words addressed to him? Could he still be hopeful? Would a miracle happen so that he would not have to forsake all he held dear to face an unknown beyond?

Binyomin listened as the rebbe continued speaking.

"As we know, when the Jews reconquered the Holy Temple that had been profaned and destroyed by the Greeks, they needed enough pure oil to light the menorah. Notice, they did not travel to distant places, but searched for the oil right there in the Temple, amidst the rubble.

"You see, not only must we not yield to despair, we also ought not to presume that salvation is to be found elsewhere. Isn't this the lesson taught to us by the Holy Seer of Lublin? One day, he came upon a Jew rushing about in the marketplace, the perspiration dripping down his face. The Seer asked the man where he was running to with such urgency. 'I'm hurrying to where I might find a business opportunity,' replied the man. The Seer asked him, 'Indeed? And how are you so sure that you'll find your opportunity elsewhere? Perhaps the best place for you is right where you are and you are running away from it?'"

The rebbe smiled as he looked directly at Binyomin. "No, leaving home to improve your lot is not always the smartest move. Sometimes, success can be discovered right where you are."

As the rebbe concluded his talk, the Chassidim commenced another round of singing and dancing. Binyomin could still hear the echo of their voices hours later as he began his walk home, but it was the rebbe's message that reverberated most loudly in his head: Miracles could happen in one's own day, in one's own dwelling, just as they had in the Maccabees' time.

As soon as he entered his home, Binyomin was greeted by Raisel's tear-streaked face. She had never before complained aloud about their plight, but on this night, she could no longer restrain her desperation.

"Do you hear the wails of the children? Their hunger woke them, poor things. Their hunger won't let them sleep."

Binyomin was no longer thinking about the rebbe's exhortation, about the wonders of the past or those that might await him in the future. Faced with his family's anguish, he sank to the floor, overcome with guilt at his failure to provide for them. He watched as his oldest son, Yankele, a frail child of six, wiped away his own tears as he tried to console his younger brother.

"Don't cry, Shloimele," Yankele kept repeating, his hand on his brother's shoulder. "When the morning comes, you'll see that Father will have brought you a gift, Chanukah money, and some food. You'll see, Shloimele." Yankele turned his head in his father's direction. "Won't he? Won't he, Father?"

"Yes, of course, Yankele," Binyomin said, as he walked to his son's side and caressed his cheeks. "Do you know what? I'll make a wooden dreidel for you – no, I will make two – one for you to sell, and the other to play with and win some money. That way, you'll have a Chanukah gift and money to share with Shloimele."

Yankele's disbelief was apparent in his large brown eyes. He knew his father was only trying to calm him, and that by morning, his promise would be forgotten. Once again, they would all wake up hungry and face another day of disappointment.

Binyomin looked tenderly at his son. He walked to a sack lying in the corner of the room and withdrew a penknife. Then he went outside and soon returned with a soft piece of wood which he placed on the table.

"Just watch," he said.

Years ago, long before he'd married, back when he was still a boy, Binyomin would steal away from school and run through the nearby forest to his secret spot at the edge of the brook, where he'd sit for hours carving branches and twigs, magically transforming them into birds and animals. On one particularly ambitious afternoon, he carved a complete chess set, with original, though recognizable, forms for the king and queen, rooks, knights, bishops and pawns. The entire shtetl was amazed by the young boy's artistry.

But that was then. Binyomin grew up, married, began a family and put aside his childish diversion. All that remained from those days was his penknife.

But on this night of Chanukah, he once again sat for hours molding, cutting, carving and sculpting. By daybreak, a wonderful dreidel had emerged from the lifeless piece of wood. Young Yankele stayed awake the entire time, his tongue twisting in his mouth along with the turns of the knife, his eyes following his father's fingers and the flying shavings of wood.

"Well, Yankele," said Binyomin, a pleased smile on his face. "Here is your Chanukah present, as promised." Binyomin demonstrated how to spin the dreidel, reminding his son of the meaning of each letter carved on each of the dreidel's four sides: *nun, gimel, heh* and *shin.*

With his slender fingers, Yankele twirled the dreidel on the dusty ground. In his imagination, he conjured his winnings every time the top landed on the letter *gimel.*

Binyomin's hands remained busy throughout the early hours. Two more dreidels followed, then a magnificent miniature menorah with two lions holding the tablets with the Ten Commandments over their heads.

"Here, Yankele," Binyomin said when it was done. "This too is your Chanukah gift."

By now, Raisel was awake as well. She stood from afar, pained to see her husband spending his time with frivolities. The previous evening he'd enjoyed himself at the rebbe's, savoring food and companionship, and now he comes home and plays with his penknife while his children go hungry?

At the appointed time, Binyomin walked slowly to shul for the morning service, the reality of his situation dawning along with the sun. Now was the time for serious decisions, to face the fact he'd have to move if he hoped to earn some money. In the meantime, his family needed to eat this very day. Binyomin cast his eyes along the road, hoping, but failing, to find someone he could ask for a loan. Yankele, tired but eager, accompanied his father, excited to show his friends the marvelous wooden dreidel and menorah his father had carved for him during the night.

In shul, the other children were awed by Yankele's remarkable objects and lined up for a chance to spin the dreidel and examine the menorah. A few of the children from wealthier families offered to buy the dreidel then and there. But they had a competitor: Yisroel Varshaver, the antiques and crafts dealer.

Yisroel Varshaver observed the children engrossed in their game. Moving closer, he was impressed by the boy's wooden carvings. He lifted the dreidel, examined it, and would not let it go.

"Where did you get this?" he asked Yankele.

"My father, sitting over there." Yankele pointed proudly in his father's direction. "He made it last night. And the menorah, too. I watched the whole time."

Yisroel returned the dreidel to Yankele and walked over to Binyomin. Would he please step outside the shul for a moment? There was something he'd like to discuss.

"I truly admire your work," Yisroel Varshaver said as he withdrew several banknotes from his pocket and handed them to Binyomin. "Consider this an advance. I think we can make good money from your creations. Do you think you can make, say, a dozen of these menorahs to start with? Then we can move on to other objects: spice boxes, snuff boxes, megillah cases…"

Binyomin stood dumfounded.

"In case you have doubts, I pay well," Yisroel Varshaver assured him. "I believe this will be a rewarding partnership for us both. What do you say?"

Binyomin never did move away from his shtetl. He went into business with Yisroel Varshaver, who found a ready market for his work. True, Binyomin never became rich, but he made a decent living, and what more could a man ask for?

The Integrity of Dance

When you picture Chassidim at a celebration, festival or holiday gathering, you picture them dancing. You imagine a circle with each man clutching the shoulders of the man in front of him, feet stomping, voices singing loud and in unison. Of course, Chassidim will assure you these images only faintly capture the rapture of the real thing. Did Chassidim invent dancing among Jews? Perhaps not. But like a fire that turns a block of ice into gaseous steam, the warmth of Chassidus frees us from our frozen inertia. Chassidism teaches that sadness is the greatest of sins; joy must be at the center of our lives. And when people are joyous, will they not lift their feet in dance?

So it did not go unnoticed when Peretz remained in his seat, feet glued to the ground, rejecting every plea to join the circle of dancers. Surely some sadness was dampening his soul, a burden blocking his access to joy.

Not long before, Peretz was like the others, struggling to earn a living, but satisfied with his lot. A devoted Chassid, he'd come to the rebbe's court on every festive occasion and many a Shabbos as well, eager to join his fellow Chassidim in fervent prayer, song and dance.

And then Peretz's enterprise began to thrive. He'd become wealthy. But running a business, especially a flourishing business, requires attention: decisions must be made, crises must be managed. As Peretz's affluence grew, so did his worries.

Mind you, Peretz was no less a committed Chassid than before, but his visits to Reb Velvele were now fewer and shorter. He simply could no longer afford the time away from his business, and when he did show up to the rebbe's, his behavior was noticeably different. For one thing, he had difficulty concentrating on the words during the silent prayer. Stray thoughts invaded his mind: the outstanding debts to his vendors, the feasibility of new ventures, strategies to maintain cash flow, troubles with his partners. He tried to focus on his devotions, but these weekday concerns invariably took center stage. When the Chassidim clasped hands to dance, he'd remain on the sidelines, his mind elsewhere. He told himself, if they had the worries I have, they wouldn't be whirling about either, lost in this carefree exuberance. Moreover, it was undignified for an established businessman to participate in such ecstatic displays. A man of his standing needed to preserve his dignity.

One holiday, as the Chassidim shook the room with their usual enthusiasm and Peretz again sat alone, absorbed in his thoughts, Reb Velvele called to his assistant.

"Tell Peretz I'd like to speak with him," he said. "In the corner of the room, where it is quieter."

"I see you're not participating in the singing and dancing," the rebbe said to Peretz. "Your worries are weighing you down."

"Yes, I've got much on mind."

"But a Chassid should dance."

Reb Peretz half nodded, and pulled on his lower lip. "The Torah does not state that dancing is a commandment."

The rebbe nodded in return. "True, Peretz. But I'm not concerned that you are violating a law. I am concerned about your soul. The body's movements reflect the state of one's inner life, and when a person, especially a Chassid, doesn't dance, that bespeaks a soul freighted with anxiety, someone overwhelmed by matters of lesser consequence."

Peretz merely raised his brows in response. So Reb Velvele told him a story.

A king once called together his team of advisors. He was taking a trip and wished to enlist a guard to watch over his treasures while he was away. Naturally, this required someone of the utmost integrity, who, of course, would be richly rewarded for his supervision. But who in his kingdom could claim such honesty? And how would he find this person?

One wise advisor offered a suggestion that pleased the king. An announcement would be made throughout the land that the king was searching for a person of the highest probity, and anyone who thought himself qualified should appear at the palace at the specified day and time.

Scores of citizens showed up on the designated day, each proclaiming his trustworthiness. The court officials directed the applicants to line up single file and proceed, one by one, into the palace. But to get to the throne room where the king awaited them, each contender had to walk alone through a long, darkened corridor strewn with gold and silver coins.

"Very well," said the king when they'd all assembled. "I will now choose the most incorruptible person among you. But first, I would like you all to get up and dance."

Only one man stood up. The rest, fearing the clinking sound of coins in their pockets, sat quietly frozen.

Reb Velvele's eyes met those of his Chassid. "Peretz, our lives are but one long corridor strewn with glittering distractions. When we busy ourselves filling our pockets, we lose our integrity. And then we are afraid to dance."

The Orphan and His Prayer Book

Y oshke released a long, heartfelt sigh that caught the attention of Yoshe Ber, sitting across from him. This was during the Days of Repentance, the ten days between Rosh Hashanah and Yom Kippur when the righteous Chassidim congregated at the Rebbe's *beis medrash* and spoke of the Day of Judgment that would soon be upon them. For on Yom Kippur the fate of even the lowliest worm is decided, as the decree of life or death is declared for all living things.

"Yoshke, sadness?"

Yoshke nodded in the direction of the elderly Yoshe Ber. He ran his hand through his beard and stammered like a child. "Yes, I am worried. Such an important day is upon us, Reb Yoshe Ber, and how unprepared I am! I am so covered with sin, so full of transgressions."

"So you'll atone," Reb Yoshe Ber interrupted. "As you know, repentance, prayer and charity avert evil decrees."

"But how can I pray?" Yoshke asked. "How can one stand before the Creator and ask for forgiveness when he is garbed in sin? Tell me, Reb Yoshe Ber, do we even have a concept of what prayer is? Can anyone claim to know how to pray to the Almighty?" Yoshke pressed his fingertips to his temple and shook his head in defeat.

"Listen to you," Reb Yoshe Ber said. "You sound like a misnagid. Is this how a Chassid talks? You worry about how to beseech the Creator. It doesn't matter how. What matters is that you pray with a full heart."

Yoshke put his hand over his chest. "I know that. My heart bursts with entreaty. But surely that is not enough."

"It *is* enough," replied Reb Yoshe Ber. "And, in fact, this brings to mind a story I heard from the old rebbe, may his memory be a blessing. A story, Yoshke, it would do you well to hear."

In a small town in Poland, a poor Jewish innkeeper, a widower, passed away, leaving behind a seven-year-old boy. A neighboring Christian couple who'd befriended the innkeeper brought the orphan into their own home and raised the boy with kindness and affection, watching over him as though he were their own son.

The years passed, and the couple eventually decided that the young orphan was old enough to learn the truth about his origins.

The boy was sitting on his bed when they entered his room holding a small package. "Your father was a Jew," they told him. "A fine, decent man, but poor. This bundle contains all of his earthly belongings. This is your inheritance."

As soon as he was alone, the boy opened the package and carefully emptied the contents onto the floor: there were just a few trinkets, including a pin, an old watch that no longer worked, and a prayer book. The boy picked up the siddur and sniffed the timeworn pages. He held the book upside down and opened it from the wrong side. The odd markings were indecipherable but vaguely familiar…he had, after all, studied some Hebrew as a small child. But the letters meant nothing to him now, and he put the book back in the box, along with the other items, placed the bundle on a high shelf, and went outside to play.

Several days later, the boy was kicking a ball with his friends when he noticed a wagon drive up to the inn. Inside was a group of Jewish men in black coats and black hats as well as several women, similarly dressed in black coats and kerchiefs. With a child's curiosity, he approached the visitors.

"Where are you going?"

Engaged in their own conversations, the travelers ignored him. The boy repeated his question.

"On a trip," one of the old Jews finally answered.

"Yes, but to where? And why are all of you dressed up in such fine clothing?"

Seeing the boy's interest was sincere, the man replied with matching seriousness, "Tomorrow is the Jewish New Year. We are going to Lizhensk to be with our rebbe, our teacher, and with Jews from all over the region, with whom we will pray for a good and blessed year." And with that, the wagon resumed its journey with a lurch.

The boy remained standing in the road, his heart beating quickly. I am one of them, he whispered to himself. I belong with them. I too should be praying for a good year. He stood motionless, watching the wagon grow smaller until it disappeared around the bend.

That evening the boy took the prayer book down from the shelf, blew away the dust, and wiped the dirt from its pages. Once more he tried to decipher the unfamiliar script. This was his language, he thought.

Several times over the coming days, he'd take the book down from the shelf and confront the letters, which remained impenetrable. He thought often of the Jews on their journey to see their rebbe and he ached to be with them.

A week later, as the young boy was sitting alone on the patch of grass in front of his home, lost in his thoughts, he looked up to see a wagon pulling up to the inn. Once again it was crowded with Jews dressed in their holiday best, among them the old man who'd answered the boy's queries.

Where were they headed this time, the boy asked.

"To the same place," the old Jew told him. "Tomorrow is Yom Kippur, the holiest day of the year. Tomorrow the fate of the world is decided, the destiny of every creature is sealed in the book of life … or death. Even the fish in the sea tremble on this sacred day. We are going to the city, to Lizhensk, to be with our brethren and our beloved rebbe to ask God for a blessed year."

"I am also a Jew!" the boy exclaimed. "Take me with you. Take me to Lizhensk. Let me pray with you."

The old man gently shook his head. "You are a child. You belong at home."

But the boy persisted. "Please, please, I must go with you."

The old Jew placed his hand on the boy's head, and saw tears welling in the child's eyes. "All right. But you will need your parents' permission first."

The child clapped his hands and gleefully ran to his house to ask if he could join the group of Jews on their holy day in Lizhensk. Unable to ignore the boy's sincerity, the couple acceded to the boy's request and hastily helped him prepare a sack of clothing and food for the trip.

The boy ran toward the wagon, but just as he was about to jump on, he called out, "Wait! Wait! Please wait for me. I've forgotten something I must take with me."

The boy dashed to his room and returned a moment later, clutching his father's siddur tightly in his hands.

He sat down in the corner of the wagon keeping a tight grip on the prayer book. His anxiety lessened, however, at the sight of the woman across from him holding the identical prayer book.

When the group finally arrived in Lizhensk, its first stop was the local shul. Overwhelmed with awe and wonder, the boy observed the sea of woolen prayer shawls, the men swaying like branches in a storm, their lips moving as if casting magical spells. Some clapped their hands as they prayed while others stood as still as soldiers. But all were somber, their expressions determined. Near the ark stood the rebbe, erect and barely moving, wrapped in a majestic, silver-edged prayer shawl that reached down to his ankles.

Taking a seat next to a withered, gray-haired man who repeatedly dabbed his eyes with a white handkerchief and exuded broken sighs, the boy heard the steady undertone of prayers coming from the women's section behind him and their moans caused him to tremble.

Feeling helpless and alone, he slowly opened his prayer book but could not stop the tears that ran down his cheeks and wet its pages. Unable to read a single line, he wished he could recite the holy words like the other boys in the room. He listened closely to the prayers of the people around him and to the chanting of the cantor, but the words vanished before he could repeat them. And what good is repeating other people's words?

The tears flowed freely now as the boy, his heart aching, picked up the prayer book and placed it on the table before him. He lifted his head, looked up toward the heavens, and cried out in Polish:

"Master of the Universe! I don't know how to pray to You. I don't know how to ask for Your blessing. My father left me this prayer book when he died, but I cannot read a word of it. But Almighty, You can. So, dear God, here is the prayer book. You choose the words. You form the prayers I am supposed to say."

After the service, the Tzaddik of Lizhensk addressed his Chassidim. His holy visage was even more radiant than usual.

"I want you all to know today was not easy. At first, our prayers did not find favor at the Holy Tribunal. Our petitions were refused. I trembled for our future. But then a young boy among us cried out with a prayer that came right from the depth of his heart. His anguished words were the most beautiful expressed anywhere on earth on this sacred day. The boy's cries reached to the very chamber of the Divine Throne. And on his account our pleas were accepted."

Yoshke, who'd sat with a wide stare and open mouth throughout Reb Yoshe Ber's telling of the tale, now sat back in his chair. A broad smile brightened his face.

"I'll be all right, then," he said. "I understand now. Each of us can only pray as best we can. And that is good enough."

Study Is Not Enough

When Chassidism was still in its infancy, the fledgling movement's critics, the misnagdim, were numerous and included many of the most respected rabbis of the era. Reb Zelig, the town rabbi of Zhitomir, was among these opponents. However, unlike others in the opposition, he rarely engaged in this dispute, not because he didn't think Chassidism deserved derision – he certainly believed it did – but because he had a more pressing use of his time, namely Torah study. For Reb Zelig, every minute not devoted to Torah learning was time squandered. And Reb Zelig squandered precious few minutes.

After the Ba'al Shem Tov passed away, the nascent movement he founded was administered by his student, Reb Dov Ber of Mezeritch. Reb Ber, too, had once been a vehement opponent of Chassidism. Like Reb Zelig, he took the exhortation to "immerse oneself in Torah day and night" with the utmost seriousness. But over time, he came to appreciate the Chassidic perspective in which devotion to Torah encompassed not only study, but also interactions with others. The simple tailor, the shoemaker, the grocer, the peddler – anyone who performs an honest day's work – is as immersed in Torah as the scholar who spends his day poring over a text.

Reb Ber hoped to convey this teaching to Reb Zelig, whose learning and piety he deeply respected, but never managed to do so. Reb Zelig made it clear to him that discussions about Chassidism were simply a waste of time…time more appropriately spent on study.

On one occasion, however, Reb Zelig had to be in Mezeritch and, as protocol directed, made a courtesy call to Mezeritch's great tzaddik, Reb Ber. He was met with a distinctly cold welcome. As a misnagid wary of Chassidic leaders, Reb Zelig was quick to express his displeasure.

"So tell me, Reb Ber," said Reb Zelig to his host. "Is this, then, the new way of Chassidism? To greet scholars with aloofness?"

"God forbid," replied Reb Ber. "But to explain my behavior, I'd like to tell you a story that will answer your question."

"A story? Thank you, but no thank you," Reb Zelig said, well aware of this Chassidic penchant for replacing reasoned argument with story-telling. "Keep your frivolous tales for your followers," he said, standing up to take his leave.

"Please," said Reb Ber, imploring his guest to have a seat. "I promise this will take but a few minutes. And I assure you, the story will be well worth your time."

Begrudgingly, Reb Zelig sat down and listened as Reb Ber began his tale.

Once, a rabbi who lived in a small shtetl had a visitor from a neighboring village. The visitor, brimming with joy, explained that his wife had just given birth to their first child, a son, and had come to ask the rabbi to serve as the *sandik*, the godfather, at the child's circumcision, to take place that Friday morning, two days hence. The rabbi was in the midst of deciphering a difficult Talmudic text and, without raising his eyes from the page, nodded his distracted consent.

When Friday morning arrived, a bitterly cold day, the villager appeared early at the rabbi's home with a coach to bring his distinguished guest to his son's bris. As usual, the rabbi was absorbed in his studies, and suggested the man find someone else to serve as godfather. The round-trip would simply take too much time.

"Please, I beg you," the man implored. He blanched at the thought of his humiliation should the rabbi not appear at the ceremony. "I've told everyone how honored I was that you, the renowned scholar of our province, had agreed to be my son's godfather. Please don't refuse me now."

The rabbi saw it would not be easy to dissuade this man. Moreover, he had, in fact, promised to attend the ceremony. And so, without much enthusiasm, he acceded. "I'll join you," he told the villager. "But you'll have to wait a few minutes until I complete my scheduled study. When I'm done, we'll go."

The appreciative man reminded the rabbi that this was a short Friday and Shabbos began early. He also noted the inclement conditions – a steady snow had begun to fall – and it would take several hours to travel back and forth. In addition, he'd promised his wife's sister who lived several miles away that he'd provide her with a coach ride to the bris.

The rabbi was no longer paying attention. He'd agreed to go, fine, but now he wished to attend to his studies. The villager waited for the rabbi – what choice did he have? Finally, the rabbi declared he was ready to leave, put on in his ceremonial finery and entered the coach. By then, a blizzard was raging. Overhanging branches, weighted down with snow, rendered the roads impassable. The horses, blinded by the snow, repeatedly stalled, too frightened to continue.

Several kilometers away, his wife's older sister, to whom a ride had been promised, was trudging to the bris by foot, determined to participate in the celebration. She tightened her shawl against the biting wind, hoping that her bother-in-law would at least provide a ride for her return trip home.

At last, the storm let up and the villager was able to steer his coach through the icy paths. The bris took place, several hours late, the parents proudly looking on as the rabbi served as *sandik*. But when it was over, the aunt was once more compelled to make her way along the treacherous roads. Her brother-in-law had committed to driving the esteemed rabbi back to his home, and could not spare the time to pick up another passenger. The woman knew she'd have to hurry if she were to make it back in time for Shabbos, which was rapidly approaching.

Despite the cold, sweat dripped down the face of the poor woman as she urged herself to walk as fast as she could. Exhausted, she finally arrived at her house, and collapsed on the bed. A blistering fever overcame her and she died three days later. The woman's three-month-old-daughter was now an orphan.

Alas, the tragedy was not yet done with, for when the younger sister, still recovering from her difficult childbirth, heard the news of her sister's death, she became inconsolably despondent and soon fell ill. After a short time, she, too, passed from the world, her infant son now an orphan as well.

Years passed. When the two motherless cousins reached the age of seventeen, they decided to marry. As is customary, the groom's father, who now lived in the town proper, invited the town rabbi to officiate at the wedding.

Well, as you might expect, the rabbi did not recognize the man, the former villager at whose son's bris he had once served as *sandik*, nor was he aware that infant was now the groom whose wedding he was now invited to perform.

The rabbi's behavior had not changed. As always, he was consumed by his books. And so, he informed his visitor that he was truly sorry, but he would not be able to perform the wedding ceremony – he simply couldn't afford the time.

The groom's father left the rabbi's home nursing a disappointment that soon turned to bitterness. Of course, he'd heard the rabbi say those same words years earlier. And it was because of the rabbi's devotion to study this young couple would walk to their wedding canopy as motherless children.

Reb Ber paused.

"A sad tale," said Reb Zelig.

"Indeed."

"And that's it? That's the story you wished to tell me?"

"Yes. But there's one more thing. Do you know who the town rabbi of this story was?"

Reb Zelig paled.

"It was me, wasn't it?" he whispered.

He started to stand up, but had to steady himself as the realization washed over him. From that day on, he never left the court of Reb Ber.

A Tale of Vengeance

Although Lublin could proudly attest to its many prestigious Torah scholars and religious leaders, it was also a city like others of its day, whose inhabitants struggled to make ends meet: laborers who worked with their shoulders, legs and hands, shopkeepers anxious to pay off their debts, mothers and fathers barely able to fund their children's education or marry off their daughters.

These commonplace concerns were not those of Zalman and Gershon. Not yet, in any case. The two young men, both recently married, were entrepreneurs. Each had established a small tailor shop and was focused on growing his business. Friends since childhood, Zalman and Gershon now competed with each other, along with all the other tailor shops in the vicinity. All their lives, they'd attended the same school, shared the same teachers, prayed in the same shul and played with the same classmates. Since their respective marriages, they had even chosen to live as neighbors.

During the long winter evenings, the two friends would meet in the *beis medrash*. Sitting across from each other in the study hall, they would work their way through a Mishnah, or push themselves to understand a difficult page of Talmud before, invariably, turning the discussion to the vagaries of their business: which fabrics were popular, which worth buying, which customers creditworthy and which not.

Now, even the best of friendships are sometimes challenged and, as many of us could attest, few challenges are as telling as those involving money; greed has a way of trumping loyalty.

In the case of Gershon and Zalman, the critical event, and the harsh changes that ensued, could be traced to a shared business decision. Given that they bought their textiles from the same outlets in the same cities, why not cut costs by pooling their purchase power? As partners, they could buy larger quantities for less than they could separately. Even transportation expenses would be reduced, as a wagon driver charged nearly the same for two passengers as for one, and the cost of room and board could be shared as well.

The idea made eminent sense, and the two friends decided to travel together to Warsaw.

For Zalman, this expedition posed little hardship. He'd married into a well-to-do family; his father-in-law was happy to put up the money for the trip and the purchase of goods. Gershon, on the other hand, had no such resources and was forced to borrow the required funds from friends and acquaintances. This took time, but, finally, he managed to obtain the necessary four hundred rubles.

Before they set off for Warsaw, Zalman and Gershon shook hands on a firm agreement: on this trip, neither would make any purchases nor develop any business arrangements without first alerting the other. This was a joint undertaking, and there'd be no independent side deals.

Still, business is business, and trust only goes so far. You wondered about the other – how could you not?

Zalman's suspicions were aroused when he awoke early one morning and saw that Gershon was missing. "Ah, so," he thought, "my dear Gershon is out doing a little wheeling and dealing on his own." Zalman dressed quickly. "Well, if that's way the way it is, then two can play the same game." He'd say his prayers, eat a quick breakfast and also pay a private visit to the marketplace.

Zalman began *davening*, pacing the floor as he recited his prayers, when he nearly tripped over something in the corner of the room. He bent down and found a small pouch. It belonged to his partner and in it were the entire four hundred rubles Gershon had brought with him. Zalman placed the pouch on the table. When his friend returned, he'd point to the pouch and offer a much-needed sermon about negligence and the importance of securing one's money with care.

The pouch rested on the table and Zalman's eyes rested on the pouch. Perhaps he ought to take the money. That would surely teach Gershon a lesson. Not to mention that the thought of four hundred extra rubles in his pocket was certainly enticing.

But Zalman's better angels restrained his impulse. How could he do such a thing to his friend, especially given how hard Gershon had struggled to get here? What was he thinking, anyhow? Would this not be sheer thievery?

The pouch remained on the table as Zalman continued to pace back and forth. And then, as though his body had reached its own conclusions, Zalman suddenly grabbed the pouch and put it in his jacket pocket. I'll return this money, and Gershon will learn a valuable lesson, he reassured himself. This was the right thing to do.

Minutes later, Gershon returned. Breathless, beads of sweat bathing his face, he ran over to Zalman.

"Did you by any chance come across my sack with the money I brought with me? I can't believe this, but it's gone! I've looked all over the place, even retraced my steps on the street." Zalman raised his hand to cover his mouth, indicating that he was in the midst of his prayers and could not speak. Instead, he shook his head from side to side.

"No? You haven't seen it? This was my last hope! I thought maybe I'd left the pouch here in the room." Gershon's face paled. "I must have dropped it somewhere. Maybe it fell out of my pocket. Or maybe it was stolen. Four hundred rubles. I'm ruined."

And with that, Gershon crumpled to the floor. Zalman hurried to resuscitate his friend. He'd return the money now. Enough was enough. But he could hear Gershon trying to tell him something as he returned to consciousness.

"This is a punishment, Zalman," Gershon whispered. "I'm sorry, dear friend, but I've been less than honest. I left early this morning to do a little business on my own. I didn't keep to our agreement. I deserve this."

Zalman stared at Gershon, his pity turning to anger. So my suspicions were right, he thought to himself. My beloved friend went out this morning to do some private, underhanded dealing, after all. So much for our mutual understanding. And what would Gershon have done had he found his, Zalman's, pouch with four hundred rubles? Would he have returned it?

Don't be stupid, Zalman told himself. Don't say anything. The world won't come to an end. Keep the money – at least for now. Later, you'll think about what do next.

And so, instead of returning the pouch, Zalman consoled his friend with false hopes. He'd find that pouch, not to worry. It was probably misplaced. If lost, someone was bound to find and return it. These words of encouragement might or might not have soothed Gershon, but they eased Zalman's conscience. Perhaps he would eventually produce the pouch, as he assured Gershon someone would.

Zalman helped his friend to his bed, said he'd be back soon, and walked out into the streets of Warsaw. Now was a good opportunity to do a little business of his own.

By the time the two young men returned to Lublin, Zalman had resolved to keep the four hundred rubles he'd stashed in his pocket. He buttressed his decision by recalling a few old transgressions that Gershon had committed against him over their long years of friendship. Yes, he thought, Gershon had it coming to him. It didn't hurt matters, either, that Zalman would now have to contend with one less competitor.

To the world, Zalman maintained his pose as a sympathetic friend, aggrieved by Gershon's financial calamity. When Gershon's creditors confronted Zalman and asked whether his traveling companion had, indeed, lost his money as he claimed, or if it was only a convenient tale concocted to forestall repaying his debt, Zalman presented his most earnest face and decried even the mere suggestion of subterfuge. Gershon was an upstanding, pious Jew, incapable of larceny.

"True," Zalman added with feigned discomfort, "Gershon did admit to me that on the day the money disappeared he was prepared to violate our agreement and purchase goods on his own clandestinely – but, surely, this does not prove that he is a thief."

Zalman was well aware that his restrained protestations only reinforced the seed of doubt in the minds of Gershon's creditors, a seed that grew into full-blown suspicion.

Gershon was determined to repay his debts until every ruble was accounted for. His only plea was that his lenders give him time to meet his obligations. Ignoring his appeals, they pressed Gershon to make good on his debt immediately. Without any other recourse, Gershon sold his small business and all its assets. But these profits were small and failed to put even in a dent in what he owed.

With a family to feed but no means with which to feed them, Gershon grew more indignant by the day, responding to his creditors' demands with fuming curses. The exchanges grew ugly, with Gershon berating their greed and lack of compassion. They, in turn, perceived Gershon's fervid reactions as further evidence of his instability; this was not the demeanor of an honorable businessman, but the behavior of a thief.

One day, a creditor whom Gershon had insulted one too many times took it upon himself to notify the local government offices of Gershon's eligibility for the military draft. As everyone knew, army service was a terrible sentence for a young Jewish man, who'd face long years of cruel hardship and anti-Jewish sentiment. The town's leaders, Zalman among them, tried to obtain Gershon's release, to no avail. Gershon would be conscripted for the full term of service. His wife would become destitute, his three small children raised as if orphans.

Gershon was by nature a delicate soul, and he suffered greatly in his new environment. The officers' gruff commands and cruel indifference, the constant brawling in the barracks, were too difficult for him to bear. Determined to keep kosher, many a day he'd simply go hungry. Night and day, Gershon worried for his wife and children, and despised those creditors who refused to show them even the most basic compassion. He nourished a particular desire for revenge against the creditor who had maliciously facilitated his conscription. But Gershon's most profound venom was reserved for Zalman, who had become extremely wealthy, and yet despite his newfound fortune, never offered to help repay his old friend's debts, or even come to his defense.

Physically exhausted and spiritually crushed, Gershon was surprised to discover that the new commander of his regiment was a decent man. The officer, for his part, had taken an interest in the young Jewish recruit and designated him as his personal attendant. This meant Gershon no longer spent his days and nights in the crude company of the other soldiers, nor was compelled to comply with the arbitrary dictates of army regulations. In the evenings, Gershon would sit with the regiment commander and enjoy discussions as equals. In the course of these conversations, Gershon shared his feelings of hatred toward the Jews of his village – the whole lot of them.

The commander was delighted by Gershon's rant against his community.

He was fundamentally a good man, with no anti-Semitic inclinations toward Jews as individuals; it was their religion he resented. A committed Catholic, the commander was convinced of the truth of his creed, and it was because of this desire to share his faith, and not because of any personal animus, that he eagerly befriended Jewish soldiers with the hope of converting them to the true religion. Now that he'd won Gershon's trust, the officer decided it was time to turn their discussions to matters of theology.

Gershon was no scholar. He was certainly not equipped to debate the finer points of religious belief. The Judaism he knew was the Judaism he learned in school, the rituals of his elders. And yet, when the officer first suggested that Gershon consider adopting the Christian faith, his response was immediate revulsion.

The regiment officer was both persistent and astute. He appealed to Gershon's weaknesses, to his feelings of betrayal at the hands of his fellow Jews. Did Gershon really feel obligated to maintain allegiance to a people that permitted such treacherous behavior against its own? The commander urged him to consider the opportunities – by converting to Christianity, doors would open to Gershon that would otherwise remain forever closed. In fact, were he to join the Catholic faith, the commander could guarantee that Gershon would soon be elevated to a high military rank.

With time, Gershon's initial reluctance faded. No longer living among Jews, his connection to the old rituals and beliefs grew weak, until at last, he yielded to the commander's entreaties.

But first, there were matters that required his attention. He could only cut his ties to the Jewish community with a clear conscience if his wife received the divorce to which she was entitled. Furthermore, Gershon insisted that the commander provide sufficient financial help to sustain his family. That taken care of, he was now prepared to use the gentile name he was given upon entering the army, destroying any and all connections to his previous life. He would even try to overcome his anger toward his creditors and erstwhile friend, Zalman.

The commander met all of Gershon's demands and kept his word: Gershon was promptly promoted to officer rank.

Gershon, at least at first, was not the typical Jewish apostate. For though he continued to harbor acrimony toward his former Jewish community, he didn't allow this ill will to bleed into a wider hatred. In fact, from time to time, he'd allow himself to drift into sweet memories of his childhood days in the Lubliner synagogue, recalling the pleasures of reading the legends of the Talmud or arguing his way through a Mishnah. Other times, he'd give himself over to reminiscences of holiday festivities. And sometimes, with a sigh and a quickening heartbeat, he'd think of his former wife and children.

But time runs its course. Images blur and evaporate. Gershon's reflections on his past grew increasingly sparse as present circumstances demanded his attention. He undertook the study of military affairs, and possessing a decent and determined mind, soon excelled in his endeavors. Gershon's abilities did not go unnoticed; his skills, along with the preferences extended to him as a result of his conversion, translated into a series of promotions in the military ranks. It was not long before Gershon was elevated to the post of regiment supervisor.

Gershon performed his work diligently and fairly. His interactions with Jewish recruits were similarly correct; he displayed neither favoritism, nor unwarranted animus.

One day, a Jewish soldier charged with a violation was brought to Gershon's office. Gershon interrogated the soldier, found him guilty as charged, and proclaimed a harsh punishment for his offense. But before he was taken away, Gershon ordered the soldier to empty his pockets and place all his belongings on the desk. The frightened soldier did as he was told and produced a small Jewish prayer book, two or three crinkled letters from his family, and an old, torn pouch containing a few rubles.

Gershon ignored the other articles as his eyes rested on the pouch, which he picked up and carefully examined, turning it inside and out. His hands began to shake. There was no doubt. This was definitely his pouch, the one he'd brought with him to Warsaw all those years ago, the one whose disappearance sparked the cruel sequence of events that led him to this room, where he now sat as a military officer and a Christian.

Gershon glared at the soldier and the terrified young man looked back, utterly bewildered by the intensity of the officer's stare.

"Where did you get this pouch?" Gershon demanded.

The soldier shrugged. What was this about?

Gershon repeated the demand.

"Years ago, I was a waiter in a Jewish restaurant in Warsaw," the soldier stammered. "On one occasion a merchant from Lublin dined there and when he prepared to leave, he said he'd like to leave me a tip for my services, but he was not carrying any change. Instead, he'd leave me this empty pouch."

"Sit down," Gershon ordered the soldier. "Tell me more. I want to hear exactly when this incident occurred. How many years ago? What time of the year? Describe this person. Tall? Short? Young? Old? Tell me all you can."

The soldier summoned his memory as best he could. He was able to recall the day he'd received the pouch because he remembered being fired exactly one week later. Closing his eyes, he conjured the features of the man who'd left him this strange gift.

Zalman, my dear friend Zalman, Gershon whispered to himself. He'd never suspected him before. All these years he'd imagined he'd lost the pouch and its contents, or, perhaps, that a pickpocket had relieved him of it, but, never that it had been stolen by his best friend. How had he failed to see it?

A bitter rage raced through his heart. The desire for retribution overwhelmed his very being. Gershon dismissed the soldier with only a warning. He now had other matters to attend to.

As the days passed, Gershon could think of little else but Lublin. He became obsessed with images of Zalman relishing a life of ease, his wealth propelled in no small measure by his own four hundred rubles. He pictured Zalman honored with a seat against the eastern wall of the synagogue with the other esteemed pillars of the community, Gershon's merciless creditors paying Zalman their obeisance.

Gershon requested a new post as the chief inspector of the city of Lublin, a position that would provide him with the administrative power to investigate, threaten and punish anyone he wished. His superiors were happy to accommodate his request. After all, Gershon had become a man of influence. He had friends in the right places and enjoyed an excellent military record. Moreover, he was a courageous convert from Judaism.

It was the week of Chanukah. The winter had been brutal, but the day Gershon was scheduled to return to Lublin was especially harsh. Snow from the previous night's blizzard lay thick on the frozen road. But Gershon would not be deterred. He paid no attention to the weather – his only thoughts were of Zalman. He could almost taste the vindication on his tongue.

But Gershon was not the only one traveling the icy roads that afternoon.

Yehuda Aryeh – the Shpoler Zeideh, as he was known to all – was also on the road that afternoon. The Shpoler Zeideh was a celebrated Chassidic master, renowned for his readiness to travel anywhere to rescue a Jew in distress.

Deep in the forest, a few kilometers outside the city, the holy rebbe asked his driver to stop the wagon for a while so he could recite the afternoon prayers. Through the cloud of breath in the glacial air, one could see the radiant glow on the Shpoler Zeideh's face as he prayed. The rebbe's assistant had to interrupt to remind him that it was Chanukah, and they ought to hurry along if they were to reach the city in time to light the menorah.

From the depths of his thoughts, the Shpoler Zeideh said to his assistant, "Yes, of course, it is nearly time to perform the great mitzvah of lighting the Chanukah lamp. And so we shall. Let us take out the Chanukah lamp and prepare it for our blessing."

"Here? On this road in the woods?"

"Yes, right here."

The rebbe stood quietly near the menorah, his head tilted slightly, as if listening to a faraway sound. A few moments later, his assistant, too, heard something in the distance: the unmistakable click-clack of a wagon. The Shpoler Zeideh nodded his head and asked the assistant to retrieve a burning twig, with which he would kindle the menorah's wick.

His voice resonant in the cold night, the rebbe began to recite the Chanukah prayers. As he reached the words, "As the miracles were performed in the days of our fathers, so shall they be in our own days," a carriage traveling along the road came to a stop.

As the Shpoler Zeideh turned toward the carriage, his eyes met those of the man inside. They stared at each other for several moments, transfixed.

Gershon sensed he could read the message in the rebbe's gaze: a plea for mercy. As he sat looking at the rebbe and the menorah's flickering flame at the rebbe's side, Gershon felt as if he were awakening from a long sleep. Recollections rushed toward him, memories of his own Chanukah celebrations – his children's delight as they gathered around the glowing lights, eagerly awaiting their holiday gifts.

As if in a trance, Gershon stepped down from his carriage and walked toward the Shpoler Zeideh.

"Tonight is Chanukah?"

"Yes, it is," the rebbe said. "And do you know what this festival is about?"

Gershon drew closer, saying nothing.

"It is the celebration of renewal. It is so easy to allow oneself to remain in one place. We all need a holiday in our lives devoted to fresh starts, a time to remind ourselves of the dangers of stagnation. Chanukah is the holiday of reinvigoration."

Gershon signaled with his hands that he expected the rebbe to say more, to say what he knew he was supposed to hear.

"Listen to me," the rebbe said. "Vindictiveness is an ugly trait. Revenge hurts the avenger, not only the avenged. I assure you, the pleasure of payback is short-lived and ultimately demeaning. There is, on the other hand, profound solace in forgiveness. The words we recite in the Chanukah prayer, 'As the miracles were performed in the days of our fathers, so shall they be in our own days,' exhort us not to harp on the past, but to turn to the present."

Gershon pursed his lips. "I was on my way to take revenge on the Jews of Lublin," he confessed. He told the rebbe the events of the past years, his loss of faith and apostasy. "Will the rebbe help me?"

The two men continued their journey together to the city of Lublin. When they arrived, the rebbe immediately called Zalman to his quarters, where Gershon was waiting. The former friends sat across from one another as the rebbe spoke.

"I have reached a judgment on how to proceed. Zalman, in recompense for what you have done, you are to give half your assets to Gershon."

Zalman acceded to the ruling without protest. As for Gershon, he remarried his former wife and lived out the rest of his days among the Jews of Lublin.

The Besht Discovers How to Celebrate the Sabbath

The Ba'al Shem Tov taught that joy is the most important aspect of genuine service to God; that sadness and fear are inimical to the fullness of the soul. The Besht even suggested that gloom is a form of idolatry, a deeply misconstrued understanding of how to engage with the divine. For this reason, Chassidim have always vehemently eschewed asceticism of any kind – even when undertaken for the sake of heaven. To be sure, one must fear the Lord, but at the same time, one must distinguish between terror and awe.

Yet this was not always the Ba'al Shem Tov's perspective. When the Ba'al Shem Tov was a young man, he worried that he was unable to observe the Sabbath with the requisite elation. How could he enjoy the day of rest when he was constantly aware of the possibility that he might transgress one of the many complex strictures of its observance? He knew how terrible it would be to violate the laws of the Shabbos, and this dilemma posed a wrenching discomfort.

Then one night the Besht had a strange dream. An angel appeared, lifted him onto its wing and brought him to the afterworld paradise of Gan Eden. There, the Besht saw two empty chairs adorned with diamonds, pearls and exquisite gems, seamed with golden threads.

"For whom are these seats prepared?" the Besht asked the angel.

"One awaits you," the angel explained "that is, if you attain genuine understanding and wisdom. The other is for a certain individual, someone you don't know."

The Besht's curiosity was piqued. Who deserved such splendor in the World to Come? And why? The angel then led the Besht out of Gan Eden and transported him down to the depths of Gehenna, where he was shown two other empty chairs, each surrounded by snakes and scorpions.

"And for whom are these seats prepared?" he asked.

"One is prepared for you ... if you do not attain genuine wisdom and understanding."

"And the other?"

"That awaits a certain individual you do not know."

The following night, the Besht had another dream, in which he met for the first time the person for whom the chair in Gan Eden was intended: an extremely wealthy but ignorant Jew who knew little Torah and was known for his boorish behavior.

The Besht was perplexed. "If I attain my seat in the afterlife, why would this man, of all men, be sitting in the neighboring chair?"

There must be more to him, the Besht concluded. So to find out what that was, he decided to spend the next Shabbos observing the man's behavior.

And what he saw astounded him. As soon as the sun set Friday evening, this man was transformed, a rapturous glee animating his every step. The Besht watched as the man finished the evening prayers and hurried home to his Shabbos table, filled with bountiful food and drink and surrounded by numerous guests, who continued to arrive throughout the evening. "Welcome and a good Shabbos to you all," the host announced. "On Shabbos we must indulge in pleasure. And so we shall."

When the sumptuous meal was nearly over, the host again called out. "Joy without song? That cannot be." And he invited all at his table to join as he sang the repertoire of traditional Shabbos melodies. And when those were sung, the host and his guests turned to tunes of all sorts, in languages other than the Holy Tongue. They sang and clapped and laughed long into the night.

"Why do you have such feasts?" the Besht asked the man.

"This is the way my father observed Shabbos," the man replied. "And so I do likewise."

The Besht was about to admonish the man for the liberties he was taking, such as singing unholy songs in a foreign language…at the Shabbos table, no less. But when he opened his mouth to castigate the man for his laxity, the power of speech escaped him. He was unable to express any words of condemnation.

He turned from the man and began backing away when he realized the reason he could not speak: had his reproach been accepted, the man would henceforth conduct his Shabbos differently. With a new fastidiousness about the laws, a solemnity would descend on his table and the joy would dissolve. The Besht continued to dream. He was now introduced to the man for whom a seat was reserved in Gehenna…his neighbor should he, the Besht, fail to achieve true understanding.

To his surprise, the man was sitting at his desk, tefillin on his forehead, absorbed in the study of Torah. The Besht observed him the entire day and noted that the man did not eat at all, but continued to pray and study the holy texts. Why would someone like this be condemned to the netherworld?

There must be more to him, the Besht concluded once again. So he decided to spend the next Shabbos observing the man's behavior.

As the sun set that Friday night, a look of consternation set over the man's face. He was irritable and muttering under his breath as he made his way to the synagogue for the evening services. Because he prayed slowly, careful to pronounce all the words and articulate every sentence of the liturgy, by the time he returned home, the Shabbos candles were long extinguished. Even as he dutifully sang the *Sholem Aleichem* melody welcoming the angels into his home and recited the Kiddush, he was distracted by fears of spilling the wine or inadvertently committing another infraction of the myriad Shabbos laws. He sat, hardly moving, throughout the meal and demanded the same of his family, lest someone accidently touch an object forbidden on the Shabbos. Hardly a word was spoken throughout the meal for how else could one be certain not to utter an unholy word, God forbid, on the day of rest? The entire dinner felt more like the cheerlessness of the meal before the Fast of Tisha B'Av than a festive Shabbos repast.

The Besht was about to admonish the man for his doleful sternness. We are commanded to delight in the Shabbos, he wanted to say, and this obsession with not violating the Shabbos was, in fact, a violation of this commandment. But as he was set to deliver this reprimand, the power of speech was taken from him. Again, he could say nothing.

And again, he quickly realized why: His reproof would be ignored. For this was a man driven by the scintilla of the law, someone who was unable to understand that his behavior distracted from actually fulfilling the law.

The Besht awoke, his dreams still vivid in his mind. The solution to his own Shabbos dilemma was resolved. It was now clear to him: constant worrying about transgressing the Shabbos is itself a transgression. He realized, as well, this principle of joy must accompany the performance of all mitzvot, and this became the central message of Chassidism, the lesson he would teach the rest of his life.

The Fifth Question

Hertske lived a life rich in both spirit and worldly success. Even as a young yeshiva student, he was sought after as a "great catch" by upstanding, wealthy men seeking promising scholars for their daughters. For not only did Hertske excel in his Torah studies, the young man also had a practical head on his shoulders – a rare commodity in the rarified world of the seminary.

Hertske married and did not disappoint. The sharp analytical skills with which he navigated difficult Talmudic passages he now applied to complex business deals; within a few short years, he'd expanded his father-in-law's respectable furniture concern into a major timber enterprise. Hertske was no less strict in fulfilling God's commandments: no financial emergency kept him from his daily Torah sessions with his study partner and no winter storm prevented him from attending communal morning prayers. He supported a dozen good causes and his generosity was celebrated throughout the town.

Hertske was also a Chassid. Not your typical Chassid, he'd acknowledge, for he balanced an appreciation of the mystical with a firm commitment to reason. In his younger years, he'd scorned the very notion of a "rational Chassid" as a blatant oxymoron; if the town of Zlotchov was a bastion of anti-Chassidism, and it was, and its yeshiva the citadel of this opposition, and it was that, too, then Hertske was the most fervent spokesman for the anti-Chassidic cause. With youthful ferocity, he lambasted the budding movement as muddled Kabbalists who willfully transgressed hallowed traditions. And their leaders, the rebbes? "A bunch of ignoramuses, charlatans who prey on the superstitious masses and can no better interpret a page of Talmud than a page of Turkish."

Then, one Shabbos morning, Hertske decided to visit the small Chassidic *shteible* of Reb Mikhel of Zlotchov, determined to witness first-hand the inanities these Chassidic rabbis passed off as wisdom. Hertske stood in the rear of the shul, his arms folded against his chest, and listened intently as Reb Mikhel addressed his Chassidim at the end of the service. The rebbe belonged to the elite band of students of the Maggid of Mezeritch, the distinguished disciple of the great Ba'al Shem Tov. On this particular morning, Reb Mikhel did not expound upon esoteric Kabbalistic mysticism but on Talmudic law. Hertske was dazzled by the rebbe's erudition, and so began his conversion from ardent misnagid to ardent Chassid.

Yes, Hertske seemed to have it all: affluence, intellectual rigor, spiritual sustenance and the respect of his community. He also had a wife, Pesel, whom he adored and who adored him in return. There was, however, one painful gap in Hertske's otherwise complete life: he and his wife were childless.

For years, Hertske and Pesel had visited fertility doctors across the region, traveling as far as Vienna and Berlin, but after too many dashed hopes, Hertske had come to terms with reality. It was God's will that he have no progeny. Well, he decided, if he could not raise children of his own, he'd help raise the children of others. With his considerable resources, Hertske established schools for impoverished students, and provided for their medical care. He cared for orphans when they were young, and when they grew up, paid all their wedding expenses.

Of course, surrogate children could not fill the void of a childless household, but Hertske had come to accept the divine judgment. Alas, such equanimity was not possible for Pesel. Her days were exercises in distraction, her nights torments of desperation. The festivals were worst of all.

"It's the bitterness itself I've come to detest," Pesel said to Hertske one night, not bothering to hide her tears. "I hate the way the holidays make me feel, but what I hate even more is that I feel as I do."

How often had she beseeched the rebbe to intercede, to plead for them, to do something for heaven's sake, only to hear the rebbe repeat that God will act in His own good time.

Several weeks before the holiday of Passover, Pesel paid yet another visit to the rebbe, again asking for his blessing.

"Why is it always me who asks for this blessing?" she demanded of Hertske when she returned home. "Never you. Of course not. You won't deign to ask for an exception from the normal course of biology. Nature is nature, right?"

"Pesel, we've discussed this a hundred times," Hertske said. "You know the esteem in which I hold Reb Mikhel. He has taught me a great deal of Torah. He's also advised me on communal and business affairs. But full devotion to the rebbe does not mean treachery to reason. No human being, not even a holy tzaddik like Reb Mikhel, can revoke the laws of nature. Let's face what we must: We cannot have children. So be it."

"So be it?" Pesel shouted. "So be it? Do you have any idea what it is like for me in shul?"

"I can imagine," Hertske said softly.

"No. You can't. Through a slit in the lace that separates the women's section from the men's, I see you lost in your prayers or arguing over a page of Talmud with your admiring friends. I don't begrudge you. I'm proud of you. But it's not like that on my side of the curtain. For me, every Shabbos, every holiday, is a day of mourning."

Pesel turned away from her husband and took a few breaths before facing him again.

"I hear a baby cry in its carriage and I want to cry too because I have no child to console. My sister rushes to tell me her little Yonason has just mastered the entire *aleph beis* and I'm astonished at how a heart can burst with so much pride and despair at the same time. The children next to me sing their prayers and I accompany them with my broken sighs. I try to concentrate on the cantor's chanting, but all I hear is the murmur of young mothers discussing diapers, baby carriages, baby shoes, schools, doctors, story books, nursing tips, who is pregnant and who is not, and I want to flee from the room. Sometimes I do."

"Pesel," Hertske said, reaching for his wife's hand. "We have so many blessings. Think of all the bickering between husbands and wives, a wretchedness we have never known. For your own sake, you must come to terms with the destiny ordained for us. This is the only way we can truly celebrate this coming Pesach."

Indeed, Passover had always been the exception to the gloom that enveloped Pesel's days. On this night, their home bustled with family, friends and needy strangers, all joyously participating in the lavish Seder. Pesel directed the presentation of the elaborate dishes, while Hertske, robed in his spotless white kittel, sat in regal splendor at the head of a long linen-covered table set with opulent china and glittering silver goblets. The Seder was filled with the spirited reading of the Haggadah, and even more spirited singing that lasted into the wee hours of the morning.

But the wheel of fortune spins to its own inscrutable rhythm and those who have become those who have not. During the previous year, the market for Hertske's timber had abruptly dried up. He was over-leveraged, and the creditors came knocking. The banks foreclosed on his properties. In less than six months, Hertske was bankrupt. Nevertheless, he stoically endured his deepening destitution, for this was God's will and he would accept whatever fate bequeathed.

When the Seder night arrived. Hertske helped set the table, as he always had. But this year there were no gleaming goblets, no fine china, and no fancy dishes. Gone, too, were the holiday guests. Still, a Seder is still a Seder, Hertske reminded himself. He was determined to create as festive a mood as he could. He prepared the pillows for his chair, arranged the matzos and vegetables on the Seder plate, and took out his well-worn Haggadah.

He poured the first glass of wine and recited the Kiddush with Chassidic fervor. Lifting the matzah, he read aloud the passage describing the bread of affliction and prepared the second of the four mandated cups of wine. Here the Haggadah instructs the son to ask his father the *ma'neshtana*, the Four Questions. Hertske hesitated. He bit his bottom lip and looked over at Pesel, who'd been observing him. Each saw the tears in the other's eyes. Hertske tried again: "And now the son asks…" But instead, he collapsed in his chair.

"I can't go on," he sighed, rocking slowly in his seat.

Pesel had never seen him weep before.

"Father in heaven," he cried out. "I'm sorry, but I can't continue with the Seder because I, Your son, have a fifth question for You. My poverty notwithstanding, I have done everything You have required for the Seder. I've cleaned the house of bread, prepared the matzos and the bitter herbs. I've set as beautiful a table as possible with the few coins at my disposal. But I cannot perform the part of the Seder that calls for the child to ask the Four Questions. Why won't You allow me to fulfill Your commandment? Master of the Universe, where is the child I need to complete my Seder?"

Pesel watched in astonishment as Hertske closed the Haggadah and put on his coat.

"To the rebbe," he said, answering her unspoken question. "I'll ask him my fifth question."

Outside, a steady drizzle had begun to fall. The Jewish quarter of Zlotchov was eerily quiet. The storefronts had been shuttered since early afternoon and the sidewalks were deserted but for the occasional young couple shuttling between their respective families, having promised, no doubt, to reverse the order of their visits the following night. The only voices one heard wafted from the dining rooms above the streets, where some children were reading the story of the redemption from slavery in Egypt, while other families were already enjoying the holiday meal.

Hertske walked for twenty minutes and had almost reached the rebbe's home when the rain, heavy now, forced him to take refuge under the nearest canopy. In an apartment directly above, an old man was reciting the passage describing the four sons and their respective responses to the Passover rituals: the wise son who inquires about the particulars of the ceremony, the wayward son who separates himself from the community, the simpleton who is confused by it all and the fourth son, so dull he is unable even to formulate a question.

This dumbstruck son – that's me, he said to himself, his tears merging with the streaks of rain. All these years, I didn't know how to question. Well, now I will not only ask, I will demand. He fastened the top button of his coat, pulled his hat down tightly and marched into the sodden streets.

The Zlotchover Rebbe showed no surprise at seeing Hertske standing in his foyer. He placed his hand on Hertske's wet shoulder and ushered him into the dining room, where the rebbe's family and guests were seated at the Seder table.

"I have a fifth question to ask—" Hertske started to say, but the rebbe held up his hand.

"Yes, I know," the tzaddik said. "As a matter of fact, your question already made an impact in heaven."

"I don't understand," Hertske said.

"Listen carefully," said the rebbe.

His hand still on Hertske's shoulder, the rebbe continued with a nod to his guests. "There's a lesson here for all of us.

"The great misfortune of your life, my dearest Hertske, is that you have no child. You confronted this adversity without complaint, as God's decree. Admirably so. We must accept our circumstances as they are, pleasant or not. But you have confused acceptance with acquiescence. You ceased to hope. Along the way, you submitted to your lot as though it were immutable."

Hertske looked toward his rebbe.

"It's a conceit to think we know the ways of the world," Reb Mikhel said. "To live life not expecting the unexpected. This surrender to fate is a rejection of faith."

Hertske bowed his head.

"And so this was your punishment: you weren't granted the child you didn't ask for. Your refusal to petition God, your ceasing to hope, led to the loss of your wealth. But tonight … ah, tonight at your Seder, at last, you asked the fifth question. And my dear precious Hertske, tonight your question has been answered."

The Rebbe's Insight

The Rebbe can only raise the ladder; the
Chassidim must do the climbing on their own.
REB MORDECAI YOSEF OF ISHBITZ

Khuna's Messiah

Self-deception is the nastiest of illnesses, warns an old Yiddish aphorism. Pity those who, without warrant, convince themselves they are extraordinarily wise or handsome or good – or the familiar hypochondriacs who continually insist they suffer from a lethal ailment. But the disease of self-deception also afflicts those who are overcome by an obsession, a bizarre belief not about themselves, but about the world. Those who are, as they say, in the throes of a *mishagas*.

Someone like Khuna.

In most ways, Khuna was no different from the other Jews who lived in the town of Kalshin. An honest merchant, solid family man, and dutifully religious Jew, Khuna struggled all day to earn a living, and spent his evenings at the synagogue, immersed in prayer and Torah study. It was in this last matter, the study habit, that Khuna distinguished himself from those around him. Ordinarily, a Chassid's regimen was focused on Torah learning, beginning with passages of Scriptures, then perusing a page of Talmud, and perhaps, if he was so inclined, dabbling in a work of Kabbalah. But Khuna ignored the standard texts – the Five Books of Moses, the Mishnah and its commentaries. Khuna was interested only in the Zohar, the esteemed, classical work of Jewish mysticism.

Alas, Khuna was no scholar, lacking both the depth and breadth of knowledge that are prerequisites for understanding this notoriously confounding text. The Zohar's profound metaphysical ideas, subtle analysis of language, and complex theosophical discussions of the *sfirot*, the divine emanations that permeate creation, were simply beyond Khuna's grasp. Despite hours spent bent over in study, Khuna's understanding of Jewish mysticism remained limited to the folk traditions of Kabbalistic lore – the existence of the *lamed vovniks*, the thirty-six people whose concealed righteousness supports the world, that the letters of Torah have the power to both create and destroy, and that the divine spark dwells even in the simplest of people. Khuna was particularly enthralled by the popular teaching that the messiah and his forerunner, Elijah, could appear at any time, in any guise: as a pious tzaddik, but also as an ignorant Jew – or, for that matter, even as a non-Jew.

Perhaps in response to the stress of mounting business pressures, Khuna took to spending more and more time at the synagogue, concentrating ever harder on his study of the Zohar, losing himself in a maze of esoteric ruminations he could not understand. Soon he began having mystical intuitions of his own. He dismissed them for the most part, until one night, an astonishing notion crystallized in his mind. In the midst of a deep sleep, he suddenly sat up in bed, possessed by the distinct knowledge that the province's military commander was actually Elijah. And the messiah was none other than the Starosta, the region's elder administrator.

Other than this singular eccentricity, Khuna conducted himself normally; if you had an ordinary conversation with the man, you'd never guess the secret he was carrying. But should the discussion turn, as it sometimes did, to the hope for the coming of the messiah, Khuna's eyes would glisten and he would put his finger to his mouth and drop his voice to a conspiratorial whisper.

"I have something startling to tell you," he'd begin. "You think the general and the Starosta are who they appear to be – gentile government officials. Well, they aren't. In fact, the general is Elijah, the forerunner of the messiah who, in turn, poses as the Starosta."

Khuna would then reveal the "proofs" of his discovery, reading various meanings into the words or actions of said officials.

"Yes, they seem ordinary," he'd tell his audience. "But don't you see these are really signals? Soon, very soon, their true missions will become clear to all."

For the townsfolk, Khuna and his fantasy became a source of endless mockery. But for Khuna's wife, these bouts of insanity were hardly amusing. She was stung by the smirks and ridicule, but even more by her husband's flight from reason. She pleaded with him to be done with this absurd notion of his, or, at the very least, to cease mentioning it to others. But Khuna would not be persuaded.

"I know people think I'm crazy," he told his wife after a particularly tearful entreaty. "But let me assure you that I'm the normal one here. You'll see. Soon enough I'll be vindicated."

Khuna's wife, frantic for help, sought out the best medical experts she could find; her adamant husband, as you'd expect, declined to accompany her on these consultations. It was just as well. These visits proved futile in any case; the doctors merely shrugged and admitted that solving mental aberrations of this kind was beyond their capabilities.

The desperate woman decided to call on the great Chassidic leader, Reb Simcha Bunim of Peshischa. Although her husband maintained that he did not require help of any kind, a visit to the great rebbe was not something he could refuse.

Khuna's wife had arranged to speak to the rebbe first in private. Dabbing her eyes with a handkerchief, she told the rebbe of her husband's idea about the messiah and the damage this was wreaking on his reputation.

"No one has any idea how to cure him of this delusion," she told the rebbe. "Please help restore him to his senses."

When it was Khuna's turn to speak with the rebbe, Reb Simcha Bunim greeted him warmly, engaging him in friendly conversation. Only after he was sure his visitor was at ease, did the rebbe steer the discussion to the sorry state of the human condition.

"Ah, such troubles," said the rebbe with a prolonged sigh. "When will we be worthy, finally, to experience the coming of the messiah?"

As if on cue, Khuna raised his hand to his mouth, his eyes assuming the wild, glazed look that mention of the messiah always provoked.

"Rebbe," Khuna said in a hushed voice, "we've already proved worthy. Yes, yes. Elijah and the messiah have already arrived."

"Really? They've arrived? And you know who they are?" the rebbe exclaimed, feigning surprise.

"Yes, I do," Khuna said. "Perhaps through my study of Kabbalah, I've been able to make this discovery. Elijah is the military commander of our region and the messiah poses as the Starosta."

The rebbe looked directly at Khuna, meeting his eyes. "Reb Khuna, since you seem to know so much, tell me who I am."

The question bewildered Khuna. "I don't understand," he stammered. "Who are you? You are of course Reb Simcha Bunim of Peshischa, the holy tzaddik of our generation."

"Well, then, Reb Khuna," said the rebbe, his eyes still fixed on Khuna's, "if I am, as you say, the tzaddik of our generation, do you not suppose that I, too, know the secret identities of the commander and the Starosta?"

Khuna nodded his head slowly, arriving at the inevitable realization. If he, a simple Jew, had discovered the confidential identities of Elijah and the messiah, then surely the great Rebbe of Peshischa must be privy to this information as well.

"I'm sure the rebbe knows who these men really are," he admitted.

"Precisely," said the rebbe. "But listen carefully. Why you have been granted this clandestine information, I cannot say. What I do know is that it is too early to unveil the true missions of these men. And you, too, Khuna, must keep this a secret. This must remain between us alone. Do you understand?"

"I do," Khuna said gravely. "Until the time is appropriate, I will not disclose what only we know." A smile crossed his face. "This is a secret known only to the Rebbe of Peshischa... and me."

Khuna kept his word. When his acquaintances tried to goad him into commenting on the doings of Elijah and the messiah, or on whether the commander or Starosta had provided any new hints of their covert identities, Khuna refused to be provoked.

"Enough with this nonsense," he'd say and move on to another subject.

As time passed, the townspeople stopped bothering to engage Khuna on the subject. He'd recovered from his obsession, they concluded, and happily welcomed him back into the community. For his part, Khuna gave no reason for them to assume otherwise, all the while relishing his self-control in keeping his momentous discovery all to himself.

Lie After Lie

The Apter Rebbe, Reb Avraham Yehoshua Heschel, was considered in his day to be The Rebbe's Rebbe. Ordinary townspeople flocked to him by the thousands, but so, too, did the great Chassidic masters, eager to hear him expound on Chassidus and Torah. They came, too, to hear his stories, tales that often seemed incredible, sheer outlandish exaggerations. Most Chassidism did not know what to make of these tales, but the Chassidic leaders could discern their deeper meanings; the most astute among them declared that no one ever spoke words as measured and precise as the Apter.

When his Chassidim pushed their way to be closer to the rebbe, jostling for a better vantage point, the Apter remarked that proximity didn't matter – those who understand will understand from afar and those who don't understand won't understand any better nearby. Everyone comprehends as best he can, he added. Indeed, when sinners came to confess their sins to the rebbe, he was known to offer encouraging but allusive words of repentance. Those who were serious about atonement would get the message.

One day, a woman came to the Apter with an odd question. She'd put starch in her dress after Purim and now wondered if she could wear the dress during Pesach. Starch products, particularly if made from wheat, are prohibited to eat on Pesach, but could one wear them? The woman seemed very concerned.

The Apter Rebbe studied her for a moment, then furrowed his brows. "Don't you have something else to ask me?"

The woman shook her head slowly, not apprehending the rebbe's meaning.

"No?" said the rebbe. "If you don't understand why I am asking you this, let me tell you a story."

There was once a Jew who ran a popular tavern. He was generous in giving credit to the locals who'd come to drink and even lent them money when they needed it. He'd also offer them his sought-after advice and listened discreetly when they told him their secrets.

One evening, an inebriated peasant approached the tavernkeeper. He was weeping. Grabbing the tavernkeeper's arm, he said, "*Zhid*, my dear Jew, you should know I am a sinner. A nothing. Not worth the earth I stand on."

"What did you do that was so terrible?" asked the tavernkeeper.

"I'm a thief. I stole a rope."

"A rope? This isn't all that terrible, is it? You can make amends. Return the rope, and I'm sure you'll be forgiven."

"Ah, but the problem is, I don't know from whom I stole it."

"Well, that's not the end of the world. Sell the rope and give the money to charity. That'll count as recompense."

"Yes, but it's not that simple, my dear *Zhid*," said the peasant with a sigh. "Tethered to the end of the rope were two oxen. When I stole that rope, I seized them as well."

"Look," the tavernkeeper said, "you can atone by giving charity. Sell the oxen and donate the money to a good cause."

"Too late. I long ago slaughtered the oxen and ate the meat."

"Well then," said the tavernkeeper. "Estimate the value of the oxen and give that amount to charity."

The peasant helped himself to another shot of vodka. "I'm afraid it's a bit more complicated. Those oxen happened to be attached to a wagon. So I pulled the wagon with me as well."

"You stole the wagon?"

"I did."

"And what did you do with it?"

"I broke it, chopped it up, and used it as firewood for my stove."

The peasant began to weep again. The tavernkeeper gently shook the man's shoulder.

"Listen to me. This is certainly not a good thing you did – stealing rope, oxen, and a wagon. But there is a God above who accepts genuine regret. What you have to do now is figure out the worth of all you took and give that money to the needy. Your regret will be genuine, compensated…and your sins forgiven."

The peasant said nothing for a few moments. Tears trickled down his face as he took another swallow. "Alas, alas. I do want to repent for my sin. Honestly. But it is not merely a matter of money involved here. You see, *Zhid*, when I stole the wagon, there was someone in it."

"Who?"

"A young child."

"A child!" exclaimed the tavernkeeper. "You kidnapped a child!" A shiver coursed through his body.

"And what became of the child?"

"Murdered."

"You—"

"I thought he'd start screaming, so I killed him."

The tavernkeeper stepped back. "A murderer! You killed an innocent child, and then tell me you want to repent for stealing a rope!"

As the Apter related this story, the woman listened, baffled. She'd come with an inquiry about wearing a freshly starched dress on Passover and the rebbe had answered with a tale about a killing. But by the time the rebbe finished his account, the woman was quaking. And then she let out a scream.

"It is true, it is true. Yes, rebbe, I killed a child! I had an illegitimate baby and was terrified of what people would say. How would I explain it?

"Oh my God, Rebbe," the woman wailed, "I am a murderer. Help me, please help me."

Thou Shalt Not Steal

The command "Thou shalt not steal" also means thou shalt not steal from thyself.

REBBE OF KOTZK

I have heard a dozen clever explanations of "Thou shalt not steal." But let me remind you, it also means "Don't steal."

REB NAFTULI OF RUPSZITZ

Yossele's wife watched as her husband gathered his needles, thread, hand mirrors and other sundries, and placed them in his rucksack. Today, he would again spend the day far away from their home in Leipnik, trudging from hamlet to hamlet, offering his meager goods for meager pennies.

Please, God, she thought, let them not sic their vicious dogs on him again. Today, please, let those young ruffians not hurl rocks at Yossele as he walks by. However horrible their poverty, her husband's daily humiliations were worse. If only there were easier ways to earn a crust of bread.

Yossele noticed the concern on his wife's face, a familiar worry that would not lift until he returned home later that evening.

"Dvoyrah, we must have faith," he told her once more. "Things will get better, you'll see. We must not despair. Miracles happen."

Yossele had faith. Surely the good Lord who provides sustenance even for the lowly worm would provide him with a livelihood that did not entail such hardships. He said goodbye to his wife and thought of the long day ahead. Miracles do happen, he assured himself as he walked along the road, even managing to hum a cheerful tune.

Yossele had been walking along his route for several hours when the postal coach galloped past. As it gained speed, a few envelopes fell from a loosened sack and dropped to the road. Yossele grabbed the fallen letters and called to the postman to halt.

"You dropped some mail!" he shouted, but it was too late; the wagon was already beyond earshot.

Yossele caught his breath and examined the envelopes in his hand – one, in particular, stood out. It was stamped with an official government seal and the words: "*Registered mail, insured for thirty thousand marks.*"

The poor man put the envelope in his inner jacket pocket and hurried after the coach. In a few minutes he'd caught up with the wagon at the small inn, where the postman had stopped to make a delivery.

"You dropped this on the road," Yossele muttered as he handed the man the letters. About the registered envelope hidden next to his chest, Yossele said nothing.

The postman was grateful to Yossele, shaking his hand and repeating his thanks.

But the moment the postal coach had continued on its way and was no longer in sight, Yossele walked to the side of the road, hid behind a bush, and removed the government missive from his jacket. He could feel his knees knocking as he managed to steady his trembling fingers long enough to open the seal. His eyes widened as he stared at the contents: freshly minted banknotes. Thirty thousand marks!

Yossele read the address on the front of the envelope. Yossele knew the name well. The money was to be delivered to the poretz, the nobleman of the neighboring village. He'd had his own unpleasant dealings with the man, a nasty character who went out of his way to make life difficult for Yossele, forbidding him from selling his wares in the nobleman's domain. Why deliver the money to that scoundrel? No, this was the miracle he'd prayed for all these years. He held a small fortune in his hands. Life would be easier now, the years of bitter struggle finally behind him. Yossele returned the envelope to his jacket pocket and hurried home.

Dvoyra's first reaction upon seeing her husband return home so early in the day, his knapsack still bulging with unsold items, was utter dread. What new tribulation today? Surely a calamity had befallen him. But the joy on her husband's face suggested otherwise.

"Well, guess what?" said Yossele, bursting through the door, barely able to contain his excitement. "Don't I always say we must never give up? That miracles do happen? Well, look at this."

He waved the envelope in his hand and told her of the windfall that had come their way.

"A miracle you call this?" Dvoyrah exclaimed. "This is not a miracle. This is theft. Pure and simple." She shook her head in disbelief. "No, Yossele, no. Go and return this money immediately. It's not yours."

"Return the money? To that good-for-nothing anti-Semite who spares no effort to embitter our lives? It would be a downright mitzvah, a genuine, righteous deed, to steal money from a man like that. Besides, I didn't even steal it from him. And, anyway, the money is insured, so he'll be reimbursed by the government."

"And stealing from the government – is that permissible too?" his wife asked.

Yossele waved away her words with a flick of his wrist. "What is thirty thousand marks to the regime? They won't even notice the loss. So relax, will you?"

But Dvoyrah would not be calmed. "Spare me the excuses," she said to her husband. "I know only one thing. The money doesn't belong to you. This isn't money you've earned. You should have returned it with the other mail. In fact, you—"

Dvoyrah suddenly stopped speaking as a new thought thundered in her head.

"Oh my God," she said, her face turning pale.

"What?" asked Yossele.

"The letters!"

"What about them?"

"Oh my God. We are in such trouble."

"But why?"

"But why? Don't you see, Yossele? When they realize the registered letter is missing and that you returned all the others? It's obvious. You're the one who took it. You're the thief."

Dvoyrah slumped into a chair and held her head in her hands. "What will we do? What?"

Yossele stood motionless, absorbing the reality of his predicament. "You're right," he finally said. "We have to hide the envelope."

Rummaging around the room, he found a hammer, pried open a floorboard, put the letter in the empty space, then carefully replaced the board.

"There," he said to wife. "We're okay now. If they come, they'll find nothing. And I'll deny everything."

Barely an hour later, the post office manager arrived at Yossele's hut, flanked by two policemen. The interrogation began at once. Why hadn't Yossele returned the government letter with the others, they demanded to know.

"What government letter?" Yossele asked, claiming to have no idea what they were talking about.

After a futile search and a barrage of hostile questions, the police were still unconvinced.

"We'll have to continue this investigation at the police station," one said, slapping a pair of handcuffs on Yossele's wrists.

Yossele adamantly continued to declare his innocence, but to no avail. As the police dragged him away, they informed Dvoyrah her husband would remain in custody until someone showed up with the missing letter.

The Jews of Leipnik soon learned of the plight of Yossele the peddler. They knew Yossele to be a forthright and decent man and couldn't imagine he was guilty of the crime with which he'd been charged. No doubt, this was the usual pretense perpetrated by the Jew-hating government. And so the community organized to bring food and succor to the arrested man's forlorn wife and children, and to consider how to free Yossele from his unjust imprisonment. The community leaders called on their best and most effective connections to the regime's officials.

But their appeals were unsuccessful – the authorities would not release Yossele. They did, however, announce a reward of five hundred marks to anyone who procured the government letter with the banknotes intact. With the return of the money, and only with its return, the regime promised, would Yossele gain his freedom.

Distraught, Dvoyrah paced the room day and night, her thoughts directed to the letter hidden beneath her feet. She'd long since decided she must return it...but to whom? If she brought it to the post office, the police would immediately conclude Yossele had been in possession of the letter all along, and who knew what punishment would await him then? No, she'd have to get the letter to the authorities some other way. But what other way?

Every path was fraught with risk, Dvoyrah thought, still pacing. She needed advice. She'd seek it from Leipnik's rabbi, Reb Baruch Ta'am Frankel, an eminent Talmudic scholar famous for his judiciousness as well as his learning. She'd personally hand Reb Baruch the envelope and explain the entire sorry story. He would know what to do.

Dvoyrah opened the floorboard, removed the parcel and made her way to the home of Reb Baruch Ta'am.

As Dvoyrah neared the rabbi's house, she heard a chorus of voices flowing from an open window. Walking nearer still, she could see Reb Baruch studying with his students. Unwilling to disturb the learning of Torah, Dvoyrah instead walked to the open window and hurled the letter inside, where it landed at the rabbi's feet.

Reb Baruch picked up the letter, noted the government seal and registration for thirty thousand marks, and reached a reasonable conclusion: The thief regretted being the cause of Yossele's unjust imprisonment and had decided to deliver the letter to the town rabbi, who would surely arrange for the release of the incarcerated Jew.

Reb Baruch finished his teaching, retreated to his office and stared out his window. What were his options? Were he to bring the letter to the postal service, he'd be subjected to an unpleasant interrogation. Naturally, they'd demand to know who gave him this packet. And what could he say? That the letter landed at his feet one afternoon, that it flew like a bird through an open window? No one would believe that story. No, they'd insist the thief was a Jew whom the rabbi was trying to protect.

On the other hand, what if he were to do nothing? That too was unacceptable. After all, a robbery had been committed and the money must be returned to its rightful owner, no matter how despicable he might be. In the meantime, poor Yossele sat in jail, an innocent and broken man.

Reb Baruch needed to think this through calmly and carefully, an impossibility in his home where he was constantly surrounded by the commotion of students, scholars and family, all vying for his attention. And so Reb Baruch decided to take a walk on the outskirts of town, in the surrounding fields, where he'd find the quiet he needed to reflect undisturbed.

As he strolled along, lost in his thoughts, Reb Baruch looked up and saw a figure ambling in the distance. When the two men drew closer, Reb Baruch recognized his good friend, the town priest. A moment's exchange revealed that the priest was also fond of taking a break from his busy day to walk alone in the countryside.

"What's the matter?" the priest asked, noting the consternation on the rabbi's face. "Is something troubling you?"

But instead of answering, Reb Baruch had a question of his own. "Tell me, people come to you for confession, do they not?"

"Yes, of course. Hearing confessions is one of my main duties."

"Can a Jew also confess to you?"

The startled priest raised his eyebrows. "Certainly. Anyone can. There's no reason a Jew can't confess."

"So, may I? Confess to you?"

"Indeed," replied the priest, hardly believing what he was hearing.

"It's also my understanding," Reb Baruch continued, "that whatever is admitted in a confession is confidential, is it not? Nothing said will ever be repeated to anyone else?"

"Absolutely," the priest replied, even more curious now. "I am sworn to secrecy, forbidden to repeat what I hear during a confession. Not to other priests, not to the authorities. To no one."

"Well then," said Reb Baruch, "I'd like to confess."

The priest was astounded. Reb Baruch, the most illustrious rabbi in the province, wished to confess to him, the town priest! Taking hold of the rabbi's arm, he said, "Yes, by all means. Come with me to the church and I will hear your confession."

"No, no," Reb Baruch protested. "Not in church. I wish to confess to you right here in this field where no one is around. On the condition that what I tell you will never leave your lips."

And so, with the priest's repeated assurance of privacy, Reb Baruch recounted the circumstances of how he came into possession of the registered letter containing the thirty thousand marks. He noted the suspicion and interrogation that would surely ensue if he, the region's leading rabbi, brought the money to the authorities.

"But you, dear friend, can return this letter with impunity. You need but report that a penitent handed you the letter during a confession and, therefore, you are not at liberty to say who it was. Your confidentiality will be respected. And an innocent man will be freed from captivity."

The priest immediately agreed to the plan, and two hours later appeared at the government office, letter in hand. As reward for returning the lost funds, the authorities handed the priest the reward of five hundred marks, and the hapless Yossele was promptly released from his cell.

The following day, the priest brought the reward to Reb Baruch, whom he deemed the more rightful recipient. Reb Baruch, in turn, declined the money and recommended it be given to the unfortunate Yossele, who had suffered greatly in jail these past months. And so it was done – the money was delivered to the poor peddler.

"Ah, so you see?" said the gleeful Yossele to his wife. "My days of trekking through dangerous villages are over. With this money, we can open a stall selling goods right here in town. Didn't I say miracles happen?"

But Dvoyrah understood matters differently. "We have been blessed, true. But the months you spent in prison, my dear Yossele? That was penance for refusing to return that money. 'Thou shalt not steal,' means what it says."

Beirish the Batlan

How would you describe a *batlan*? An incompetent comes close. Perhaps reliably unreliable is even better. But *our* batlan, we should emphasize, though certainly inept, was also a kindly, well-meaning fellow.

Since childhood, the only home Beirish had ever known was the court of Rabbi Ber of Mezeritch. The young man's parents had died when he was twelve years old, and with no relatives, he was taken in by the renowned Chassidic master. And so Beirish grew up listening to the teachings and observing the practices of the holy Reb Ber who had inherited the mantle of leadership from his teacher, none other than the Ba'al Shem Tov, the founder of Chassidism.

The court of Reb Ber encompassed the entire ambit of Beirish's world. His favorite hours were those spent in the study hall, where he eagerly soaked in the magical tales and cunning gossip of the Chassidim who flocked to their rebbe and who would, on occasion, hand a few coins to the young orphan before making their way home.

It's true Beirish was a callow youngster, bereft of any marketable skills or understanding of the world, but, as we've said, he was also a decent young man who never complained and made no demands. And why should he? After all, his needs were few and were, in any event, taken care of.

But time does not stand still. Beirish was now well past the age of eighteen, the age when young Chassidic men were expected to find a wife and begin a family. Yet Beirish the batlan had no interest in marriage.

The years passed, until one day, the rebbe called Beirish into his office.

"Beirish," the rebbe began, "it is time you married. I'm aware you have no interest in doing so, but this is not a healthy situation. You cannot remain single for the rest of your days. The Torah enjoins us to find a mate and build a home. You do understand, don't you?"

Beirish lifted his shoulders and lowered his head. In fact, he didn't understand why he must marry. But Beirish was not one to ask questions, certainly not of the great tzaddik, Reb Ber.

"If the rebbe says so," he replied.

"You know," said the rebbe, "the Talmud notes that it is human nature for a person to search for a lost item, and that is also the case with regard to a spouse. You need to *seek* your mate. This will not be an easy undertaking for you, I understand. You are inexperienced in the ways of the world – a bit of a batlan, as I'm sure you know your friends call you."

Beirish gave the rebbe a puzzled look.

"Here's my advice," said the rebbe. "The first match proposed to you – accept it. I assure you it will work out. Now, go forth, and may your search bring you success."

Anxious but obedient, Beirish bade his farewells, placed his meager possessions in his rucksack, and embarked on his first journey into the world beyond the rebbe's court.

After a good day's walk, he happened upon a Jewish-run kretchma. In need of a place to spend the night, he entered the inn and quietly sat down in a corner. He retrieved a small religious book from his sack and began to read. Beirish became absorbed in the fine print before he sensed a pair of eyes on him. Looking up, Beirish found an outstretched arm and an open calloused hand.

"*Sholem Aleichem*," the man said. But before Beirish could return the greeting, the man began to bombard him with questions: Who are you? From where are you coming? Where are you going? The gruffness of the man's voice matched the callouses on his hands. Nor was there any mistaking the snicker in his tone.

The guileless Beirish answered each question dutifully and honestly. He explained that his rebbe had told him to set out on the road to find what he was looking for but hadn't told him where to go.

"And what precisely is it you seek?" asked the man, taking another long swig of whiskey from his glass.

"A wife," said Beirish.

"A wife!" Beirish's inquisitor broke into a wide a smile and flashed a wink to his friends, who were intently observing the exchange from a table across the room. Soon they gathered around Beirish, enjoying the game.

"Our little Chassid here," said the boor to his friends, "is looking for a mate." To Beirish, he said, "Well, your search is over. I have a match for you."

Another swallow from the glass and the man pointed to a girl dressed in peasant clothes, wiping bottles and placing them on the shelves behind the bar. She gave no notice of the drunken patrons.

"She's the owner's daughter. He's not here at the moment. She'd make an excellent wife for you. A fine, upstanding Jewish girl."

Beirish remained silent, confused.

"She's divorced," one of the assembled men contributed.

"But it wasn't her fault," added another. "She divorced the guy. A no-good bum."

"Ah, but a fine man like you," the first man said. "She'd be a lucky woman."

Beirish didn't know what to say.

"Well, yes or no?" said the man. "Do you or do you not agree to this match?"

Beirish took another look at the young woman, who was still busy cleaning whiskey glasses. He shut his eyes. This was all so strange. But the rebbe had said he was to accept the first marriage proposal to come his way.

Beirish nodded his consent.

"Marvelous!" announced the inebriated peasant. A broad smile lined his face as he walked over to the young woman.

Beirish observed him whisper into her ear and saw her shake her head emphatically in response. He whispered in her ear again, and this time the girl laughed loud enough for all to hear. The game was on.

The other men quickly caught on to what was afoot and set about their tasks. Within a few minutes, four poles had been produced and a tablecloth placed on top.

"An instant canopy!" the men declared as they nudged, prodded, and nearly dragged the perplexed Beirish to the hastily built khupa and someone contributed a cheap ring which he placed in Beirish's hand. His bride stood beside him, barely stifling her grin. Beirish felt as though he were Daniel in the lions' den. He was unable to speak.

"Well, what are you waiting for?" his chief tormentor urged. "Pronounce the marriage vow. You know the required phrase: 'You are consecrated to me with this ring according to the laws of Moses and Israel.' C'mon, on with it."

Beirish managed to recite the marriage formula: *Harei aht mikudeshes lee*, "you are consecrated to me..."

Cheers erupted. "Mazel tov, Mazel tov! Here's to your marriage!"

The din of boisterous merriment filled the room. From all quarters came cries of "This calls for another round of drink!"

Amidst the intoxicated festivity, the celebrants barely noticed that the saloonkeeper had returned. At first, he was bewildered by all the revelry. But when he noticed the makeshift canopy, the befuddled young Chassid standing alone in the center of the room, and his daughter, who'd returned to wiping the counters but for some reason was laughing, he construed what had taken place.

Though no great scholar, the saloonkeeper was more learned than the others, and unlike his customers, understood the gravity of what had transpired in his tavern that day. Oblivious or not, the young man had willingly pronounced – with the appropriate phrasing – a marriage vow to his daughter, and had done so before witnesses. As for his daughter, she had publicly accepted the ring. Whether he liked it or not, a genuine wedding had been performed. Alas, this was no jest – one did not jest about the legality of a marriage.

The furious saloonkeeper glared at his daughter and approached his new son-in-law.

"Look, young man. I'm sorry these fools here put you up to this nonsense. You do recognize, I hope, this was all a gag, don't you? A practical joke. Unfortunately, the fact is you are legally married to my daughter. This, of course, can't be. The two of you married? Ridiculous. And as preposterous as it might seem, you must now go through with a legal divorce. Remain here and I'll assemble a court that will legitimate the divorce proceedings. I won't be long."

Beirish merely looked down at his shoes with his usual, confounded stare. The rebbe had told him to marry the first woman proposed to him, and that's what he'd done. The rebbe had said nothing about a divorce, and without the rebbe's permission, he would not proceed.

"I won't agree to a divorce," Beirish said.

"What do you mean you won't agree to a divorce? Of course you will. Let's get on with it."

"I can't," Beirish repeated.

"Can't? What can't?"

Beirish, guileless as always, explained that he could not undertake such a decision without his rebbe's directive.

After many minutes of intense pleading, and seeing the young man's obstinacy could not be overcome, the saloonkeeper lifted his palms and shook his head.

"This is absolutely ludicrous, but if you insist, we shall go and have the divorce executed at your rebbe's court."

Reb Ber listened carefully as the saloonkeeper explained the hoax played on poor Beirish.

"I'd appreciate it if the rebbe would expedite this divorce as quickly as possible," the saloonkeeper said. "For my daughter's sake."

Reb Ber nodded a few times before replying. "You're right, of course, about this wedding being a charade. But you're correct that prank or no prank, a legal divorce is necessary if the two are to go their separate ways."

"Excellent," sighed the saloonkeeper in relief.

"But it will come at a price," the rebbe added.

"Price? What price?"

"You're asking your son-in-law to divorce your daughter. This is your idea, not his. So it will cost you."

"Cost me? What?"

"Let us say five thousand rendel."

"Five thousand rendel!" The saloonkeeper flailed his arms in the air. "This is outrageous! These drunken buffoons perform a circus in my saloon and now I must hand over an enormous sum of money to this clueless batlan?"

Reb Ber looked over at Beirish, who was waiting patiently for instructions on what to do or say.

"Beirish," said the rebbe, "my suggestion is you do not divorce your wife unless her father presents you with five thousand rendel. Nothing less."

Seeing there would be no convincing the rebbe or Beirish to do otherwise, the saloonkeeper begrudgingly wrote a promissory note for the funds and handed it to Beirish.

"All right, then," said the rebbe. "We can now get on with the divorce proceedings. Let the court assemble."

Within an hour, the proceedings were complete. But as the saloonkeeper prepared to leave the rebbe's office, Reb Ber asked that he remain a moment longer.

"It dawns on me," said the rebbe. "Your daughter seems to be a fine girl."

"A fine girl she is," said her father.

"It isn't good for a young woman to be alone," said the rebbe.

"No, it is not," the saloonkeeper agreed.

"Well," said Reb Ber, "I think I have a match for her."

"Yes?"

"A fine young man. As a fine young woman deserves."

The saloonkeeper stole a look at his now twice divorced daughter. She was not getting any younger, either. A suitable match would not be easy to come by.

"And who might that be?" the saloonkeeper asked.

"He's a pious young man. Of good character. And, I might add, he is not a poor fellow, either. I understand he's got a bit of money to his name."

The saloonkeeper liked what he was hearing.

Reb Ber pressed on, no longer bothering to conceal his smile,

"Yes, this young man is worth at least five thousand rendel."

"The rebbe can't be serious!" the saloonkeeper said, stealing a look at Beirish.

"But why not?" Reb Ber replied.

"Yes, why not?" the saloonkeeper's daughter echoed.

And so a wedding canopy was prepared once more.

A Mother's Lullaby

They were the only Jewish family in a hamlet of peasants, a small family compared to most: Perele, an attractive woman of valor, her son, Shmuelche and daughter Shprintza. And, yes, a husband, of whom the less said the better. It's true that his wheat business brought in a decent living, but it was also true that he spent his nights carousing with the local farmers and had no interest in providing his children with even a modicum of Jewish learning. The man's father, a well-to-do saloonkeeper who lived in a nearby town, pleaded with his son to join him there so the children would have a more refined circle of friends and a chance to study the sacred texts of their tradition. Perele, too, beseeched her husband to leave his boorish life behind and begin anew. But he steadfastly refused. He was pleased with his life. Did he not enjoy a steady income? Were the children not happy with their playmates? Why ask for more?

But soon the day came, as it was bound to, when the husband returned home to an empty household and the consequences of his stubbornness.

For what could one expect of Perele? Long before the day she left she'd retreated into a dreary and isolated existence. She passed her days in loneliness, bearing her husband's absences in quiet, without friends in whom to confide. That is, until two men entered her life and changed her destiny.

The first was the local priest, who made no pretense about his goal: to convert Perele to Christianity. As you'd imagine, Perele's first impulse was to throw the man out along with his outrageous agenda, but she never did. In fact, she cherished his visits. He was a gentle, charming man and Perele looked forward to the good cheer he brought into her cheerless home. The priest inquired with genuine interest about her life, related news of the world and appreciated her thoughtful comments. When the conversation turned, as it sometimes did, to the possibility of conversion, he'd note Perele's agitation and delicately drop the subject. And yet, as time passed, the priest managed to plant the seeds of conversion in Perele's mind, a prospect reinforced by the appearance of Perele's second visitor.

Ivan was a strapping fellow – tall, blond and muscular – with the typical features of the farmer stock from which he was derived. He also had sufficient wit to invent one pretext after another for calling at the home of the Jewess. But the real reason for these visits was that he'd fallen in love with Perele. Ivan would stop by regularly with bags of almonds and other delicacies for the family, and make a point of spending time with the children, marching about the house in the military formation he'd learned as a soldier, carrying little Shprintza on his broad shoulders while a gleeful Shmuelche followed in tow, trying to match Ivan step for step. Perele would busy herself with housework and pretend to ignore Ivan's antics, all the while stealing glances in his direction as she quietly hummed along with his countryside tunes.

As Ivan's visits became more frequent, the need to make excuses decreased; Ivan no longer bothered to hide his romantic intentions. And however much Perele wished she could banish him from her home, she welcomed the days he'd stop by and could hardly hide her disappointment on the days he did not.

At first, Perele was torn by conflicting emotions. Was she not a daughter of her people, a committed Jew, a married woman? Yes, but married to a man who was physically and emotionally absent. And how could she deny the longing in her heart for Ivan? The priest's arguments seemed increasingly persuasive, at least worthy of consideration. Distraught by her inner turmoil and where it might lead, she once more begged her husband to pull up stakes and move to his father's town, where they could rebuild their lives in a wholesome Jewish community. But Perele's husband responded angrily at having to discuss the matter yet again. Where they lived was their home and would remain so, he shouted with finality.

Perele was less dismissive now to the priest's assurances that life as a Christian promised great rewards in both this world and the next. And she no longer vigorously protested Ivan's advances, reconciling herself to the jumble of anxiety and desire his presence provoked.

Ivan suffered no such hesitation. "Come, live with me," he pleaded with Perele. "Forsake this awful life of yours and your callous husband. Become a Christian and marry me. I promise you a life so much more pleasant and joyful than the one you have now."

At last, Perele assented. Planning her escape would be easy enough. Her husband was already away from home for long stretches and she could pack her few belongings without suspicion. As for the children, Ivan agreed she could bring along Shprintza, but not Shmuelche, who would stay with his father and remain a Jew.

All was readied for the afternoon when Ivan's wagon drew up to the front of Perele's house. With tears streaming, Perele hugged her son, exhorting him to be a good boy and never to forget her.

"Shmuelche, listen to me," she said, giving the boy a final kiss before entering the waiting carriage. "Leave here. Leave this village and go live with your grandfather in town. I've made all the necessary arrangements."

With her heart aching, she wrapped her arms more tightly around her daughter and kept her eyes on Shmuelche for as long she could while the wagon made its way toward the church.

The first months were blissful. Ivan proved to be a devoted husband, showering Perele with gifts, along with his affection. Theirs was a happy home, where mandolin players regularly assembled for festive evenings of music and dance. Ivan, too, basked in his newfound celebrity as the man who had rescued a Jewess and her child with the truth of Christian salvation.

Shprintza, now called Maria, made new friends and adapted quickly to her surroundings. Perele managed the transition as well.

Though some chores remained onerous – she was still nauseated by the pork she prepared for dinner, for example – she valiantly lived up to her husband's expectations. She was even diligent about accompanying Ivan to Sunday Mass at the local church, where she dutifully fell to her knees in obeisance before the statue of the Holy Mother. She taught her little Maria the catechism and expected that before long, the child would be freed from any lingering memories of her Jewish past.

Still, Perele had not forgotten her son. She was pleased to learn that he had indeed moved to the neighboring town to live with his grandfather. But because thinking about Shmuelche inevitably ushered in waves of sadness, she redirected her attention to the bustling activities in her home.

Perele was content. Her new life pleased her. And she believed it would so remain.

But lives rarely remain the same. A new priest arrived in the region, an ardent anti-Semite whose weekly sermons preached unvarnished venom toward the Jews. Perele would kneel in her pew and listen to his hateful words, her heart racing, her dark eyes filling with tears as she recalled the morning of a pogrom when, as a small child, she watched a wild mob enter the synagogue and pitilessly beat the congregants. She could still hear her mother's voice ordering her to hide in the synagogue attic, warning, "Do you see, Perele, how the blood boils in these people? Do you see how violent they can be?"

Her mother's words echoed in her mind as she listened to the priest's invective. Perele looked around at her fellow congregants and saw the same murderous looks on their faces. She resolved never again to return to church.

Ivan was deeply displeased by her decision. And so a rift developed between the two, a divide that showed no sign of closing. Perele's once devoted, clean-living husband was changing. Now he regularly came home drunk and, on occasion, even beat her, calling her a worthless Jewess. Perele would withdraw to a corner of the house, her daughter huddled at her side, and the tears flowing from both their eyes as Perele tried to comfort Maria with the old Jewish lullaby she used to sing to her as a child.

With each passing day, the strife between Perele and Ivan grew increasingly bitter, until one morning Ivan left home and never returned. Where could Perele turn now? She'd burned all her bridges. Her neighbors despised her and the feelings were mutual. She certainly couldn't expect a warm welcome from members of her former faith. She and her daughter were alone, utterly alone, with no means of sustenance. And Shmuelche? He would be a young man by now, sturdy and smart and living…where? Did he ever think of her? But then, she'd tell herself, surely it was better that he not know his mother's fate, how she'd been cast out and humiliated, how she'd become a starving beggar, a stranger everywhere.

Shmuelche was ten years old when his mother and sister drove off in a wagon to begin their new lives. He arrived at his grandfather's home unable to read the Hebrew alphabet, ignorant of any of the prayers, with hardly any knowledge of the Bible or Jewish holidays. But Shmuelche had a good head on his shoulders and under his grandfather's tender guidance, he excelled in his studies. By the time he turned twelve, a year before his bar mitzvah, he could navigate his way through a page of Talmud.

Yet Shmuelche's social life did not progress as well as his studies. He was always self-conscious, always aware he was different from his peers. He'd overhear the murmuring behind his back, and on several occasions he'd hear his mother's name whispered along with the name Ivan. He tried to understand why his mother had left him. He invented explanations, concoctions that toggled from a young's boy fantasies to a young boy's dread. His father, who had come to live with him and his grandfather, was suffering from a deep depression and refused to speak with anyone. When Shmuelche would ask his grandfather what had happened to his mother, the old man would only say, "She is no longer. When you will be older, you will learn all."

No one dared tell Shmuelche of the tragic events of his childhood, but eventually no one needed to. As he approached his sixteenth year, he slowly pieced together his sad history. Finally, he understood why his friends sometimes kept their distance from him, why his conversations with adults were accompanied by studied sighs. Shmuelche had expected to feel a measure of relief upon learning the details of his past; instead, he felt lonelier than ever.

On days when his pangs of isolation were most intense, he'd recede to the *beis medrash*, where he'd recite the words of the Talmud in a mournful melody. He startled himself when he recognized the melody as none other than the lullaby his mother had once sung to him as a child. Overcome with yearning, he'd bury his head in his hands and allow himself to weep without restraint.

These spasms of tearful shudders were becoming too frequent for the young man. Shmuelche was terrified he might collapse into the same horrible depression that consumed his father. There was only one possible solution to his growing despondency: He would have to travel afar to escape the hovering whispers that were ever-present in his grandfather's town.

Shmuelche bade his farewells, threw his belongings into a rucksack and headed off in the direction of Hungary. At the suggestion of some local scholars, he decided he would go to the town of Khalev and visit the court of its renowned Chassidic rebbe.

In Khalev, Shmuelche quickly acclimated to his new surroundings, and again excelled in his Torah studies. He was careful to tell no one of his troubled origins and his new friends had the good sense not to press him on the matter. Neither did he reveal his history to his teachers, though the more sensitive among them detected the abiding sadness that clung to their young student. Shmuelche did not even disclose his woes to the rebbe, convinced that he didn't need to. Somehow, he thought, the rebbe must know the reason for his melancholy.

Music became a special bond between Shmuelche and the Chassidic master. Among Chassidim everywhere, the Khaliver Rebbe was deemed the Prince of Song, in recognition of his wondrous compositions and teachings about the mystical meanings of melody. Often, when the rebbe would sing his beautiful tunes, he'd approach Shmuelche and ask the young man to sing along with him.

"A song has the power to lift a soul," the rebbe explained to Shmuelche. "Each human emotion has its own distinct song, even if sung in different languages with different words. There is a song, too, that accompanies the birth and nurturing of every child. This song belongs to the mother and her child, and no one can ever take it away from them."

The meaning of the rebbe's words was unclear to Shmuelche, but he suspected that they were connected to the lullaby he'd find himself humming when he studied Torah.

Shmuelche remained in Khalev for several years, expanding his grasp of Torah and Chassidic thought. His fine mind, along with his exemplary character, attracted the attention of fathers from the region's most prominent families, who now sought out Shmuelche as a husband for their daughters. Shmuelche shooed away the matchmakers. "I'm not ready to marry," he repeated month after month. At first, the matchmakers blamed his reluctance to marry on his studiousness. But as his adamant disinterest showed no signs of abating, suspicions arose. Why would an upstanding Chassidic boy already past the age of twenty refuse to entertain a marriage proposal? Rumors spread. No doubt the boy's lack of interest had to do with his mysterious past.

Shmuelche realized his situation would only become more impossible. It was unseemly for a serious young man to remain single, but were he to agree to marry, his future in-laws would certainly be entitled to learn of his family and lineage. They would, he knew, be horrified to discover that he was the son of a mother who'd converted to Christianity, a *meshumedess*. The word alone made him shiver, for what greater ignominy was there than this? No, no, he promised himself. No one must ever learn his humiliating history.

One might think that Shmuelche harbored hatred toward his mother. And yet, nothing was further from the truth. Despite the fact that his mother had abandoned him and her faith, along with her husband who now lived in a cloud of darkness, Shmuelche felt no rage toward her. When he thought of his mother, he was overcome not with anger, but with pity. He was certain life had not gone well for her, and he wished he could be at her side. How he missed them all – his mother and his little sister Shprintza, his beloved grandfather, even his suffering father.

What of his own future? Would he be alone forever? Again, he heard the whispers behind his back, the misgivings and curiosity about this foreign young man who would not marry and was given to spells of sullen silence.

To still his anguish, Shmuelche threw himself into his Talmudic studies with more devotion than ever. "*Abaye omer*," he'd recite, hoping to lose himself in the argument of a Talmudic sage. But minutes later, he'd become aware that his chanting had shifted to his mother's lullaby, the tether to his childhood. He'd cover his face to conceal his tears, and bolt from the *beis medrash* without warning.

One day, as this scene again unfolded, Shmuelche was surprised to feel a hand on his shoulder.

"That is a beautiful melody," the rebbe said.

"It's a lullaby I heard as a child," said Shmuelche.

"I recognized it as a song of yearning," said the rebbe. "The melody belongs to its singer, who beckons."

Shmuelche's eyes widened, captive.

"Listen to me," the rebbe said, his voice firm and direct. "Your song begs to return to its creator. You see, a song, too, can be lost and become a wanderer, like its singer."

"What is the rebbe telling me?" Shmuelche asked, his own voice halting.

"Shmuelche, when a melody roams and its author is adrift, the two need to be reunited. Bring the song home and bring solace to its singer's life. Only then will your own wandering come to an end."

The rebbe stood silent for a moment, then asked, "Shmuelche, do you understand what I am saying?"

"I do," he whispered. Shmuelche feared what awaited him, but he also knew this was the only way out of his anguish. "Will the rebbe give me his blessing?"

The next morning, Shmuelche gazed one final time at the books in the study hall that had given him such pleasure these last years. Once more, he strapped his pack on his shoulders and began his journey, this time in the direction from where he'd come.

After several long days, Shmuelche began to recognize his surroundings. His heart quickened as his eyes fell upon the vaguely familiar houses and road signs, the clothes and mannerisms of the locals. Yet it was the distinctive scents of the countryside that brought back the most vivid memories – his mother's entreaties, his father's absences, the sense that his was a fractured family. What was he looking for? What could he possibly expect to find? Did he really want to see his mother living the life of a gentile village housewife?

"Please stop here," Shmuelche said to the wagon driver.

They were in front of the tavern that Shmuelche had slept in the first night he'd departed from his grandfather's village so many years before. He slowly walked up the path, stopping for a moment to gather himself. The tavern door suddenly flung open and a young girl darted out, a look of great fright on her face. The tavern owner ran after her, shouting, "Out! Out! Little peasant thief! I catch you here again and I'll kill you. Do you hear?" Noticing Shmuelche, the innkeeper muttered by way of explanation: "Urchin, trying to steal food."

Shmuelche recognized the man and lowered his hat over his eyes to avoid being recognized in turn; he wasn't sure of his plans and wanted to preserve his anonymity for the moment. Cold and exhausted, Shmuelche gratefully warmed his hands in front of the fireplace, then stretched out in the corner of the room and fell into a fitful sleep.

At first, Shmuelche thought the voices he was hearing were coming from his dreams, but when he opened an eyelid, he traced the sounds to two beggars chatting nearby. They were discussing where in this region vagabonds like themselves could expect a charitable gift.

"I hear an old Jewish saloonkeeper in town has a reputation for giving alms to beggars, and substantial donations at that. And I have his address."

Shmuelche immediately recognized the address as his grandfather's.

"Too late," said the second beggar.

"What do you mean 'too late'?" asked the first.

"The man's dead. Died about half a year ago."

"Really? What a shame. I was hoping—"

"Tragic, that man's story."

The first beggar sat still for a few breaths, then asked, "So what happened to his wealth? Who has it now?"

"Don't get your hopes up," replied the second. "It's a complicated business. His son, it seems, is incapable of managing money, or anything else, if you know what I mean. All the assets were left to the grandson."

"And where is he?"

"No one knows. He left home years ago and has not been seen or heard from since."

Shmuelche let out a loud cry, grabbed his rucksack and dashed outside, running as fast as he could wherever his feet would carry him.

Sheets of snow fell from the sky, but Shmuelche continued to run, oblivious to the freezing temperature and howling wind. He pushed himself to go on, to gain distance from the crushing news of his grandfather's death. Where could he turn now?

"Alone! Utterly alone!" he shouted into the wind, until, overcome with exhaustion, he collapsed on the wet ground. There, huddled on the forest floor, he began to sing the lullaby that had comforted him all his life.

But wait! He was not the only one singing! Shmuelche stopped his humming for a moment. No, he was not dreaming. In the distance, someone was singing the very same lullaby. He stood up, as if in a trance, and walked toward an older woman's voice, quivering with sighs. As he neared its source, he could hear another voice, that of a young girl, softer, singing in harmony.

Shmuelche hid behind a nearby a tree.

"Why, mother, did he strike me?" the girl was asking. "Why did he chase me out like a stray dog? I'd only gone to the kitchen to ask for a piece of bread so you and I would have something to eat. Only a single piece of bread."

Shmuelche could now see the two figures clearly. An old woman dressed in rags and a young girl, her pale face streaked with dirt and tears, sitting at her side. The old woman was stroking the girl's matted hair as she sang the lullaby.

Shmuelche could hear the thumping of his heart. He took a deep breath and walked toward the woman, singing the melody with her.

Perele looked toward the approaching young man and her singing stopped. Her mournful eyes met her son's. For a moment, they could only stare at each other, frozen in the shock of recognition.

"Mamma?" Shmuelche cried out.

"Shmuelche!" Perele whispered.

It Takes a Thief to Catch a Thief

Yankov was a partner in a growing business enterprise so successful it had begun trading with countries beyond its own borders. Still, despite his considerable financial achievements, Yankov was a stalwart Chassid, disappointed that his business affairs deprived him of spending more time in his rebbe's court. Indeed, he was pleased that his fellow Chassidim never esteemed his financial success, nor gave him priority seating or special honors; if anything, they considered wealth a challenge, even an impediment, to leading an elevated life. How different it was in town, where all routinely deferred to the prosperous businessmen.

But of late, those close to him noticed a concerned look on Yankov's face when he returned from a visit to the rebbe: the pursed lips, the narrowed eyebrows, the long stares into the distance. At the office, he'd walk about shaking his head, lost in his private thoughts.

On one occasion, when Yankov came back from a stay with the Chassidim once again distracted, his partner grabbed him by the lapels. "Enough, Yankov. Get a hold of yourself. Customers are waiting and you sit here not knowing which world you're in."

This partner, a bit of a maskil, considered himself enlightened; as far as he could tell, his partner's visits to the rebbe were clearly the cause of Yankov's distress.

"You've got to stop going there," he admonished Yankov. "These Chassidim and that rebbe of yours are turning your head around."

Yankov squinted at his partner as though seeing him for the first time. "Stop going to the rebbe? Are you serious? In fact—"

"In fact what?"

"In fact," Yankov said with a sudden resolve, "I'm going back to the rebbe right now. There's something I need to discuss with him."

"You can't be serious," his partner said.

But Yankov had already dashed outside, where his readied wagon awaited him.

When he arrived at the rebbe's court, he asked for a private audience, and was soon ushered into the rebbe's room. At the rebbe's invitation, he took a seat and began to speak, but then halted.

"Yes?" the rebbe said, waiting.

"I'm not sure how to say this," Yankov managed, scratching his chin. "So I suppose I'll just come out with it: I stole – not from someone else's pocket, but from my own. From my business. Well, I suppose that means from someone else too...my partner. Not just once, either. I've done this over the past few years. Helped myself to a little extra from the profits without notifying him. But now..."

Yankov stopped talking for a moment and wiped his eyes before continuing.

"When I'm with the rebbe and the other Chassidim, I'm reminded how little one's material fortune matters. Every time I leave here, I leave with a heavy heart. I know it's time to confess. But I don't know to whom or how.

"And so, I'd like the rebbe's advice. How do I repent for this transgression? And how do I pay back what I owe my partner without him learning of my embezzlement?"

The rebbe listened intently as Yankov spoke, not interrupting with even a word, until Yankov was finished.

"Did your partner ever give any indication that he was suspicious of your activities?" the rebbe asked.

"Never."

"Interesting," said the rebbe. "About repentance, we'll speak another time. But for now, return to your place of work, and tell your partner in no uncertain terms that he must stop stealing from the business."

"What?" Yankov exclaimed. "Is the rebbe suggesting that my partner is stealing from me? I came here to tell the rebbe that I've been stealing from *him*!"

"Yankov, I suggest you do as I say. Tell your partner you know about his thievery. And if he denies any such wrongdoing, engage a competent bookkeeper to review the accounts. I predict you'll discover your partner has stolen considerably more from you than you have from him."

Bewildered, Yankov returned to his village and immediately went to his office as the rebbe had instructed. He confronted his partner, insisting he cease his thievery at once. His partner, naturally, replied that his insinuation was completely outrageous. Yankov said nothing in response, but following the rebbe's instructions, procured a bookkeeper to review the business's transactions. What the bookkeeper discovered only mildly surprised Yankov. Indeed, his partner had been skimming steadily from their business for several years.

After presenting his partner with the glaring evidence of his pilferage, Yankov knew he had to tell him the full truth.

"I must admit," Yankov said quietly, "I've been no angel myself. I too engaged in a bit of deception these past years."

"Really?" his partner responded dryly. "As If I didn't know."

"You did? Well, so what now?" Yankov said.

The partner extended his hand. "I think now that we're both aware of each other's duplicity, it's time to stop."

Yankov returned to the rebbe to relate all that had transpired.

"But please tell me, how did the rebbe surmise that my partner was stealing as well?"

The rebbe chuckled. "Believe me," he said, "this did not require a great feat of clairvoyance. Only a little insight. But to explain, let me tell you a little anecdote."

Once, two friends, a blind person and a sighted person, were buying some cherries at the marketplace, which they agreed to share equally. "You eat one cherry, then I'll eat one," the sighted man told his friend. But later, when the blind man reached into the bag and accidentally withdrew two cherries instead of one, he noted that his partner didn't say a word. Interesting, he mused to himself and proceeded to take two cherries at a time instead of one.

After a little while, the blind man said to his friend, "Please turn and face me." When his friend did as he asked, the blind man suddenly smacked him across the face.

"What was that about?" his partner yelped.

"I smacked you because you're a cheater," said the blind man. "I can't see, but you can. And you clearly noticed I was taking two cherries instead of one, not as we agreed. Yet you said nothing. And I know you too well to attribute your silence to your great charitableness. No, if you didn't complain, it's only because every time I took two cherries, you were probably taking four. That's why you deserved to be smacked."

The rebbe looked up at Yankov and smiled. "Your partner is no fool. And given what you told me, it was highly unlikely he hadn't noticed you were filching from the business these past years. Yet he said nothing. The reason was obvious. He must have been stealing even more from you."

The Rebbe's Mind and the Maskil's Heart

Reb Ahron was not only among the wealthiest men in the Galicia region of Poland, he was also learned in Torah and diligent in its observance. Furthermore, Reb Ahron was a man of the world, fluent in several languages, respected not only by his fellow Jews, but by his non-Jewish neighbors as well.

The time had come for Reb Ahron to marry off his only daughter, Bluma. As one might expect, proposals for matches streamed his way from the best of families. Reb Ahron ignored them all. What mattered to him when considering a potential son-in-law was not wealth or ancestry but the young man's personal achievements. Was the fellow a scholar? Was he clever? Disciplined?

Moyshe met all these criteria. Although poor, with unremarkable lineage, he was hailed as extraordinary by his teachers and fellow students alike. Moyshe's brilliance, they agreed, was reinforced by an equally prodigious devotion to his studies. And so, Reb Ahron, after completing the requisite inquiries, arranged for the marriage of Moyshe to his beloved daughter.

Reb Ahron was happy to provide a substantial dowry that enabled his new son-in-law to apply himself to his Torah studies without worrying about a livelihood. Moyshe met his father-in-law's highest expectations.

His erudition in rabbinical texts deepened. He was the most dedicated of students, disdaining any wasted minutes that kept him from his studies. It was because of this commitment to learning, Moyshe explained, that he had such little patience with Chassidism.

"All those hours squandered listening to the rebbe's talks, the useless mystical exercises, those precious minutes frittered away singing and dancing and storytelling."

On the holidays, when he begrudgingly accompanied his father-in-law to the Shinover Rebbe, Moyshe rarely joined in the festivities. Instead, he retreated to the *beis medrash* where, alone in the study hall, he immersed himself in a page of Talmud or in unraveling a legal conundrum posed by Maimonides.

Moyshe's peers tried their best to convince him of the worthiness of the Chassidic way of life. They appealed to his intellect, to his piety, to his sensitivities, but their appeals were of no avail. The Chassidim did not interest him.

The Maskilim, on the other hand, did.

The Maskilim were supporters of the Haskalah, the movement of "Jewish Enlightenment" that developed alongside, and in bitter competition with, Chassidism. The Haskalah made inroads into Jewish communities across Europe, pressing for broader assimilation of Jews into the society at large, a greater emphasis on secular studies, and the relaxation – or complete abrogation – of Jewish law in daily life. The Maskilim wanted the Jews to embrace modernity and this, they insisted, entailed a commitment to rationalism and the rejection of mysticism.

Moyshe's reputation as an outstanding intellect made him a prime target for conversion to the cause of the Haskalah. And so the Maskilim sought him out.

At first, the Maskilim restricted their conversations with Moyshe to the intricacies of Jewish law, only slowly expanding into questions of theology and faith. Pleased with his interest, they introduced him to the major Haskalah writers of the day: Peretz Smalinsky, Abraham Mapu, Isaac Ber Levenson. Thirsting to learn more, he undertook the study of foreign languages and soon mastered Latin and German well enough to read the great works of Western civilization in their original languages.

Moyshe conducted these intellectual trespasses in utmost secrecy. Overtly, he was the same faithful student of Torah who participated in all public rituals. But Chassidim have sensitive noses. They smelled something awry with Moyshe, something no doubt related to his frequent conversations with the Maskilim.

The rumors about Moyshe soon reached the ears of his father-in-law. Reb Ahron certainly had no interest in subsidizing the makings of another maskil. Furious, he presented his son-in-law with an ultimatum: either Moyshe cease his friendship with these heretics, or he'd receive not another groshen. Moreover, Reb Ahron warned, he'd make life downright unpleasant for Moyshe should he persist with this nonsense.

In truth, Reb Ahron did not know how deep Moyshe's attraction to the sacrilegious ideas of the Haskalah ran. He wasn't aware that, in fact, Moyshe had already decided to leave the shtetl. He didn't know of Moyshe's plan to move to Vienna, where he'd begin his academic studies and pursue a career in the law or medicine.

After months of keeping his secret, the time to act had arrived. Moyshe told his wife of his decision. Would she join him in Vienna? Join him in his new, non-observant life?

"Absolutely not," Bluma answered.

"So be it," said Moyshe.

He packed his belongings, and on a beautiful spring morning, left his young wife and village to make his way to the new world of Vienna.

Upon arrival, Moyshe exchanged his Jewish name for a German one, replaced his traditional clothing with a contemporary European wardrobe, registered in the academy and began his introduction to secular culture.

What he kept was his trademark commitment to study. This determination, along with his keen mind, helped him matriculate with honors in a remarkably short time. His new peers soon recognized his outstanding capabilities and welcomed him into the city's scholarly elite.

Word of Moyshe's new life trickled back to the shtetl. By then, it was clear this was no mere youthful experiment, no passing phase – Moyshe had made his choice and would not be returning. And what of Bluma, his forlorn wife? Moyshe had absconded without granting her a divorce. Bluma was now an *agunah*, condemned to a state of legal limbo – alone, yet legally married.

On multiple occasions, Reb Ahron sent emissaries to Vienna to ask Moyshe to divorce his wife and set her free to find another man. Moyshe refused every appeal, proudly displaying his scorn for Reb Ahron and the entire religious community from which he'd escaped. Hadn't he been the victim of their intolerance? Hadn't they harangued him when he strayed from their oppressive strictures? "Why should I make life easier for any on you?" he'd say to the messengers. Call it revenge, if you wish, but he would not concede to a writ of divorce.

Increasingly despondent, Reb Ahron himself journeyed to Vienna to confront his son-in-law.

A meeting was arranged and Reb Ahron immediately made his intentions clear. "If it's money you're holding out for," he said, "despicable though it may be, I'll pay you what you want. Do what you will with your life. But have the decency to free my daughter from this shackle."

Moyshe shook his head, relishing his sadistic refusal. "The answer is – and always will be – no."

Reb Ahron returned home, his heart heavy with despair. What could he do to change the mind of his obstinate son-in-law? Perhaps his rebbe could offer some advice. And so, with his daughter at his side, Reb Ahron went to visit the Rebbe of Shinov.

The rebbe listened carefully as Reb Ahron explained the situation. After a long moment of thought, the rebbe raised his eyebrows, nodded his headed slowly and asked his assistant to bring ink and paper. The rebbe wrote a few lines, placed the sheet of paper in an envelope, and turned to Bluma.

"Take this envelope and bring it with you to Vienna. Give it to your husband. I hope this will make a difference."

Reb Ahron looked toward his rebbe, disappointed. "Does the rebbe truly believe this will help? This man has never had the slightest regard for Chassidism or Chassidic rebbes. Indeed, he cares not a whit about anything we deem holy. Can a letter change anything? Please, rebbe, we are desperate."

"I know, I know," said the Shinover Rebbe. "Believe me, I understand your anxiety. I'm well aware of how Moyshe scoffs at religious tradition. But he was once a scholar of Jewish law, was he not? He will understand what I wrote. Perhaps it will help. We shall see."

Bluma set forth immediately for Vienna.

"Well, well, look who is here," Moyshe said when he answered the knock at his door. "Don't bother. The answer is still no."

Bluma ignored her husband's words and placed the rebbe's letter on Moyshe's desk.

"It's for you, from the Rebbe of Shinov."

"Oh my!" Moyshe responded with mock solemnity. "A letter for me from the holy Rebbe of Shinov." He looked at the envelope and burst out in a loud cackle.

Bluma's voice remained steady. "I'm staying at the hotel down the street. You can contact me there."

She did not have to wait long. Early the next morning, a man knocked at her door with a message from Moyshe. Would she please assemble a *beis din*, a court of three rabbis, to preside over divorce proceedings? The sooner, the better.

Startled, Bluma hurried to where the Jewish court presided and arranged for the judges, along with a scribe to draw up the document. Word was sent to Moyshe that all was ready.

Bluma barely recognized Moyshe when he arrived. She'd never seen him so pale. He appeared nearer to death than to life. Acknowledging her with blinking, watery eyes, he respectfully took his place in front of the rabbinical panel.

The ceremony proceeded without a hitch. When it was over, Moyshe issued a long sigh that very much sounded like a sigh of relief, as if a stone had been lifted from his heart. The color returned to his face.

He looked up at the rabbis and his now former wife and answered their inquisitive faces.

"As soon as my wife departed from my quarters yesterday, I took the letter she brought and turned to the receptacle at my side. But as I was about to trash the letter, I was struck by a curiosity. What could the rebbe be asking of me? Why not have a look? It was but a few lines. The rebbe reminded me that in Jewish law there are only two ways a Jewish wife can be freed of her husband: through divorce or the husband's death. That was my choice: divorce Bluma or have her freed by my death.

"I laughed at the rebbe's thinly veiled threat, and heaved the letter into the rubbish bin.

"Several hours later, I felt a pain surge across my chest, accompanied by a dizziness the likes of which I'd never before experienced. I lay down, but the walls continued to undulate. I began to sweat profusely. The doctor I sent for examined me at length and declared me gravely ill. Unfortunately, he was unable to determine the cause of my illness, or its cure.

"I lay shivering on my bed, my deathbed I was certain, and the rebbe's letter came to mind. And I shivered even more.

"I understood what I had to do to avoid dying. Now I understand a lot more as well."

The Rebbe's Foresight

*It is more difficult to be a leader than a prophet:
A prophet need only see the future, but a leader
must see the present in which he lives – and that is
a greater challenge.*

REB NAFTULI OF RUPSZITZ

A Lapse of Memory

While several of the Besht's students were widely esteemed in their day, in some cases, their legacies have, inexplicably, been neglected. Reb Yaakov is one such disciple. All we know of the man, gleaned from a handful of tales, is that he was extremely dear to the Besht and was often chosen to accompany the tzaddik on his mysterious journeys.

We also know that the Ba'al Shem Tov instructed Reb Yaakov that after his death, he should travel from city to city, from village to village, teaching and telling stories about Chassidism. "For how long?" Reb Yaakov asked. The Ba'al Shem Tov assured him, "A time will come when it will be clear that your mission is fulfilled."

And so, when the Ba'al Shem Tov passed to the next world, Reb Yaakov immediately began his travels as directed, relating the wondrous tales of his teacher, many of which he'd witnessed himself. No wonder then, that Reb Yaakov was crowned with the title, "The Master of Stories."

During one of his journeys, Reb Yaakov traveled to the city of Konigsberg in East Prussia. There lived a wealthy Jew, respected for his munificence. No less than ten young men lived in his home studying Torah full-time, all their needs provided for by their benefactor. Along with his generosity, this gentleman was also dedicated to performing mitzvot, good deeds. He was delighted to invite Reb Yaakov to be a guest in his home.

When his host learned that Reb Yaakov had been a student of the recently deceased Ba'al Shem Tov, he was eager to hear firsthand accounts of the holy tzaddik, whose reputation extended across the land. Would Reb Yaakov relate a few stories about the Besht that Friday night at the *tish*, the communal table where members of the community gathered after finishing their own family meals?

Friday night arrived, and along with it, the *tish*. After Torah had been discussed and the Shabbos melodies sung, the wealthy patron turned to Reb Yaakov and asked him to regale the assembled with a story about the Besht. All instantly turned their attention to the guest.

Reb Yaakov wrapped his fingers around his beard, nodded, and began: "One time, as I recall...."

But he could recall nothing. A fog had settled in his brain. Not a single anecdote or Torah insight came to mind. How was this possible? He'd personally witnessed hundreds of incredible events involving the Ba'al Shem Tov, and had heard tales of hundreds more. He'd told these stories countless times. But now nothing came to mind.

His host raised his eyebrows and waited, but all Reb Yaakov could do was shrug his shoulders.

"I'm terribly sorry," he murmured. "For some reason I can't seem to remember anything this night. But surely tomorrow—"

"Yes, tomorrow, after services," the rich man said, giving his guest the benefit of the doubt. "We will gather again and hear a story about your celebrated teacher."

But the next day, as Reb Yaakov tried to recall an incident – any incident – involving the Besht, his memory was again vacant. Reb Yaakov looked over at his disappointed host.

"At *shalush seudas*," he said. Surely, by the third Shabbos meal, his memory would return, and he'd be able to provide a recollection of the saintly Ba'al Shem Tov.

When no recollection presented itself even at the third meal, his host didn't know what to think. A refined and considerate man, he didn't wish to press his guest too strongly and cause him further humiliation. On the other hand, he began to wonder if, in fact, this Reb Yaakov might not be a fraud, an imposter posing as a student of the Ba'al Shem Tov to receive honor and money. How else to explain why he could not relate even one personal anecdote about his supposed teacher?

Reb Yaakov himself was utterly baffled. When surrounded by others, his mind was unaccountably blank. Yet as soon as he returned to the solitude of his room, he was greeted by a cascade of memories.

A few days later, a crestfallen Reb Yaakov bade farewell to his host, and again apologized for failing to tell him anything about the Ba'al Shem Tov. Alas, he could offer no reasonable explanation. The Koenigsberger gentleman nonetheless gave Reb Yaakov a donation, along with a grim-faced goodbye.

But the moment Reb Yaakov stepped into his small coach, he was suddenly struck with a memory of the Besht so vivid, it was as though he were observing the events then and there. He jumped down from the wagon and ran after his host. "Please, one moment!" he shouted. "I suddenly remember a story about the Besht. Please allow me to tell it to you."

The host, somewhat skeptical, but still eager to hear about the holy Ba'al Shem Tov, invited Reb Yaakov back into his house and bade him to recount his tale. In an excited gush of words, Reb Yaakov began his story.

It was a wintry evening, which also happened to be the Polish holiday of Wigilia, the evening before Christmas, when the local gentiles gather for prayer and devotion. It was also a holiday when Jews were best advised to stay inside their homes.

It was on this evening that I was summoned by the Ba'al Shem Tov and instructed to harness the horses and prepare a wagon. We were to embark on a journey. When? Where? I knew better than to ask. The sudden announcement of an expedition was not new to me; periodically, the Besht would ask me to accompany him on some mission or other. I rarely could fathom the reasons for these excursions, but understood they were of great importance.

"Although the evening was bitterly cold, and the danger for Jews to travel on the Kaiser's roadways particularly fraught, if the Besht said we must travel, then surely we must."

Reb Yaakov slowed his speech, reassured his recollection would not escape him now.

As soon as we reached the main road, the Besht asked the coach driver to turn his back to his horses and with *kefitzas haderekh*, the miraculous "shortening of the journey" for which the Besht was renowned, we soon entered the town of Brody. When we rode through the city's main marketplace, I noticed that the streets, usually brimming with Jews, were entirely deserted. As we traveled on, I saw that all the Jewish houses were darkened, their windows tightly shuttered. This was, remember, the evening of Wigilia, on which priests preached hatred of the Jews and the gentile townspeople responded in kind.

As we drove down a particular boulevard, the Besht suddenly asked the driver to stop. "Go knock on that door," he said to me, pointing to one of the houses. "Ask the residents to let us in." I knocked as instructed, but received no answer. I knocked again. Still nothing. I knocked yet again, this time pleading in Yiddish that we be let in. At last, the door opened a crack, and an elderly, frightened woman asked what we wanted. "We'd like to stay in your home for a short while," I said, and the woman quickly ushered us in, wondering aloud what in heaven's name Jews were doing on the road that night.

When the holy Besht entered the house, he quickly asked me to help open the shutters so that he could look out into the street. The poor woman was terrified by the Besht's request; if he could look directly out to the street, those on the street could look directly at him.

Soon, a huge Christian procession began making its way down our street. We could see the burning lamps held high and the marchers carrying wooden relics and crosses. A priest dressed in full religious regalia led the parade, which soon reached our house.

And there, right before us, the priest stopped and a small stage was placed on the ground. The priest stepped onto this platform, and began his ceremony. The entire crowd lowered their heads as he recited his benediction. The Besht looked directly at the priest as he delivered his sermon, and then, turning to me, said, "Yaakov, go out there and tell the priest that Israel Ba'al Shem wishes to speak with him."

The elderly woman wailed in disbelief. "For God's sake," she begged, "please do not do this. Can't you hear how they are calling all Jews Judas? Don't you know how ready they are to inflict bodily harm on us this night? You are putting your life in danger."

This woman was clearly unaware of the holiness of the man standing in her room. As for me, I knew the mysterious ways of my teacher and felt no fear.

I walked out into the midst of the assembled people who formed a path for me. I made my way directly to the priest, stepped up on the podium, and whispered in his ear that the Ba'al Shem Tov wished to have a word with him.

I was astonished when the priest immediately called to his assistant, instructed him to continue with the service, and followed me back to the house.

The priest and the Besht retired to a separate room, where they remained for quite a while. When they emerged, the priest returned to the procession and the Besht signaled to me that we could now begin our journey home.

The Konigsberg gentleman waited to hear more, but Reb Yaakov said no more.

"But what did the two speak about?" he demanded

Reb Yaakov shrugged. "What did they speak about? I have no idea."

"But surely—"

Reb Yaakov shrugged once more, shaking his head. "To tell you the truth, I have no idea what this trip to Brody was about. But this is the story about the Besht that came to mind, and so it is the story I have told you."

The Koenigsberger patron's eyes widened. He remained transfixed for several moments and then rose from his chair and embraced Reb Yaakov.

"Thank you, thank you so much," he exclaimed, his face now radiant. "You have no idea…" He returned to his chair. "My dear Reb Yaakov, now it is my turn. Let me tell you how your story ends. And how it began."

Not far from the town of Medzhybizh, there lived a fine Jew whose son was, shall we say, wayward. The young man was well versed in Torah and secular subjects as well; it was, however, the latter that held his interest. Over the years, he veered further and further from Jewish tradition. He began studying Christianity and soon converted. The young man's commitment to Christianity deepened and eventually he became a priest.

The father traveled to Medzhybizh to speak with the Ba'al Shem Tov and begged him to meet with his son and return him to his people. The Ba'al Shem Tov, however, could offer no solace. He explained to the father that everyone has the power to choose the life they wish to live and this is the path his son has chosen. The embittered father said to the Besht, "If you cannot get him to repent, then I ask you to curse him. If he wishes to remain a priest, then better he should not live at all."

The Ba'al Shem Tov sent word to the priest that he wished to meet with him. And out of respect, this newly ordained priest consented to meet with the holy rabbi. The Ba'al Shem Tov engaged the young man in a theological discussion, but soon realized his efforts at persuasion would not succeed.

"Listen to me," the Besht said. "Your father asked me to curse you if you insist on remaining a Christian, a priest no less. You should also know my imprecations are not idle. They will come to pass. But I will not curse you. I will not pray for your harm. Why? Because I believe every person can repent. It is never too late to reconsider one's decisions. In the meantime, I want to tell you this: do not harm your former people. Do not stir hatred toward them or seek their misfortune. Because if you do, my curse will follow you wherever you go and your truncated life will be miserable."

The priest nodded solemnly. "I understand. I will do as you ask."

Some years later, this man was appointed chief priest of Brody, a city with many Jewish inhabitants. He kept his promise to the Ba'al Shem Tov and never spouted anti-Semitic rhetoric from the pulpit, nor provoked hostility toward the Jews in his personal remarks.

But on one occasion – this was during the holiday of Chanukah – his attitude abruptly changed. Some minor event concerning the Jews had irked him that day, and when he observed them celebrating their ancient miracle, his irritation turned venomous. "Joyous, are you today?"

he whispered. "Well, the Christian holiday of Wigilia is approaching. We'll see how you celebrate your miracles once I let loose my devoted flock and they turn into wolves."

Forgetting his promise to the Ba'al Shem Tov, the priest prepared a vengeful anti-Semitic holiday sermon aimed at stirring the ready bigotry of his followers. He led the procession down Brody's main street and had just begun his sermon when a Jew suddenly appeared at his side, whispering in his ear that the Ba'al Shem Tov wished to speak with him immediately.

A shudder ran through him as he stared at the sermon in his hand and recalled his promise to the Besht. Without hesitation, he followed the Jew to the house where the Besht awaited him. Entering the room, he sank to his knees, overcome with fear along with a mixture of sadness, confusion and regret. Was he really about to unleash violence on the Jews ... *his* Jews, *his* people? He knew the time had come to foreswear his apostasy and return to the Judaism of his youth. He begged the Ba'al Shem Tov to instruct him on what to do next.

The two spent many minutes in that room. The Besht soothed the shaken man and gently suggested the step he'd need to undertake to fully repent. The erstwhile convert thanked the Besht for his advice and assured him he would follow his recommendations. But before leaving, he asked, "How will I know if my repentance is complete?"

The Besht raised a finger into the air and replied: "When someone tells you your own story, you will know that your repentance has been accepted."

The Koenigsberger gentleman leaned toward his guest and said, "Perhaps now you can better understand my disappointment when you, who'd known the Besht personally, could not recall any story of the Holy Master. But you now also understand how great is my joy at hearing your tale.

"The priest? Yes, that was me. Hearing your story – my story – I know the tribulation of my repentance is finally over. I have completed what I have been asked to do. I can now rest."

Reb Yaakov rose from his chair.

"My dear friend," he began, "I, too, have fulfilled a mission by telling you this story. Now I too can rest."

The Pious Thief

There lived in Belz a Jew named Yaakov Itche who, like many Jews in the town, had seven or eight children – a formidable number of mouths to feed. Yaakov Itche got by. He certainly didn't live a life of luxury and would have liked to spend more hours in the *beis medrash* studying Torah or listening to the teachings of his rebbe, the great Maggid, but his modest textile business sustained his family sufficiently and afforded him time for his religious and communal activities.

As did other Chassidim, Yaakov Itche became a different man on Shabbos. He dressed in his best clothing, prayed and sang with his fellow Chassidim, and together with them, nurtured his soul from the fountain of the rebbe's insights. On Shabbos, he was even able to forget about the new competitor who'd recently opened up a store directly across the street and was making serious inroads into his customer base. He put such weekday concerns on hold; on the day of rest, better to tend to matters of the soul.

But the reality of his dwindling livelihood could not be so easily ignored. Even his dependable customers now did their shopping at his competitor's store and too many days went by without a single customer crossing his threshold. In better times, Yaakov Itche was able to find a few minutes between sales to study a page of Mishnah, but now he could spend his day studying entire chapters.

Yaakov Itche would come home now without a coin in his pocket, and when his wife Malka greeted him with an inquisitive look, he'd lower his head and mutter that he had nothing. Another useless day. Once more, the children would go to sleep hungry. Yaakov Itche retreated to his room, where he tried to lose himself in his studies.

Yaakov Itche was a pious man. He interpreted events as God's decrees and did not believe he was owed an easy life. He didn't even have complaints against his competitor, who, after all, was engaged in legitimate business rivalry. True, his poverty was bitter, but surely it was part of some larger plan leading to an ultimate good. This is what one ought to believe, and so he did.

But this comforting sentiment grew hollow when he confronted the faces of his hungry children. How many weeks had it been since they'd tasted a piece of meat? How many nights had they gone to bed with rumbling in their empty stomachs? As for Malka, the night finally arrived when she decided she had no choice but to speak plainly to her husband.

"Why not sell your business to your competitor and start something new?" she asked.

Yaakov Itche did sell his business. But the meager revenue from the sale brought home nothing more than some meat for the Shabbos meal. With no alternatives at hand, Yaakov Itche spent the following weeks studying the Talmud and its commentaries, and learning Torah with his children, insisting, as always, that one must accept one's plight with equanimity.

Weeks went by this way. Then months. The townsfolk were aware of Yaakov Itche's penury. All he had left, they said one to another, were his good heart and good character. Still, they'd add, were these not a person's most important assets? And anyway, they'd conclude before moving on to a different topic, Yaakov Itche was not the first and would surely not be the last person whose fortunes had gone sour. Sometimes, that was simply the way it is.

But such philosophizing cannot pacify a mother of starving children. Malka implored her husband to go to the rebbe, pour out his heart, and ask his advice.

At first, Yaakov Itche ignored his wife's plea. Only the boorish bother the Rebbe with mundane concerns about income and physical well-being; a true Chassid turns to his rebbe for help in matters of spiritual growth and religious understanding. As the days passed, however, Yaakov Itche realized he could not ignore the needs of his children and torment his well-meaning wife, so he put on his patched-up Shabbos coat and went to see his rebbe.

The rebbe read the *kvittel*, Yaakov Itche's note describing his pressing poverty – no doubt due to his spiritual failings, he wrote – along with a request that the rebbe pray on his behalf.

The holy rebbe put the note aside and, turning to Yaakov Itche, spoke in a gentle voice.

"We know that sometimes a man does not succeed in business because his business is not appropriate for him. But it's also true that a person can succeed in a business that does not initially seem suitable. Success can come from the most unexpected sources.

"Reb Yaakov Itche," the rebbe continued, speaking more deliberately and slowly. "Sometimes it is fated that a man succeed only through sin. That he act dishonestly to arrive at a decent, honest living."

Reb Yaakov Itche said nothing, not following the rebbe's meaning.

"I'm afraid that is your current situation," the rebbe continued. "This is what you should do."

"What? What should I do?"

"I know it will not be easy."

"Please, Rebbe, I do not understand you."

"Become a thief."

"A thief?!" Yaakov Itche's eyes widened in disbelief. He was a man of probity, a devoted Chassid, and his rebbe was suggesting that he become a burglar? How could this be?

When Yaakov Itche arrived home, Malka immediately demanded a report on what had transpired at the rebbe's.

"What did he suggest you do?" she asked, wringing her hands.

Yaakov Itche looked her in the eyes, his mouth trembling, but no words formed. He turned away, unable to repeat what he'd heard. Instead, he shook his head and retired to his room, where he recited Psalms and yielded to tearful sobs.

The next day, Malka stood before her husband, frantic. She'd run out of places to borrow money and could no longer stand putting the children to bed famished.

"Please, Yaakov Itche. You know I try my best not to complain and on most nights, I don't. All your learning, all the rewards of the next world that await you – that's all fine. But it all pales in the face of our hungry children. Is it not true that *pekuakh nefesh*, the command to save a life in danger, trumps all other religious demands? You must do something."

"All right," he whispered to himself as much as to Malka. He knew his wife was right.

"I'll get us some money."

Late that night, Yaakov Itche made his way into town dressed in his tattered Shabbos coat and the Shabbos sable hat that still remained from his better days, to underscore, if only to himself, that he was, in fact, fulfilling a mitzvah.

He walked with surprising steadiness, repeating to himself that what he was about to do was permissible. His own rebbe had said so.

At the first store he encountered, Yaakov Itche took a deep breath and looked around to make sure he was alone. He tried the door and was astonished at how easily it unlocked. He crept inside and opened a drawer in the back of the room. To his astonishment, it held tens of bank notes. Yaakov Itche helped himself to only one, leaving the others in place, and went home.

In the morning, he gave Malka the banknote, instructing her not to spend it on luxuries like butter and meat, but only on necessities such as bread. He then went to his room to study.

When the owner arrived at his stall the next morning and noticed the door ajar, he immediately surmised that a burglar had visited his store. Seeing the open drawer, he also assumed that all its contents were stolen, but a quick count confirmed that only a single banknote was missing. How strange!

Reports of this odd robbery soon became the talk of the town.

A couple of weeks went by and hunger again visited the home of Yaakov Itche. Malka's sighs accompanied the moans of their hungry children, and once more Yaakov Itche promised he'd have a bit of money for her the next morning. Several hours after nightfall, he again dressed in his holiday finery and walked into town.

As on the previous night, he had little difficulty gaining entrance to another kiosk. He located the cash drawer, removed a single banknote, leaving the others in place, and exited.

Over the course of the following months, he repeated this pattern again and again. In the marketplace, Jews and gentiles alike buzzed with talk about the mysterious thief who stole only the barest minimum when he could take so much more. Who might he be? Theories were plentiful. Curiosity, no less than the desire to bring the thief to justice, motivated several townspeople to volunteer as guards. They'd gladly forgo a night's sleep to catch the burglar and discover his identity. Yet, despite their many nights patrolling the town, no one ever saw the man.

Not a few concluded they were wasting their time. This thief was not human at all, but some sort of ghost, a phantom impervious to detection.

Soon, word of this elusive, so-called honest thief reached the local poretz. Overwhelmed with curiosity, he decided to patrol the area himself. As fate would have it, the night he was set to serve as guard was the night Yaakov Itche decided to strike again.

Dressed in his usual finery, Yaakov Itche made his way into town. Once more, he approached a stall and once more, managed to open its door without much effort. As was his custom, he removed only a single banknote and was preparing to leave when he heard a shout from behind him.

"Aha!"

Yaakov Itche turned around to find himself facing a large, muscular man blocking the entrance, dressed in the uniform of a town guard.

"So, you are the famous thief we've all been talking about," the man said. "Well, your thieving escapades are over. You've been caught. Now come with me to the police."

Noting the man's size and official attire, Yaakov Itche realized there was no possibility of escape.

"I only steal because I'm desperate to feed my family," he pleaded.

The guard took hold of Yaakov Itche. "I'm not interested in your sob stories. Come along, we're going to the police station."

"I promise I am not a thief by nature," Yaakov Itche implored. "I've been driven to this profession strictly by necessity. But if you let me go, I promise to never do it again."

"Okay," the guard said. "Let's see. You're clearly an excellent thief, but apparently one with some honesty about you. So I'll let you go...if you accept this offer. I've heard from very reliable sources – don't ask for details – the poretz has won a huge sum of money in a recent lottery. I have also learned – again, I can't reveal my sources – that he keeps this money in the third drawer of the desk in his boardroom. Apparently, no one in his household knows where this money is kept. Here is what I propose: the two of us will go to the poretz's house and I'll wait up the road. You make your way into the house and steal the money, which the two of us will divide equally, then go our separate ways."

Yaakov Itche repeated once more he wasn't a real thief and certainly wasn't interested in stealing such a huge sum of money, but seeing as how the guard would not let him leave unless he agreed, and concerned, too, about the *khillul Hashem*, the shame his arrest would bring to the Jewish community, Yaakov Itche agreed to the proposal.

That night, the poretz, maintaining his identity as just another guard, waited down the road as Yaakov Itche made his way to the house. Just a few minutes later, he saw Yaakov Itche returning toward him.

"Good news," Yaakov Itche said.

"You got the money?"

"No."

"No? So what's the good news?"

"I didn't have to steal it."

The poretz shook his head. "I'm not following. What happened?"

"When I got into the house," said Yaakov Itche, "I happened to overhear two people talking on the other side of a wall. One asked if the poison was ready. The other said that it was. The first then said, 'Tomorrow afternoon, before I bring the poretz his tea, I'll put the poison in. It'll take but a couple of minutes for it to do its work. And then we can help ourselves to the loot in that drawer. No one will ever know about the money or our robbery. It's perfect.'"

The poretz, taken aback, looked away for a moment before responding. "Interesting, but I still don't understand why you didn't take the money."

"Because now we don't need to," said Yaakov Itche. "I'll inform the poretz about the planned assassination and I'm sure I'll receive a reward in return, which we'll share."

The poretz, still posing as a guard, agreed to let Yaakov Itche go home for the night.

In the morning, one of the poretz's messengers appeared at Yaakov Itche's and asked that he return with him to the nobleman's home. Yaakov Itche followed behind the man, terrified about what awaited him: it was possible, indeed probable, that the guard had informed the poretz about his plan to steal his money, and who knew what punishment he'd receive as a result? Finally, they reached the residence. With a shudder and a prayer on his lips, Yaakov Itche entered the poretz's study.

The poretz embraced Yaakov Itche, who immediately recognized him as the guard from the previous evening.

"Yes, that was me," the poretz said with a smile. "The plot you told me about turned out to be true. Indeed, they were planning to kill me and take the money. You saved my life."

Yaakov Itche was at once astonished and relieved.

"I see you are an honest man, indeed," the poretz said. "I wasn't sure, but now I'm convinced you wouldn't steal if you didn't have to, and won't steal even if you could be wealthy as a result."

The poretz withdrew an envelope from his pocket.

"Here, take this. A reward, you might say. There is enough here for you to open a legitimate business. In fact, there's enough here to provide for you and your family for the rest of your life." The poretz looked up at Yaakov Itche and added with a smile, "Without ever having to steal again."

A Cautionary Note

This story takes place in those years, and there were many, when the Polish poretz, the provincial nobleman, had complete control over the lives of the citizens in his domain. The peasants worked his land and earned their keep by his sufferance. A merciless poretz could draw the blood from the marrow of his people; if he was a drunk or a sadist – and neither was unusual – his population lived in terror. In fact, it was not unheard of for a poretz to decree capital punishment for even minor offenses.

The Jews who leased the poretz's taverns, the innkeepers, were especially dependent on their nobleman's character. A decent poretz could ensure a decent livelihood for his Jewish innkeeper, whereas a mean-spirited poretz meant misery.

Yisroel had the misfortune of working for a particularly loathsome poretz. The nobleman demanded unusually high rents from his kretchma operators and punished the failure to pay on time with imprisonment in his private dungeon, and not only for the tardy tavernkeeper, but for his entire family. Some who'd been thrust into this poretz's pit never emerged.

One terrible day, Yisroel was unable to garner enough money to pay his monthly fee. Within hours, the poretz's henchmen arrived at Yisroel's door to deposit him, his wife and infant son into the tiny, damp cell, where they were sentenced to remain for months without appeal.

To add to their wretchedness, the poretz appointed the drunkard Janek to be their guard. Janek despised Yisroel because he'd sometimes refused to give him credit to purchase additional shots of vodka, and he relished the opportunity to treat Yisroel and his family with spiteful malice. A particular favorite pastime of Janek's was to shout into the small hole that constituted the dungeon's window: "Srulik, you still alive? Come, I have cake and wine for you!" Then, when Yisroel would reach up for the family's daily ration of bread and water, Janek would spill the water on the floor. He'd follow this stunt by tearing the ration of stale bread into small pieces, which he hurled to the ground so that Yisroel had no choice but to get on his hands and knees to gather the crumbs to feed his hungry wife and child.

Janek considered these antics hilarious.

The leaders of the Jewish community petitioned the poretz to have some mercy on Yisroel or, at least, allow his wife and child to return home.

"Let them all rot," was the poretz's reply.

But Yisroel's gentile neighbor Piotr would not let his friend rot. He was a kindly man who felt a close attachment to Yisroel and his family, visiting the prison regularly to learn how Yisroel fared and, when possible, smuggling in food for the couple along with milk for the child.

On one visit when the two friends were able to snatch some conversation, Yisroel told Piotr that the situation had become impossible and he couldn't hold out much longer.

"Our little Dovid'l is running a dangerous fever. The baby's lips are parched and that drunkard Janek won't even bring the bit of water the poretz allows us. I don't think the child can survive like this much longer."

"I have a plan to get you out of here," Piotr whispered. He looked around and, seeing no one, removed a flask of whiskey from his pocket and pushed it through the small cell hole. "Take this," he said. "It's powerful whiskey. The strongest around."

Piotr lowered his voice further and spoke quickly. "Listen, here's what you do. Late tonight, when everyone in the village is asleep, call over Janek and show him the whiskey bottle. Say it somehow got into your possession, or you always had it with you … it doesn't matter. Just make sure to offer Janek a drink. I assure you that drunkard will grab the flask from you and not return it. In fact, I wager that he'll drink it all in one sitting. And with this whiskey? I can also assure you he'll be asleep in no time.

"And don't worry, I'll be there watching the whole time. When I'm sure he's knocked out, I'll take the key from his pocket and open your cell."

Yisroel interrupted, "But where could—"

Piotr kept talking. "I'll have prepared a wagon with two fast horses and a competent driver to take you and your family far away from here. Far enough so that you'll be beyond the poretz's jurisdiction. There you'll be able to begin your life anew."

"It's a good idea," Yisroel said, "but I can't do it. Our Dovid'l is deathly ill. A long trip like that would certainly kill him."

"And what do you think?" Piotr countered. "That little Dovid'l will survive here in this cold prison? Without milk, without water? No, better you and your wife escape. And when they discover the child here, I will volunteer to raise him and convince the poretz to give him to me. Once you are established safely elsewhere, I'll send you little Dovid'l. I give you my word." Yisroel agreed and was about to say something else when he saw Janek approaching the cell. The two friends bade each other a hasty goodbye.

The next hours were interminable for Yisroel. His heartbeat galloped as he waited anxiously for nightfall to begin the execution of Piotr's scheme.

As Piotr predicted, Janek grabbed the flask of whiskey as soon as it was proffered, drank it all down in quick gulps and fell sound asleep, allowing Piotr to retrieve the key and unlock the prison door. The waiting wagon dashed off at high speed and was soon outside the boundaries of the poretz's domain.

When Janek woke from his inebriated slumber he strolled over to the cell and let out a loud scream.

"They're gone!"

His cries reached the home of the poretz, who came running to the dungeon. Where were the prisoners? He seethed at the dereliction of his guards and furiously demanded these Jews be apprehended.

When Janek informed him that the Jews had left their child behind, the poretz rubbed his hands against each other while his lips formed a cruel sneer. "Excellent, bring me the kid. I'll take care of it as it deserves to be taken care of."

Just then, Piotr appeared.

"Dear poretz, I have a better idea. You want truly sweet revenge on these Jews? Let me have the boy. I have no children of my own and I'll raise him as a Christian – what wonderful retribution that would be."

The poretz thought this a superb suggestion and had the child handed over to Piotr.

Piotr had always adored little Dovid'l and he and his wife tended to the sick child with care and compassion. The baby regained his health and soon his cooing and giggles lit up their home.

Despite his deepening attachment to the child, Piotr intended to keep his word: as soon as he heard from Yisroel, he'd return the child to his parents.

Two years passed and then the letter came. It began with a heartfelt thanks to Piotr for his brave help in arranging their freedom. Yisroel also wrote of his deep gratitude for his friend's generosity in caring for his child. But now, Yisroel was happy to inform Piotr, he could relieve him of that burden.

> *Thank God, I'm living beyond the reach of your poretz. I'm earning a respectable living managing a new kretchma for a nobleman who is principled and fair. Enclosed are a few rubles that should cover the expenses for Dovid'l's trip. As you can imagine, we can't wait to see him.*

Piotr was thrust into emotional turmoil. He was a man of his word and he'd made a promise. Moreover, Yisroel was his friend. But when Dovid'l would call out "Daddy," and crawl up to his lap, the idea of parting with the child seemed unbearable. The child had transformed their home into one of joy. When Piotr showed Yisroel's letter to his wife, she immediately shook her head: no way would she give up the child. He was everything to her.

Piotr did not respond to Yisroel's letter.

As the months dragged on and he'd heard nothing from Piotr, Yisroel reached the conclusion that Dovid'l had died back in that prison and that his friend hadn't written back to spare him this painful information. By then, Yisroel and his wife had been blessed with two more children, and they tried their best to put the memory of Dovid'l behind them.

Years passed. Dovid'l – or Stefan as he was now called – grew into a happy twelve-year-old, popular with his peasant cohorts. Tall and healthy, he had flushed cheeks, bright eyes and a sharp mind.

One afternoon, Stefan and one of his friends got into an argument that soon escalated into a scuffle. Punches were traded, with Stefan landing the harder blows and drawing blood. He had pinned his adversary to the ground when his exasperated friend cried out: "Let go of me, you Jew!"

Stefan could tell from his friend's tone this was not just an idle taunt, but had the ring of truth. Stefan gripped his friend tighter.

"What are you saying? I won't let you budge until you explain what you mean, calling me a Jew."

"Well, you are a Jew," his friend said in a muffled voice. "Everyone knows you're a Jew. What do you think, dummy? That Piotr is your real father? Now, let me go."

Stefan stood up. He knew his friend wasn't making this up. Tears welled up in his eyes as he ran home as fast as his legs would carry him.

"Tell me the truth," he demanded of Piotr as soon as he entered the house. "I need to know. Are you my father? My real father? Am I a Jew?"

"What are you talking about?" Piotr answered, hoping Stefan wouldn't notice how his lips trembled as he spoke. "Of course you are our son. What is this nonsense? You are a good Christian boy."

But over the coming days, Stefan would not stop pestering Piotr, detecting the hesitation in his voice. Every day, he'd ask Piotr to assure him that he was his real father.

After many such exchanges, Piotr could no longer lie to the boy. He knew he had no choice but to tell him the circumstances by which he'd come to their home. He told him his name was Dovid, or Dovid'l as he'd once been called. He told him his parents were still alive, living somewhere beyond the poretz's reach.

For the next several weeks, Dovid'l could think of nothing other than the fact that he was Jewish and his parents alive. Restless and confused, he became obsessed with the idea of leaving home to find them.

Piotr sat Dovid'l down for a talk. He expressed his love for the boy and his hope that he wouldn't forsake him. He also pointed out that should Dovid'l run away, the poretz would consider Piotr complicit.

"The nobleman's wrath would be unforgiving. I just want you to be aware of the consequences," he told the boy.

Dovid'l agonized over his dilemma. Although he was determined to leave his hamlet and reclaim his life as a Jew, he loved the two people who had raised him and could not bear the thought of causing them any suffering. He spent his nights sleepless, until at last he came up with a plan: As he no longer wished to live in his present home, he'd offer to remain on the poretz's property and work for his keep. By telling the poretz the decision was his own, that he no longer considered himself the couple's child, they would not incur the poretz's wrath.

The next day, when Dovid'l went to see the poretz, the nobleman was thrilled with the boy's proposal. His hatred for Yisroel had not abated over the years, nor had his desire for revenge. And here was Yisroel's son, asking for work.

"A fine idea," he said to the boy with a glint in his eye. "Yes, you will do labor for me. But you must begin now."

Within hours, the poretz had assigned Dovid'l to the most degrading, difficult work he could think of: cleaning out stalls, scrubbing latrines, lugging heavy stones in the field.

Dovid'l dutifully accepted his chores, but while he toiled, he plotted his flight. He was comforted knowing that if his strategy succeeded, Piotr could not be blamed for his disappearance.

Piotr visited Dovid'l regularly, and his heart ached when he saw the menial burdens Stefan was forced to endure. Even though he was aware that the boy had chosen this path, Piotr decided that he must help the boy flee the poretz's clutches, just as he had once done for his father.

One morning, Piotr learned that the poretz would be embarking later that day on a trip to the town of Zlotchov. And so, Piotr made his way to the poretz's estate, where he soon found Dovid'l in a barn pitching hay. He passed a few rubles into the boy's hand and said, "This afternoon you can leave. The poretz is going to Zlotchov. I've made the necessary arrangements. Someone will help you hide in the back of one of the accompanying wagons. Once you arrive in Zlotchov you can run away. The poretz has no dominion there. You'll be beyond his control."

Dovid'l and Piotr embraced.

"Thank you. I won't forget you," Dovid'l whispered.

"Good luck," Piotr said, as he stepped away and turned around so the boy would not see the tears running down his face.

Zlotchov was teeming with Jews. Never had Dovid'l seen so many. As soon as the wagons reached Zlotchov and he was sure he'd not been detected, Dovid'l leaped from the wagon, realizing he was free. And now, walking the streets of this town, he was surrounded by Jews. His fellow Jews. He walked and walked but hadn't a clue about what he might do next.

The thought occurred to him to go see the rabbi of the town, but when he asked Jewish passers-by for directions, they looked at him askance and refused to answer. He spoke no Yiddish. He knew no Hebrew. He was dressed in gentile peasant clothes that marked him an outsider. What business was it of his where their rabbi lived?

Finally, he managed to find one man who agreed to give him the address and soon Dovid'l arrived at the court of the tzaddik Reb Mikhel. He was shocked when one of the rabbi's assistants waved him in to the rabbi's private study. "What brings you here?" asked the rabbi, and suddenly Dovid'l found himself pouring out his entire story: his parents' imprisonment, his life as Piotr's son, his desire to return to the Jewish faith.

The rebbe welcomed the boy and invited him to remain in his home. For the coming weeks, the rebbe himself attended to the boy's education, teaching him how to read Hebrew and the fundamentals of Jewish practice.

Dovid'l drank in the rebbe's lessons like a thirsty wanderer in the desert. He proved to be extremely bright and in no time had learned how to read Hebrew and soon understood much of what he read as well. The rebbe, pleased with the boy's progress, found him a tutor to further his studies.

"I'm putting you in charge of an exceptional young man," the rebbe instructed. "A lost Jewish soul. Teach him Bible, Talmud and the importance of being a mensch." The tutor was equally astounded by Dovid'l's diligence and abilities. When Dovid'l turned thirteen, Reb Mikhel strapped the tefillin on the young man and celebrated the bar mitzvah feast as if it were his own son's celebration. Dovid'l's bar mitzvah discourse on an obscure matter of Jewish law impressed the learned in the audience, who were still discussing it weeks later.

By the time he was seventeen, Dovid'l was an accomplished scholar. One day, the rebbe asked Dovid'l to join him in his room. There was something to discuss.

"Dovid'l," the rebbe began, "you were brought up as a gentile and spent your childhood as a gentile. Of course, this was not the result of your choosing. But we are taught that the activities of one's body affect one's soul. You spent many years eating non-kosher, violating the Sabbath and the holidays, praying in a Christian church. It would be a good idea to clean that slate, blameless though you are for its cause. For we are taught that in so doing, our previous actions are not only erased but also transformed into positive deeds – a transgression repented counts as a *zkhus*, a merit."

Now his eyes met Dovid'l's.

"I want you to take the wanderer's stick in your hand," the rebbe continued. "As you know, many of the most righteous Chassidic masters undertook a year of exile. You are old enough to bear this burden.

"Take to the road for one year. And heed these instructions. Where you sleep, you will not spend the day, and where you spend the day, you will not sleep. But, if you arrive somewhere where they ask you to stay, do so."

The rebbe paused and lifted his finger in the air, signaling he had more to say. He leaned closer to the young man.

"Dovid'l, you know you will soon be eighteen years old. We say, 'at eighteen, the canopy.' Yes, it is time for you to marry. So here is my further instruction: Accept the first match proposed to you."

Dovid'l took a deep breath and nodded. "I'm ready to begin my journey today," he said.

But as he turned to leave, Reb Mikhel asked that he wait for a moment. "There's something I must give you before you go."

The rebbe reached into his drawer and removed a small folded and sealed piece of paper.

"Take this, Dovid'l, and sew it into your *talis kuton*, the fringed garment we wear under our jackets. And remember this: when, with mazel, you accept a marriage proposal and become a groom, remove this piece of paper and read what is written there. Do you follow?"

"I do," Dovid'l assured the rebbe. He received the tzaddik's blessings, said farewell to his companions and set out on his travels.

Dovid'l wandered where his feet took him, from hamlet to hamlet, from village to village, never sleeping where he spent the day, nor spending the day where he'd spent the night. He was continuously cold and hungry and weary. But the greatest hardship for him was not having a place to sit and study Torah nor the opportunity to pray with a minyan. Still, Dovid'l dutifully, even happily, accepted these privations if they would make amends in the cosmic balance for his past transgressions.

Near the end of his year of wandering, Dovid'l stopped off at a kretchma not far from the city of Brod. The Jewish tavernkeeper was a gentle soul who provided Dovid'l with a warm meal and a quiet place to sleep. In the morning, as Dovid'l prepared to resume his journey, the tavernkeeper approached the young man and suggested he remain at the tavern for a few days.

"Rest a bit. You're clearly exhausted from your travels. You'll eat and sleep, and regain your strength. Then you can move on to wherever it is you're going."

Dovid'l recalled his rebbe's instruction to accept any invitation and agreed to the tavernkeeper's offer. He thanked the man and withdrew to a corner, opened his Talmud, and immersed himself in its pages.

At first, Dovid'l paid no attention to the voices coming from the next room. But then, almost involuntarily, he deciphered words of Torah. Someone was explaining a passage of Talmud and two children were responding. But the teacher was getting it all wrong! He was mistranslating phrases and utterly misunderstanding the point of the argument. Dovid'l didn't wish to intercede, but also felt an obligation to correct the misinformation.

He looked into the room and saw a young man, no older than himself, instructing two eager children, the children of the tavernkeeper, presumably. In a friendly, unassuming manner, Dovid'l excused his interruption and demonstrated the correct reading of the text.

"What?" the tutor sneered. "You think you know this material better than I do? You of all people – a vagabond, a tramp!"

The tavernkeeper overheard the commotion. He had long suspected that his children's tutor was not as educated as he claimed. He could also see that his new lodger had a great deal of knowledge as well as a kind demeanor. The tavernkeeper counted out a sum of money and handed it to the tutor. "I thank you for your services," he said, "but I don't think we'll be needing them any longer. This should cover your projected income for the coming year."

After the tutor had left, the tavernkeeper asked Dovid'l if he'd like the tutoring job, and Dovid'l agreed.

The children responded well to Dovid'l's lessons and, in turn, Dovid'l grew close to the children.

After several weeks, the tavernkeeper brought his children with him to see the Rav, the town rabbi, who tested them on their studies. When the examination was over, the Rav told the tavernkeeper he was amazed at their progress. Clearly they must be studying with someone new.

"Indeed," the tavernkeeper replied. "They have a new instructor. A wonderful young man."

"Well," the Rav said, "let me assure you, this tutor is also a scholar. He'd taught the children insights only someone steeped in Torah learning could. I'd very much like to meet him."

When Dovid'l arrived at the Rav's home it took but a few introductory moments before the two were engaged in an animated discussion about some difficult Talmudic passage.

"You have a genuine treasure in your home," he told the tavernkeeper when they again met.

"Don't I know," the tavernkeeper agreed. "I've had the pleasure of watching this young man up close and I'm tremendously impressed."

The tavernkeeper had a sixteen-year-old daughter and he observed Dovid'l with yet another aim in mind. This young man would be an outstanding choice for a son-in-law, he realized. Here was a match he ought not squander. And so when he asked Dovid'l if he'd like to marry his daughter, he dearly hoped the answer would be in the affirmative.

Dovid'l remembered his rebbe telling him to accept the first match to come his way and didn't consider long before saying yes to the tavernkeeper.

But the tavernkeeper was not the only one who had an eye on Dovid'l as a future son-in-law. Ever since he met with Dovid'l, the Rav thought the young man would be an excellent match for *his* daughter. When the tavernkeeper next visited, the Rav told his guest there was a matter he'd like to discuss with him.

"Would you mind serving as the matchmaker for my daughter?" the Rav asked.

"Certainly," the tavernkeeper answered. "Who is the groom you have in mind?"

"Dovid, your tutor."

"Rav," said the tavernkeeper, collecting himself after a long moment of silence, "that's why I came here today – to invite you to the engagement ceremony of my daughter…to Dovid'l."

It was the Rav's turn to be taken aback. "Well, I am obviously disappointed. But it seems he was destined to be a member of your household. I promise to be at your celebration, along with my entire family."

All the honored dignitaries of the shtetl and the surrounding hamlets gathered at the kretchma for the engagement party. The tavernkeeper prepared a sumptuous feast for his guests, thankful for his good fortune at having found such a fine young man for his daughter. As the groom, Dovid'l sat next to the Rav and delivered the customary discourse on Torah.

When they were ready to proceed with the traditional breaking of a plate to finalize the engagement, Dovid'l suddenly remembered the piece of paper sewn into his *talis kuton* that the Zlotchover tzaddik told him to read before getting engaged.

He excused himself, went into a small room, and closed the door behind him. He removed the garment and, with a trembling hand, withdrew the letter and cut open its seal. His hands shaking, he read what the rebbe had written: *"Haya k'zos b'Yisroel, azh a brueder zal khasana huben mitt a schvester?"* – "Has ever it occurred in Israel that a brother should marry his sister?"

It made no sense. He read the sentence again and again and then once more. What was the meaning of this?

By now, the guests were growing anxious, wondering where the groom had gone. What was he doing all this time? A few, along with the Rav and the tavernkeeper, decided to find him and make sure all was well. And soon enough they found Dovid'l in a small room at the back of the inn, sitting on a chair, a piece of paper in his hand, shaking his head back and forth slowly, clearly puzzled and distraught.

Dovid'l handed the paper to the Rav. The Rav read the sentence carefully, and then asked all the others, except the tavernkeeper, to leave the room.

"Dovid," the Rav said, "I have to ask you a few questions. I need to know the truth about your history. Where did you come from? How did you end up here? Why were you carrying this paper?"

Dovid'l told the Rav how his parents had left him in the care of a gentile neighbor in whose home he was raised. And he explained how he came to study in the court of Reb Mikhel of Zlotchov, who'd given him this note and instructed him to read it before becoming a groom.

Standing nearby and following every word, the tavernkeeper turned pale and grabbed hold of a chair so as not to faint. His lips quivered and his breaths came short and rapidly.

"Dovid'l!" he exclaimed, rushing to embrace the boy. "My Dovid'l!"

The wedding feast did not go to waste. The Rav was delighted when Dovid'l agreed to be engaged to his daughter and everyone sat down to food and drink to celebrate.

The Rav, with a broad smile, said to the tavernkeeper, "Didn't I tell you this young man was destined to be part of your family?"

The Blessing of a Drunk

Bitter was the day Stanislaw Wyszynski became commissar of Krosno and its environs. The Jews were now ordered to pay an additional tax beyond their already heavy financial burden, and those who could not afford the payments were turned out of their homes. Club-wielding ruffians attacked Jews without fear, aged Chassidim being a favorite target of their relentless taunts.

At first, the Chassidim of Krosno sought to alleviate their misfortune through the customary means: a day of fasting and prayer, further appeals to the commissar and then to his superiors, who, unfortunately, proved no more sympathetic to their plight. No one was surprised when Reb Abish, the most respected Chassid in Krosno, said the time had come to try bribery. The Chassidim of Krosno were by no means wealthy, but they agreed to pool the little funds they had. Perhaps, once again, avarice would trump malice.

With the money raised by the desperate community in his pocket, Reb Abish, along with two of his fellow Chassidim, made his way to the tavern where Commissar Wyszynski was known to revel in his nightly rounds of drinking.

"Please accept this donation in recognition of our civic devotion," Reb Abish said to the commissar, placing a stack of bills on the table next to his playing cards.

Wyszynski looked straight at Reb Abish and twirled his horse-shoe moustache. A snarl creased his ruddy face.

"This will pay for tonight's vodka," he said, laughing. "But you accursed Christ killers must be stupid if you think I can be bribed by the likes of you. I have better ways to get your pitiful zlotys. Now get the hell out of here before I chase you out with my whip."

Even more despondent than before, the Chassidim of Krosno decided to seek the blessing of the esteemed rebbe, the Tzaddik of Dinov. Yet while the Dinover Rebbe listened with a broken heart to the travails of his Chassidim, he offered little solace.

"I fear my prayers will be of no avail," he told them.

The Chassidim stood forlorn when suddenly the tzaddik raised his head, his eyes shining like a ray of light across a cloudy night.

"And why not?" he said, apparently answering his own question. "You need the blessing of Naftuli Geiger."

The Chassidim had never heard the name before. Was he one of the *lamed vovniks*, the thirty-six people in every generation whose covert righteousness sustains the world? The rebbe said only that he might be found in the village of Yavenik and wished them success.

The next morning, with unwavering trust in their rebbe's words, Reb Abish and his two compatriots arrived in the tiny hamlet, one of many that dotted the Chassidic landscape of Polish Galicia, and headed immediately to the local *shteible* where fellow Chassidim gathered to pray. Yet when they asked where they might find one Naftuli Geiger, they were greeted with blank stares. No one seemed to have any idea whom he might be. Their inquiries in shuls, schools and the marketplace were equally fruitless. With heavy hearts, the Chassidim trudged to the local kretchma to spend the night.

The roadside inn was deserted except for a group of gentile villagers drinking in the drab dining room. The fatigued Chassidim sat at a table of their own and ordered tea. Aware that their strange presence demanded an explanation, they said they were looking for a Jew by the name of Naftuli Geiger. Not one of the peasants recognized the name. No one, that is, except for a one-armed man sitting alone at the far side of the room.

"They mean Tadik," he said, and gave the Chassidim directions to Tadik's shack on the outskirts of town.

The others in the room were incredulous. "Tadik? That good-for-nothing drunk is a Jew?"

The Chassidim were even more astounded. Why would the rebbe send them to receive a blessing from an alcoholic lout? Most likely, they decided, Tadik was a clandestinely devout Jew who only appeared inebriated, but, in fact, spent his evenings at home studying Torah and fulfilling its commandments.

When they reached his humble dwelling, however, they were not met with the sound of a Jew chanting sacred scriptures, but with silence. Only a small light in the back signaled that anyone was home. Peering inside, the Chassidim could see that Tadik was asleep in a corner, surrounded by empty whiskey bottles and stale vomit. Seeing the door was open, the Chassidim entered the foul-smelling hut, determined to complete their mission. Trying to wake Tadik was like trying to teach Kabbalah to a goat, but the Chassidim pulled and prodded and finally cajoled him to open an eye.

"Who in God's hell are you people?" he wheezed.

"We're here to receive your blessing," Reb Abish said.

"You ask for a blessing?" Tadik growled. "You come to mock me? A swig of dog's blood is what you'll get. Now go away and let me be." He turned to the wall.

"We've been sent here by our rebbe," Reb Abish continued. "We cannot leave without your blessing."

"Okay, I bless you. Now good-bye."

But the Chassidim hadn't come all this way to be cast off by a pitiful inebriate. "You need to concentrate," they said.

"Damn," Tadik said, managing to sit up. And in a voice suddenly steady and sober, he said, "Fine. Father in Heaven: On my behalf, may the Jews of Krosno be spared further humiliation and pain." Turning to his visitors, he asked, "Will you now leave me to my sleep?"

The crowd at the Krosno station descended on Reb Abish and his colleagues the moment they stepped onto the platform, everyone shouting the good news. Commissar Wyszynski had been implicated in an extortion scandal and dragged off in handcuffs. His appointed successor had promised to install an honest administration that would immediately abolish Wyszynski's draconian anti-Jewish laws.

Relieved, but bewildered by the course of events, Reb Abish traveled the next day to the rebbe, hoping to learn what had transpired. Naturally, the Dinover Rebbe was delighted to hear about the turn of events in Krosno, but sighed when told of Naftuli's condition.

"I was hoping he might have changed," the rebbe said. "No doubt you're wondering why I sent you to him. I will tell you."

A dozen Chassidim crowded around the rebbe's table to hear the story of Naftuli Geiger.

"Naftuli's father was a Chassid of my father, the holy Bnei Yissoscher, may he rest in peace," the rebbe began.

Naftuli would often join his father when he came to us for the holidays. The young man was certainly not a gifted Talmud student, but he was kind and devoted. He worked at a textile factory outside the city of Rzeszow, and one day the young daughter of the local poretz, the region's overseer, came to purchase some fabric. She took a liking to Naftuli and was soon making repeat visits to the warehouse after store hours. It was not long before the affection turned mutual. The visits led to secluded walks and clandestine trysts, and you might guess where this eventually led. The young woman told her father she wanted Naftuli as her husband.

"My son-in-law a Jew? Impossible!" the poretz declared. He couldn't fathom why his daughter would be interested in a Jew, let alone one with neither money nor education. But his daughter was obstinate; the boy was her true love, she insisted. The poretz finally relented, and one brisk morning showed up at the warehouse and invited Naftuli to accompany him on a ride in his carriage.

"Let me get straight to the point," the poretz said. "I can't imagine why, but it seems my daughter is determined to marry you."

Naftuli began to tell him that the feelings of affection were reciprocated, but the poretz interrupted him. "Your sentiments are of no interest to me. You can be sure, however, that no Jew will be my son-in-law. You will, therefore, convert to Christianity. Do you have a Polish name?"

"My nursemaid called me Tadik," Naftuli said uncomfortably.

"Tadik, short for Thadeus. Fine. Let's get this over with quickly. You will be married in a few days. I will see to all the necessary arrangements."

Without another word, the coach returned the shaken young man to the mill.

Tadik faced an excruciating decision. On the one hand, he was very fond of this girl as she was of him and his life would certainly be easier if he married her. Would he ever have this opportunity again? To live a life of leisure, to give orders, not take them, to ride in ornate coaches, not walk the roads with dogs and goats? But could he really abandon his people? Affection is one thing, but to marry out of his faith? Still, hadn't Jewish rituals become rote, tedious, meaningless exercises for him? Conversion would be arduous, but, Naftuli concluded, with time he'd settle into his new life.

Three days later, two heavyset men showed up at Naftuli's workplace and ushered him into a waiting carriage. A half-hour later, they arrived at a church a few miles outside town, and Naftuli was brought up to a small room in the attic. One of the men leaned in close and whispered into his ear.

"Tomorrow morning the priest arrives and administers the necessary rites, and you will be converted to the Holy Roman Church. In the afternoon you will be married. They've even prepared a wedding suit for you."

The two men left Naftuli sitting on a bed, locking the door behind them. At seven o'clock the next morning, the priest knocked on the attic door, turned his key and entered the room, only to find it empty. For the previous night, alone in the dark, Naftuli had been forced to confront himself. What was he doing in this Christian house of worship? How could he mouth words he didn't believe in? Was material comfort so important to him that he'd betray his people and his heritage? No, this was beyond the limit. Skillfully fashioning a rope from the bed sheets, Naftuli secured the cord to the window and in the dead of night, made his escape.

The repercussions were swift and severe. Word went out that no one was to hire Naftuli Geiger, forcing him to move beyond the long reach of the poretz. Eventually, Naftuli made his way to Yavenik, where he kept a low profile and used his Polish name.

In the early days after his escape from the church, he'd attended a few services at the synagogue, but felt disconnected, a loner. He became an outsider in both the Jewish and gentile worlds. Alone in bars, staring at the stale bread on his plate, Naftuli took to drink and drink took to him.

The rebbe exhaled slowly. "How I wish this story had a happier ending for Naftuli. For now... well, Reb Abish, you saw for yourself."

"But why did you send me to him for a benediction?" Reb Abish demanded. "Why would his blessing matter?"

"We are taught not to take lightly the blessings of the ordinary person," the Dinover Rebbe said, "even the sinner, though most of us mumble our thanks for their good wishes, paying them no mind. But we should. You see, Chassidism also teaches that an unrewarded deed bestows on the doer of that deed power to affect events. We can never be certain who bears this power, nor is the bearer himself aware of his spiritual strength. The blessing of a drunk lost in an intoxicated haze might carry more weight than the blessing of the holiest tzaddik in the world.

"When Naftuli turned his back on apostasy and a life of ease, the heavens conferred upon him a special gift: should he offer a benediction, it would be fulfilled. But it never dawned on him to bless anyone for anything. That is, not until a group of Chassidim from Krosno appeared one day at his shack."

With that, the rebbe pointed to the clock on the wall. It was time for afternoon prayers.

A Good Deed Thwarted

Rebbe Meyer of Premishlan used to say that only because of his charity was he confident he'd be admitted to heaven. The prosecutors in the Next World could always claim his learning, his prayers, his fulfillment of the commandments – all lacked pure intent. They could accuse him of a hidden agenda, of mixed motives. But when it came to charity, Reb Meyer knew, motive didn't matter. What counted was that you provided for those in need, whatever your reasons.

So it's not surprising that while Chassidim came to Reb Meyer seeking his advice and blessings for all sorts of matters – family affairs, business decisions, health concerns – the poor, too, flocked to him, knowing they could rely on a donation.

Elyah the wagon driver was one such regular visitor. An impoverished father of six, he'd show up every Friday to ask Reb Meyer for money to purchase challah, wine and perhaps even meat for his Shabbos table. Reb Meyer gave him what he could.

Elyah, you should understand, was an incompetent, and, truth be told, a rather lazy incompetent, at that. Noting how their rebbe always helped him, Reb Meyer's Chassidim initially sought to assist him as well. And so, they'd hire Elyah even though he drove a creaky wagon pulled by a skinny horse as lethargic as its driver. Even the whip could not provoke the horse to move, and when the wagon went up a hill, the horse would kick its legs and sway its nose as if to say, "What's the rush? We'll get there eventually." No wonder, trips with Elyah invariably took an hour longer than they would with anyone else. Worse, he refused to drive if the weather was even slightly inclement; a threatening cloud or moderate wind was enough to make him plead mercy for his mare and take the day off. Eventually, even those who wished to patronize Elyah no longer sought his services, and he was compelled to turn to the public coffers and to the rebbe to feed his family.

On one occasion, the Chassidim mentioned Elyah's indolence to their rebbe.

"Maybe if the rebbe stopped subsidizing the man, he'd work harder to make a living on his own."

But Reb Meyer only replied with a shrug, "What do you want from my reliable friend? Elyah helps make sure I give charity and purchase a little place in the Next World."

One afternoon in the middle of the week, Elyah appeared in the rebbe's room.

"Rebbe," the wagon driver said, explaining the unusual timing of this visit, "because of the huge blizzard and icy conditions that have descended on us these past weeks, a young man from Lemberg has been forced to stay in our home. Well, it seems he's cast a favorable eye on my eldest daughter. He's even announced his desire to marry the girl. But he expects a dowry of at least fifty kerblech. I, of course, don't have that kind of money and was hoping the rebbe would help me."

Rebbe Meyer began rummaging through his drawer. Finding nothing of value, he called to his wife.

"Do you have your shawl? I'd like to use it as security for a loan."

"Sorry, but I already gave my shawl last week to someone as security so you'd have money to give to the poor." She darted a look at the visitor. "Including Elyah, for his Shabbos meals."

"Do we have anything else of value in the house?" asked the rebbe.

"Nothing at all," his wife said, shaking her head as she left the room.

The rebbe instructed Elyah to call on Reb Baruch, the richest man in the town, and ask him to pay the rebbe a visit. When Reb Baruch entered the room, the rebbe immediately asked if he could lend him fifty kerblech. Reb Baruch was accustomed to such sudden requests from the rebbe and considered it an honor to comply. But this time, his face soured.

"Alas, I am unable to help," he murmured. "Because of the great frost of the past weeks, my business has come to a standstill. Perhaps in a week or two I could come up with the money."

Determined to raise the funds, the Premishlaner Rebbe sent for several other well-to-do townsfolk who could usually be relied upon for donations. But all excused themselves, noting that circumstances made it impossible for them to help at this time.

Rebbe Meyer returned to his desk and sat quietly, reflecting. Elyah, who had been waiting patiently in the rebbe's study all this time, fixed his eyes on the rebbe, certain he was thinking about whom he might turn to next. But after several minutes, the rebbe looked directly at Elyah.

"I don't approve of this match," the rebbe declared. "This fellow is not an appropriate choice for your daughter."

Elyah began to formulate his puzzlement, but the rebbe's shake of his head was enough to end the matter. Though perhaps unlearned, Elyah was firm in his Chassidic devotion and knew better than to second-guess the rebbe. He returned home, resigned to forgoing the possibility of this match for his daughter.

A few days later, when the weather had turned milder and the roads were once more hospitable, two police officials from Lemberg arrived at Elyah's door. They took hold of the visitor and handcuffed him, revealing only that they were bringing him back to Lemberg. The townspeople soon learned the police had been pursuing this young man for some time. He was a scam artist who had already swindled several unsuspecting families by asserting his interest in marrying a girl, receiving a dowry and then absconding with the funds.

When his Chassidim heard what had transpired, they praised their rebbe's miraculous foresight.

"No, don't think my deduction is proof of some supernatural powers on my part," he told them. "What came to my mind was the teaching that when a person is determined to perform a good deed, the divine helps him in his quest. Well, I tried! I pursued every avenue I could to get this money for Elyah...yet I failed. And so, I concluded that the reason I was unable to complete this mitzvah was that the effort ought *not* succeed, that the match must be ill advised."

The Light of the Menorah

Persecution had always been the natural state of the Jew in exile, and it hardly mattered whether one's country was at war or at peace. But there was this difference: during times of peace, Jewish communities could at least maintain contact with one another. If Jews in one district were beset with dire sanctions, the Jews of a neighboring district would come to their assistance, engaging their *shtadlunim*, the Jewish dignitaries who enjoyed good standing with government officials, to serve as advocates. During times of war, however, these connections evaporated. The military officials who administered what little order remained barely bothered with even the pretense of justice.

It was during one such period of mayhem that Menashe disappeared.

The bitter conflict between Napoleon and Russia had been raging for months. Civilian travel within Russia was treacherous for all, but especially for Jews, for whom such journeys were fraught with danger even in the most tranquil of times. But what can one do if his livelihood depends on traveling from region to region, from city to city? The merchant Menashe, with a family to feed, had little choice but to accept the risks of his trade – war or no war.

He undertook these business trips each year soon after the High Holidays, making his way from his shtetl to the distant, unwelcoming regions of Russia beyond. The success of these ventures often depended upon personal connections and sheer guile. Indeed, despite the edicts of the Czar, Menashe had, at times, even sneaked into cities where Jews were denied entry.

This year, he knew, his journey would be especially perilous. Before taking to the road, he fortified himself by receiving the good wishes of his rebbe, the holy Tzaddik of Liadi.

On the day of his departure, he bade farewell to his wife with more anxiety than usual.

Every few days, by mail or word of mouth, Menashe's wife received word from her husband, notifying her of his whereabouts and activities. She was delighted when a letter arrived from Petersburg, dated the second day of Chanukah, informing her that his business dealings had gone well and with God's help, he'd be returning home soon.

Then she heard nothing more.

Days passed, then weeks, and still not a word. Her small children stared out the window, awaiting the gifts their father always brought when he returned from his far-away travels. But there was no sign of Menashe. No posts, no regards, no reports of chance encounters. Months passed. It was as though he'd disappeared into thin air.

Had these been normal times, the *shtadlunim* would have traveled to Petersburg to make inquiries, but with the country at war, such a venture would be useless. Officials in Petersburg, a Czarist capital city, had more pressing issues to contend with than missing Jews. As for Menashe's wife, she sent urgent letters to every agency that might prove helpful, but received replies from none. Not knowing where to turn next, she sought the advice of Reb Schneur Zalman of Lubavitch.

"I'm a veritable *agunah*," she told the rebbe, referring to her status as an abandoned – but still legally married – woman. "As for my children, they're suffering as though they're orphans."

The rebbe consoled the woman and assured her that, with God's help, her husband would return home safely.

Spring passed, then summer and autumn too, and soon the winter winds were already announcing their presence. The war continued to rage, the Russian forces losing one battle after the next. These were days of great travail for the entire population, and, as usual, especially for Jews.

Still, a man must earn a living. The previous year, it was Menashe who had traveled through the embattled region; this year, Tzvi Hirsch would face the same challenge. Like Menashe, Tzvi Hirsch was a devoted Chassid of the Lubavitcher Rebbe, and sought the sage's blessing before commencing his trip.

As Tzvi Hirsch prepared to leave the room, he heard the rebbe calling to him.

"Tzvi Hirsch, you said you'd be gone for several months, yes? That you expect to be away during Chanukah?"

"Yes, I'll still be on the road," Tzvi Hirsch replied.

As in years past, he'd planned his itinerary so he could celebrate Chanukah in a town inhabited by Jews and, if possible, with other Chassidim. But why was the rebbe asking about this now?

"I want to remind you," the rebbe continued, "the essence of the mitzvah of lighting the menorah is *pirsumei nisa*, the public proclamation of the Chanukah miracle. That is why we try to put our menorah near a window so its light will be visible to the world."

"Yes, of course," Tzvi Hirsch said. "I always place my menorah near the window in my house."

"Good," said the rebbe. "But remember, the performance of *pirsumei nisa* isn't limited to one's own home. One must ensure the menorah is visible in whatever location one finds oneself. May you have a safe, successful trip."

Tzvi Hirsch was a considerably more successful merchant than Menashe, for whom every ruble was a struggle. Tzvi Hirsch's formidable connections allowed him to walk through doors closed to other Jews and to sojourn in royal cities like Petersburg, from which Jews were officially barred. But this was wartime, and all the thoroughfares were controlled by hostile military personnel. Meanwhile, a heavy snow had blanketed the roads, rendering the main arteries impassable.

On the eve of the first night of Chanukah, Tzvi Hirsch found himself stranded in a God-forsaken, isolated village, where he doubted even one Jew could be found. Given the weather conditions, he had no choice but to resign himself to spending the coming days at the local inn.

Alone in his room, Reb Tzvi Hirsch welcomed the holiday of Chanukah, reciting the traditional liturgy that recalls the miracles of the past and expresses the hope that they will recur in our own day. At the end of prayers, he removed a menorah from his bag, and prepared to place it on a chair across from a mezuzah affixed to a doorpost, forgetting for a moment he'd find no mezuzah in this gentile inn. Casting about for an appropriate spot, he suddenly remembered the rebbe's exhortation to light the lamp in public view.

And so, Tzvi Hirsch dutifully set up his menorah near the window of his shabby room. Who would see these wicks' modest flames? The storm had intensified during the past few hours; no one in his right mind would dare extend a finger into the howling wind, let alone hazard a walk outside. But Tzvi Hirsch set aside his puzzlement and kindled the menorah with all the zeal he could muster. A surge of homesickness overwhelmed him as he thought about the joyful Chanukah celebrations at the court of the rebbe. Fighting pangs of loneliness, he pulled a chair up next to the menorah, and began singing a Chassidic melody.

The second night of Chanukah was no different. Tzvi Hirsch lit the two wicks in front of the window as an unrelenting gale lashed against the pane. Once more, he sat across from his menorah and immersed himself in Chassidic song and prayer. So absorbed was he in his devotions that he failed to notice the door open, or the man who'd quietly entered his room.

The unobserved visitor was immaculately dressed in a military officer's outfit, his jacket bedecked with medals. He stared silently at the Jew swaying slowly in his chair, oblivious to his surroundings.

When Tzvi Hirsch finally opened his eyes, he lurched from his seat, and quickly removed his cap in reflexive obeisance. But the officer merely smiled, and readily accepted Tzvi Hirsch's invitation to have a seat.

"Allow me to explain my presence here," the officer said. "I came to this province on military leave. I'm staying in a room nearby. Last night I noticed a peculiar light coming from your room. A mere flicker, hardly enough to yield warmth or even light. I thought, How strange! And when tonight, I saw two such glimmers from this room,

I asked myself, What is going on in there? I knocked on the door and receiving no reply, let myself in. And what do I see? A Jew busying himself with a small lamp. And so I ask myself, What is a Jew doing in this remote part of the country? And what is he doing with this little lamp of his?"

"I will explain," said Tzvi Hirsch, speaking in a sophisticated Russian that matched the officer's. He recounted the history of the holiday, the Maccabees' valiant battle for freedom, the ritual lighting of the candelabrum, one additional light each night, progressing to eight, in commemoration of the discovery of a small flask of pure oil that miraculously burned in the destroyed Temple for eight days.

"So, the Jew is innocent after all!"

"What Jew?" asked Tzvi Hirsch. "Innocent of what?"

"He did tell us the truth."

"Sir, what Jew? The truth about what?"

The officer leaned back in his chair. "I am a military judge in the military court in Petersburg," he said. "Last year – around this time, in fact – we were presented with a Jew arrested as a spy. His name was Menashe, as I recall. The evidence pointing to his guilt was substantial. For one thing, he was found in Petersburg, where Jews are not permitted entry. For another, he was carrying false papers. And then there was this business with the lights. He we seen kindling his lamp near a window, one night one candle, two on the next night and so on. We concluded this was a signal to the enemy, a code communicating the number of battalions arriving into the city.

"The Jew admitted he was in the city illegally, but insisted he was there only to conduct some business and certainly not to spy. What about the lamp, the lights in the window? He said this was a ritual belonging to the Jewish holiday of Chanukah.

"He didn't convince the court, although, to tell the truth, we weren't inclined to believe his account. The man was sentenced to a ten-year prison term."

"What happens now?" Tzvi Hirsch asked, astonished.

"Well," said the officer, "I see now we should have listened more judiciously to what the Jew had to say. As soon as I return from my furlough, I'll see to it he is given his freedom."

When Tzvi Hirsch returned to his town, he was greeted by the news that Menashe was already in his own home, reunited with his family. Not even Menashe knew what had prompted his sudden release. But each year, when Tzvi Hirsch lit the menorah he made sure not only to proclaim the miracle of Chanukah that had occurred two millennia earlier, but also the miracle that occurred in his own day.

Character and Compassion

Why don't we pronounce a blessing before we
perform the mitzvah of giving charity? Because
first feed the hungry – our piety can wait.

REB TZVI ELIMELECH OF DINOV

Why Rothschild
Became Rothschild

Rabbi Zvi Hirsch Horowitz of Chertkov – known to all as Reb Heschele – was celebrated in his village and beyond as a master scholar and teacher, but this renown did not translate into a steady income. Although his meager financial circumstances were of little concern to him – his primary interests being religious study and practice – he was also realistic: he had daughters to marry off, and weddings and dowries were costly affairs. And so, Reb Heschele prudently put kopeck after kopeck into a fund dedicated to meet those future expenses. When he'd accumulated a sufficient number of these coins, he'd exchange them for a gold ducat. He followed this procedure diligently, year after year, until he eventually accrued the sum of five hundred gold coins, sufficient for his family's needs.

Reb Heschele kept these precious ducats, his life's savings, in a small bag hidden away in a double-bolted drawer within a drawer in an old wooden desk. He'd check on this hiding place but once each year, on the day before Passover. On this day, religious Jews comb every crevice and scour every nook of their homes in an effort to remove any trace of leavened food, which is forbidden to them during the weeklong festival. On this occasion only, Reb Heschele would peer quickly into the secreted drawer, then secure it once again with two protective locks.

For many years, Reb Heschele was assisted in his rabbinical work by a devoted student, Meyer Amschel Rothschild. The accolades for this young attendant came easily: Amschel was bright, energetic, judicious and eager to learn from his mentor. And although Reb Heschele would miss the young man, he was delighted when a match proposal for Amschel was announced.

The bride hailed from a respected, prosperous family in the nearby town of Sniatin, and was reputed to possess all the qualities the promising Amschel richly deserved. Reb Heschele gladly gave his blessing when Amschel informed him he'd be moving to his bride's hometown to embark on a business venture. And Reb Heschele was delighted to hear, not long after, that the young man's business was thriving.

But that same year misfortune would arrive in Reb Heschele's home. When the rabbi performed his annual pre-Passover search for leavened bread and opened the locked drawer, he saw to his horror that the purse containing his gold coins was missing. In utter disbelief, he stood staring at the empty drawer. All those years of saving…vanished! The money so carefully sequestered to pay for his now grown daughters' marriages…stolen!

Reb Heschele, his voice trembling, called to his wife and children to inform them of the news. Who could be the thief? There was only one possibility, his family concluded: Only Meyer Amschel Rothschild knew the whereabouts of this cache.

"Notice how quickly since leaving our small village the young man has achieved success," Reb Heschele's wife said bitterly. "Yes, with a little capital advance from Reb Heschele's life savings, he's doing very well for himself."

Reb Heschele shook his head in disbelief at his wife's verdict. This couldn't be. Not Meyer Amschel. The young man was earnest, devoted, and patently honest. But Reb Heschele could offer no reasonable alternative.

"You must go to Sniatin as soon as the holiday is over," his wife implored. "I know it won't be easy, but you must demand that Amschel return the money he's stolen."

So the day after Passover, with a heavy heart, Reb Heschele made his way to the home of his erstwhile assistant.

The rabbi's distress was evident as he told Amschel what had befallen him. "My entire savings, all those years …." His voice caught in his throat as he uttered the words he had come to deliver. "They suspect you, Amschel. After all, who but you knew the whereabouts of this sack of coins?"

A cold shiver coursed through Amschel. He looked at his mentor, then looked away and lowered his eyes. His body rocked back and forth as he slowly nodded his head. "Yes," he said, his voice barely audible. "It is true. I confess. I took the money. The temptation was too strong. The evil urge won his battle."

Amschel finally looked up at Reb Heschele. "I want to repay you. At this moment I can only give you two hundred gold ducats, but I promise to repay the entire sum over time, all of it until the last kopeck." He bowed his head again. "I'm sorry."

Reb Heschele returned home with his emotions in turmoil: relief that he would have sufficient funds to marry off his daughters, disheartened that his beloved assistant would succumb to this thievery, but gratified that Amschel had admitted his transgression and offered full restitution.

The years passed, and Amschel Rothschild became a man of eminent wealth and a pillar of the Jewish community. Reb Heschele's children were all happily married, the remainder of the debt long since paid off.

One day, a peasant from Chertkov entered the local saloon.

"What is the most expensive whiskey you have?" he demanded of the saloonkeeper. "Whatever it is, that's what I want."

When it came time to pay, the peasant reached into his pocket and presented a broad smile, along with a gold coin.

"Lucky me. Look what I found," he said.

The saloonkeeper knew better. People don't lose gold coins and people don't find them. But having no proof to the contrary, he said nothing and dutifully gave the man his change.

A few days later, the peasant returned to the saloon, this time with a cohort of fellow drinkers in tow. The lot drank their full and when the bill arrived, the peasant declared that the drinks were on him and paid the entire bill with another gold coin. Again, he met the incredulous stare of the saloonkeeper.

"A gift," the peasant explained, laughing. "A wonderful gift."

The saloonkeeper's doubts were confirmed: the man was clearly a thief. He related his suspicions to the police, recounting how this poor peasant had appeared twice with gold coins, offering fanciful stories of how he'd procured them.

The police shared the saloonkeeper's misgivings and advised him to set a trap should the man return.

"Get him good and drunk," they suggested. "And when he is sufficiently inebriated, have a clever fellow befriend the man, engage him in conversation and, hopefully, elicit the truth about those gold ducats."

The saloonkeeper decided that his neighbor was just the man for the job.

A week later, the peasant returned. The saloonkeeper scanned the bottles behind him and selected for his eager patron the strongest liquor on the shelf. A second and third round followed and before long, the peasant was leaning back in his chair, utterly intoxicated. As planned, the saloonkeeper had invited his neighbor to chat with the drunk, and an alcoholic camaraderie quickly developed between them. Soon, the peasant was explaining how he'd come by his new fortune.

"Many years ago, my wife worked for this rabbi," he recounted. "Well, the Jews have this custom, you see, of getting rid of all their bread before their Passover holiday. Don't ask me details, I don't know. But they do this search all over the house. Anyway, my wife, she's helping them with this big cleaning job in preparation for their holiday, scrubbing, washing, when she notices something interesting. In the rabbi's office there's this drawer that's always locked. Two locks, in fact. Well, it makes her curious."

The tipsy peasant paused a moment to down another round of whiskey before continuing his tale. "So this year my wife keeps her eyes peeled, you know what I mean? She's watching when the rabbi opens the drawer and keeps watching to see where he puts the keys to those locks. My wife, she tells me what she observed."

"And you suggest?" his new friend asks.

"The obvious," says the drunk. "And you know what she finds in that drawer? A sack with five hundred gold coins! You heard me…five hundred gold ducats. I couldn't believe my eyes when she showed me what she'd brought home."

The drunk leaned forward in his seat. "Listen, my friend," he continued, clearly pleased with himself. "I'm no fool. They notice me spending those coins after a robbery like that, no way I'm not suspected of a crime. But I have patience. I bury the sack under this big rock in my backyard and I wait. But now it's been long enough. Now I'm ready to enjoy life."

The peasant erupted in a loud laugh and called for another round.

Within hours, the police uncovered the peasant's hiding place, along with the sack containing nearly all the five hundred unspent ducats. By the end of the day, the money had been returned to a stunned Reb Heschele.

Rebbe Heschele immediately set out for Sniatin, bringing the five hundred ducats to return to Amschel, and an apology for holding him responsible for the larceny all these years. Only one question occupied Reb Heschele's mind as he made his journey: Why had Amschel confessed to a crime he hadn't committed?

Soon, the two men were sitting across from each other in Amschel's elegant sitting room.

"It was the pain on your face," Amschel said. "I saw the agony you were undergoing at the loss of your savings. I knew how devastated you were because you would not have the means to pay for your daughters' marriages. And so I asked myself, 'how can I alleviate my teacher's suffering?'"

"So you admitted to a robbery of which you were innocent?"

"I did," said Amschel. "You can imagine how it felt to be judged a thief – especially in your eyes. And even worse, as the thief of *your* money. But I also observed your grief and could bear that even less. So I took responsibility for the theft."

Reb Heschele remained speechless for a few moments, his eyes moist with tears. He took Amschel's hand in his. "Let me bless you," he said, his voice clear and unbroken. "In return for this act of generosity, this generosity of money, yes, but especially this generosity of spirit, may you and your children and your children's children never want for material comfort, but enjoy lasting wealth through the generations."

And, as we know, so it came to be.

The Once and Future Bride

"The prince of Vienna" was how many Jews referred to Reb Shimshon Vienner. One of the wealthiest Jews of his day, Reb Shimshon was renowned not only for his extraordinary learning and wisdom, but for his close relationships with government officials. Yet it was Reb Shimshon's remarkable history that made his success even more striking.

We can pick up his story with the visit by an esteemed member of a Jewish community to the local yeshiva – a well-to-do visitor seeking an appropriate son-in-law for his only daughter. The Rosh Yeshiva proudly presented one of his prize students, still in his early teens. Shimshon was young, perhaps, but he was also a gifted scholar of excellent character. The visitor, much taken by the young man's qualities, suggested Shimshon meet his daughter – if the two consented, they would marry.

A short time later, the would-be father-in-law introduced Shimshon to his modest, learned and comely daughter. The attraction was mutual and the two youngsters nodded their consent to the hovering question. They wished to be wed.

Shimshon returned to the yeshiva and began preparing the learned discourse he'd deliver at the forthcoming engagement party. The girl's father was delighted, a delight that was augmented when the night arrived and the community's leading Torah scholars were thoroughly impressed with the young man's analytical skills, declaring Shimshon a genuine prodigy.

A date was set for the wedding to take place in three weeks.

The wedding would be a major event and the entire town was abuzz with anticipation. After all, their foremost citizen, respected far and wide for his noble spirit and generosity, was marrying off his only daughter to an outstanding young Torah scholar. Preparations for the affair became fodder for endless speculation, as though the townspeople themselves were intimate members of the wedding party.

When the festive night arrived, the townsfolk flocked to the wedding hall bedecked in their finery, their shared elation on magnificent display. Relatives, friends and strangers danced to the lively music while children scampered underfoot, relishing the delicacies laid out on the tables. Young and old, scholars and the unlearned, rich and poor – the joy was visible on every face.

On every face but the groom's. Dressed in a custom tailored frock coat and a brand new fur hat, Shimshon sat quietly at the groom's table, surrounded by illustrious rabbis and his future wife's family, acutely aware of how alone he was in this world. He'd been orphaned as a child and had no siblings. How he missed his father and mother this night. Shimshon tried to redirect his attention to more pleasant thoughts: to the family life he'd enjoy in the future, the comforts and security of marriage, but all he could think of was his parents. When he was asked to explain a difficult Talmudic passage, he was delighted to lose himself in the intricacies of the legal discussion.

Soon strange hands were leading him to the canopy, where he was joined by his bride. He noted her elegant white dress and, as though through a mist, her gleaming eyes and lovely face. Yes, he thought, she was beautiful; their life together would bring them both much happiness.

The guests jostled for a closer look at the young couple, positioning themselves for an optimum view of the ceremony. A lucky few managed to grasp the canopy poles, while the others raised their lit candles, heralding the bride and groom. The flames cast dancing shadows on the walls as the spectators held their torches aloft. With the wedding hall packed beyond capacity, sober voices warned the crowd to exercise caution but, alas, their warnings went unheeded. Suddenly, a voice shouted that a dress had caught fire. And then more screams: "Fire! Fire!"

Within moments, the blaze had spread. Women shrieked as their elaborate dresses were set aflame. The wooden tables heaped with food were now crumbling like firewood. The music stopped, replaced by anguished wailing. Panic set in. Many fainted from the heat and smoke, while those who could, rushed to the narrow exits. The wedding hall had become a devouring pyre, that continued on a relentless path, igniting the straw roofs of the neighboring houses. The flames consumed one house after another.

Shimshon reached out to grab his soon-to-be wife and escape the inferno, but could not find her in the dense smoke. He called out her name, but his voice was lost amidst the screams and commotion.

Desperate, waiting as long as he could, he began to run and managed to find his way to the street. He ran as far and as fast as he could, and when he could run no longer, he collapsed on the cold earth, the groans of agony still audible in the distance.

Numb, he lay on the ground and only slowly did the full impact of what had transpired force its way into his consciousness. Weeping and half-limping, Shimshon returned to the embers of the wedding hall to search amidst the desolation for survivors. His in-laws, he quickly learned, had perished with the rest. But what of his bride? Had anyone seen her? Did anyone know if she'd survived – or if she had not? No one could say for sure, but all agreed it was reasonable to presume the worst.

Shimshon searched on. For days he rummaged through the wreckage, visiting the few neighboring houses that were still standing, making inquiries. No, nothing definitive, he was told over and over again, but one could safely assume.

Shimshon returned to the yeshiva and immersed himself in his studies as never before. Learning Torah was the only activity that crowded out thoughts of the calamity that was to have been his wedding day. Despite his determination, tortured memories often engulfed his young soul. He thought of his bride; the uncertainty about her fate gave him no rest.

The years passed and Shimshon became one of the top students in the yeshiva, the pride of the faculty. Again, talk turned to finding him a suitable bride. The young man understood that remaining single was not an option. But Shimshon had no interest in marriage. Not yet.

Shimshon knew he could not realistically sustain his refusal to marry. One day he'd have to accede. And that day soon arrived with the visit of a learned and wealthy man from Vienna seeking a suitable match for his daughter. Was there a student in the yeshiva who would meet his high standards?

The Rosh Yeshiva called for Shimshon.

"Enough," said the Rosh Yeshiva. "Enough suffering. Enough loneliness. It's time for you to get on with your life."

Shimshon shrugged, pulled on his now abundant beard and insisted he was not ready.

"But you are," countered the Rosh Yeshiva. "It's not as if you'll somehow be more ready in the future. This is a wonderful opportunity and you should accept the offer."

There was no mistaking the Rosh Yeshiva's confidence in the wisdom of this match. After another round of protest, Shimshon accepted the proposal. He would make the trip to Vienna.

Wedding preparations were soon set into motion, along with the doubt in Shimshon's heart. As the wedding date approached, he grew increasingly restless. Should he accept the rational conclusion that his former bride had died in the conflagration and once and for all put it all behind him? There was no alternative. And yet, the disquiet would not leave him. Shimshon decided to speak openly to his future father-in-law. He would tell him the details of that fateful night. And ask one remaining favor.

It was the Jewish custom that on the day before a wedding, a feast was held for the poor. At this affair, the esteemed gentlemen and ladies of the wedding party served the needy the best foods and choicest delicacies, and also provided substantial donations at the conclusion of the meal. As one might imagine, the grander the wedding, the more bountiful the reception for the poor.

The upcoming wedding promised to be a particularly magnificent event, and all the destitute of the province hoped to attend. After all, not only did the bride's father have considerable wealth, he also had a reputation for outstanding generosity.

Shimshon's one request of his future father-in-law was to see the list of the names of the needy who attended the pre-wedding feast. The future father-in-law agreed; a pointless exercise, he thought, but if it put the young man's doubts to rest, it would be worth the effort.

From all corners of the region they came: the blind, the crippled, the lame, the elderly, the orphans, the emotionally disturbed, the homeless and poverty-stricken – all eager to be regaled with a splendid meal and charitable gift. As they entered the banquet, the men and women identified themselves to an usher who registered each name.

Shimshon, the young groom, sat at the dais, along with his penurious guests, and delivered a brief talk on a relevant Torah theme. As the festivities wound to a close, the usher handed Shimshon the list of names.

As Shimshon perused the entries, his face blanched. He held the paper in his now trembling hand, his heartbeat quickening. Here was her name! She was alive! And here in this room to celebrate his forthcoming wedding…to another.

Shimshon gathered himself and asked that the young woman join him and his future father-in-law in a private room.

"Who are you?" they asked the thin, anxious girl. "Where do you come from?"

She spoke quietly, her eyes cast downward. Years ago, she said, she'd stood under a wedding canopy, about to marry an upstanding young man, when tragedy struck. Her parents, along with many others, had burned to death. As for her groom…she could not say. She herself had managed to escape the flames but vowed never to return to that accursed town, to inquire about or listen to any talk of that accursed night. To survive, she'd become a servant in a wealthy home. And there she'd worked all these years until several weeks ago. The man of the household was nice enough, but the same could not be said of his wife, who treated her badly and with whom she'd had a serious row. She quit her job and was roaming about, hungry, not knowing where to go. Someone told her about a splendid wedding to take place in Vienna and how the poor would be treated to a wholesome meal and charity.

"What do you want from me?" she asked, frightened. "Why have you called me into this room? Am I accused of anything? I promise, I've done nothing wrong."

Shimshon looked at the young woman, his eyes unblinking. He bit his fingers and said nothing for an eternal moment before he allowed himself a long, deep breath.

"I want to ask you something. A question I asked you once before."

The girl looked up. "Before? I don't think we—"

"Will you marry me?"

The girl stared at him, the recognition dawning. "Shimshon," she whispered. "It's you." She nodded her head, an unrestrained tear falling on her cheek.

The would-be father-in law saw the transfixed look on their faces and understood what a fine son-in-law he'd be losing – a young man willing to forego a marriage into wealth and comfort in favor of marrying a poor orphan.

He sighed and turned to Shimshon. "You know we had a wedding planned for tomorrow. Hundreds of guests have already arrived. The musicians, the lavish provisions, all readied." His own daughter, he knew, would have little difficulty finding another suitable husband. The would-be-father-in-law now clapped his hands. "Yes, we have our groom." He then gestured to the young girl. "And we have our bride. So let us go and celebrate a wedding."

Who Are You to Judge?

Someone asks you for a donation. Can you spare a few coins? You look at the person and wonder: Does he really deserve help? Is he an imposter? What will he do with the money? Is he who he claims to be?

The Rebbe of Tzanz was known never to go to sleep while there was still money in his house, money he could distribute to the poor. And when someone appeared at his door asking for a donation, he never probed the person's background. They said they were in need? That was enough.

His Chassidim once warned the rebbe about a particular beggar, whom they claimed did not deserve a single penny, considering he had a reputation as a drunk and a sinner. Nonetheless, the rebbe gave the man a coin of significant value when he came knocking at his door. When his followers heard about it, they demanded an explanation.

"In the first place," the rebbe began, "the Torah instructs us to give to the poor. Nowhere does it instruct us to launch an investigation into a person's habits and personal history. Moreover, what makes you think that you can determine who truly deserves charity and who doesn't? Sometimes one's suspicions come from the 'evil side' that interferes with the performance of a mitzvah."

When his Chassidim still seemed unconvinced, the rebbe said he'd demonstrate his point with a story.

We've all heard about the journeys of the brothers Reb Zusha and Reb Elimelech, the two great tzaddikim of the earliest years of Chassidism. They would undertake long solitary years on the road where they'd encounter forsaken Jews living in remote hamlets and share words of encouragement and Torah with them.

On some occasions, Reb Zusha traveled alone without his brother. He made it a policy to never ask anyone for charity or sustenance. If someone offered him food, he'd accept it, but to ask for help, he believed, would be a sign of deficient faith on his part; if the good Lord didn't want him to die of starvation, He'd send someone to make sure he was fed.

On one of his many journeys, Reb Zusha arrived in a distant town and, as was his custom, went directly to the local *beis medrash*. It had been two days since he'd eaten a morsel. He took a seat at the back of the room and was soon immersed in his books. None of the young men who'd come to pray and study paid him any attention. No one offered him a meal or a place to sleep. But despite his mounting hunger, Reb Zusha would not ask anyone even for a piece of bread. He stayed in the town for two full days; on the morning of the third day, weak and famished, he resumed his journey.

As Reb Zusha was walking down the road, a man noticed him from a distance, and wondered what this unfamiliar Jew was doing trudging alone along this back road. When he greeted Reb Zusha, he could immediately see he was pale and exhausted. The man promptly introduced himself as Nuteh, and explained that he was an arenda, the lessee of a tavern in a nearby town. He invited Reb Zusha to accompany him to his home where he'd be happy to give him food and drink.

When they arrived at his house, Nuteh's wife presented Reb Zusha with a plateful of food, but the tzaddik would not sit down to eat before washing his hands and reciting the required benediction with his usual fervor. Nuteh and his wife surmised their guest was no ordinary man but someone of unusual piety.

When Reb Zusha had finished his meal, he thanked his hosts and began preparing to resume his travels when Nuteh asked him if he would consider staying. True, the house was small, but there was enough to eat and as for a place to sleep, they'd certainly find some suitable accommodation.

"Alas," Nuteh added, "this wouldn't be a problem if I could afford to purchase the large house the poretz has put up for sale. There, I assure you, yours would be the finest room."

Reb Zusha agreed to stay and blessed his host that his upcoming business deal would garner enough money to purchase the nobleman's house. To Nuteh's surprise, his business soon yielded a huge profit, enabling him to purchase the house he'd been eyeing for some time.

As promised, Nuteh allocated a choice room for Reb Zusha who spent his days teaching Torah and praying with the local Jews who called on the honored guest.

Some time later, a merchant arrived at Nuteh's house to undertake some business. As Nuteh was giving the man a tour of his home, the merchant happened to notice Reb Zusha bent over his books in the study and did a double-take. "What is *he* doing here?" the visitor asked Nuteh when they were alone, his voice low but pressing.

"And why not?" Nuteh replied, recounting how he'd met the hungry man walking along the road, and how he and his wife had asked him to stay and were so impressed with the stranger's righteousness.

The businessman shook his head and narrowed his brows. "Get rid of him. I'm telling you this in the friendliest way I can. Get rid of him now before you regret it."

"But why?"

"I know this man. He's a thief. A swindler."

"This pious man? I'm afraid you must be mistaken."

"Pious? Please." The merchant shook his head again, this time more vigorously. "I'm telling you, he's trouble. Take my advice and ask him to leave immediately."

"Impossible," Nuteh replied. Despite the merchant's certainty, he refused to believe that his learned guest was, in fact, a fraud.

But a few weeks later, another salesman came to Nuteh's home and when Nuteh introduced him to Reb Zusha, he, too, called Nuteh aside with an urgent piece of information.

"Why do you allow this man in your home?" he asked.

"Who? My wonderful guest?" Nuteh said, discomforted by the salesman's suspicious tone.

"I know this man," the salesman said. "He abandoned his wife and children. Not only that, he ratted on some Jews in his town and they drove him away."

"This can't be."

"But it is," said the salesman. "My suggestion? Ask him to leave at once."

This scenario repeated a few times more. A visitor on some business trip would stop by Nuteh's house, espy his guest and inform Nuteh of some untoward behavior committed by his boarder. "An unsavory character," they would mutter. "A charlatan." Although neither Nuteh nor his wife had witnessed any behavior that would support these accusations, these aspersions took their cumulative effect. The couple decided it'd be best if they asked their guest to leave.

With all the delicacy he could manage, Nuteh explained to Reb Zusha the time had come for him to go. The tzaddik did not wait for an explanation, but instead thanked his hosts for their extended hospitality, gathered his few possessions, and promptly went on his way.

Just as Nuteh's good luck had unexpectedly appeared along with Reb Zusha, his financial success departed when his guest returned to the road. His business ventures began to collapse. He now faced mounting demands for cash and was forced to sell his assets. Before long, Nuteh had no choice but to sell the house he had once so delighted in. The downward spiral continued until he was left with nothing. His wife would live with her family, while Nuteh was forced to take the stick and walk the road.

Sleeping now with other beggars, Nuteh sometimes thought about his past. When he approached a rich man for food, he'd recall the days when he himself gave charity with a broad hand. And when he'd have these thoughts, he'd also think of the sojourner whom he'd abruptly asked to leave, sure now his wealth had been due to that man's blessing and, certain too, that his current poverty was a punishment for accepting the *loshen hora*, the unsubstantiated gossip, about him.

Nuteh drifted from place to place until his roaming landed him in the town of Hanipol. There he heard about a local Chassidic rebbe to whom Jews traveled many miles to seek his benediction and advice.

And so Nuteh decided that he too would go to see this holy man; perhaps he might give him a blessing as well.

As soon as he entered the tzaddik's room, Nuteh recognized him as the traveler who'd stayed in his home all those years ago. The tzaddik, too, immediately recognized his former host.

In a rush of words, Nuteh related to Reb Zusha his sad story, how his good fortune came to a sudden end when the tzaddik left his home. He asked the rebbe to bless him and restore him to his former position of wealth.

Reb Zusha did not reply immediately, his eyes cast to the man's side. He then turned to meet Nuteh's eager face.

"Reb Nuteh, yours is a complicated affair. The heavens took note when you invited me, a hungry stranger, to your home and hosted me with such generosity. For this munificence, the powers above decreed that you would be rewarded with good fortune both in this world and the next.

"But Satan was appalled by this decision. True, he acknowledged, you were hospitable and kind, but should this reap such huge recompense? Both riches in this world followed by the splendor of the World to Come?

"Satan was determined to prove you were undeserving of this destiny. And so one day he visited you, impersonating a merchant. He later arrived as a salesman, then as various visitors, each inventing malicious slurs about me. Eventually, you accepted their slanderous lies and sent me away, proving Satan's case. And so, he managed to have this part of your reward revoked. Henceforth, your lot in this world would be one of severe hardship."

A shudder enveloped Nuteh.

"This life of misery is now my destiny?"

"I'm afraid so," the rebbe said sadly, a sigh hovering above his words. "No one, not even me, has the power to override this decree."

The tzaddik then lifted his face and brightened. "But Reb Nuteh, know this too. While Satan was able to take the good fortunes of this world from you, he was not able to overrule the promise of everlasting good fortune in the next world. That too is your future."

Addressing his Chassidim, the Tzanzer Rebbe continued, "As you see, the motivation to think ill of someone who seeks charity might seem like reasonable discernment but, in fact does not come from a good place. That's why we must redouble our resolve to ignore these suspicions. Here is a better rule: When asked for help, give it."

How Reb Leib Sarah's Got His Name

While most Chassidic rebbes are known by the names of the towns in which they lived – the Belzer Rebbe, the Chernobler Rebbe, the Berditchever Rebbe – others are known by their first names – Reb Elimelech, Reb Zusha, Reb Schmelke. And still others by the names of their books – the *Yishmakh Moshe*, the *Bnei Yissoscher*, the *Sfas Emes*. But one rebbe has the unusual legacy of being referred to by the name of his mother: Reb Leib Sarah's. This story tells why.

In a hamlet near the town of Rovna there lived a Jew who ran the local kretchma. This tavernkeeper was a simple but pious man who toiled day and night to earn his living.

He was blessed with a fine daughter named Sarah'le who was also an outstanding beauty. But as she grew older, it became clear that her beauty was not an unmitigated blessing. If they had lived in the city, his daughter would have multiple eligible suitors. But in their tiny hamlet, the only men Sarah'le ever saw were the patrons of her father's tavern: hard-drinking peasants who took every opportunity to tease and try to pinch her.

"Sarah'le, listen to me," her father said to her one night. "You know we are at the mercy of the poretz, the young, volatile nobleman who rules our lives. Without this kretchma, I have no resources, no income. You've become a beautiful young woman and I'm sure it is difficult for you to be surrounded by boorish, leering men. I know this won't be easy, but I have to ask you to make yourself as invisible here as you can, and when you must show yourself in public, to conceal your face as much as possible."

Sarah'le's eyes welled up as she nodded. She could see her father's anguish as he spoke.

From that day on, she avoided the rooms in which the drinkers congregated and when she needed to go to the market, she hurried through the streets, hiding her face as best she could.

And yet, talk of Sarah'le's beauty soon reached the ears of the poretz, who decided to pay the kretchma a visit. When he arrived late one evening, he sat down expansively at the largest table and loudly ordered several drinks.

"And Moyshke," he called out to the tavernkeeper. "Have your daughter serve them to me."

"Actually, my daughter isn't feeling well today," the tavernkeeper stammered.

"I said I want your daughter to bring my drinks," the poretz repeated.

"I'm afraid at the moment she's not dressed appropriately to serve the gentleman," the tavernkeeper implored.

The poretz smacked his riding whip on his well-polished boot. "Moyshke, do not forget you are my innkeeper. This kretchma belongs to me. You do what I say. And I say I want your daughter to serve me my drink. No more excuses. Let her come here now and let's see if she's as lovely as people say."

As there was no way of dissuading the poretz, the hapless tavernkeeper instructed his daughter to bring the man his libations. In the meantime, he stood at the side of the room praying she not find favor in the poretz's eyes.

But when Sarah'le handed the poretz his drink and turned to leave, he insisted she remain at the table.

"They raved about your looks. Well, you're even prettier than they said."

He'd like to have a conversation with her, he said.

Soon, the poretz became a regular patron of the kretchma, insisting not only that Sarah'le serve him, but that she spend time talking with him as well. The tavernkeeper observed the poretz's visits with growing unease; no good would come of this, he knew. Sarah'le, no less afraid, pleaded with her father that she not be made to serve the poretz.

Yet her father could only offer a disheartened shrug. He knew that if he angered the poretz, he risked losing the lease on the kretchma.

One evening, as the poretz sat imbibing drink after drink, he proposed to Sarah'le that they go for a walk. When she refused, he grabbed her by the neck and tried to drag her outside. Sarah'le resisted and pushed him away. The poretz, wobbly from his bout of drinking, fell to the ground. His cronies burst into laughter at the sight of him splayed on the floor, the victim of a young girl's shove.

The humiliated poretz quickly sobered up and walked over to Sarah'le, his whip raised high in his hand.

"Obstinate Jewess! You will pay for this," he sputtered. And without looking around, he stormed out of the inn.

Although the poretz no longer visited the kretchma, the tavernkeeper anxiety was not allayed. He knew the nobleman's pride would not let the matter rest. He'd want his revenge.

And indeed, a few days later, the tavernkeeper's fears were confirmed when he overheard one of the poretz's minions whisper to another: "This clueless Jew has no idea what awaits him. We're to come here tomorrow night with the poretz to kidnap his daughter and bring her back to the master's house. A priest will be there to convert the Jewess and then the poretz will wed the girl."

A feeling of panic rose in the tavernkeeper's throat. What could he do?

He thought of Reb Yossel who lived at the edge of town. Perhaps the old man could suggest some way to avoid the impending catastrophe.

Reb Yossel was the only learned Jew in the village, having arrived long ago as a young tutor for the few Jewish children in the area. Those children had all since grown up and left for other parts of the country, as had Reb Yossel's own children. A widower for many years now, he lived alone in a small hut, subsisting on small donations from the few Jewish villagers, content to spend his remaining years studying Torah.

When the tavernkeeper arrived at Reb Yossel's home and explained the dire situation, Reb Yossel stroked his long grey beard and pressed his lips together, lost in thought. "Here's what I suggest," Reb Yossel said after a long pause. "You say the poretz plans to kidnap and marry Sarah'le tomorrow night. Clearly, we need to preempt him. You have to get her married to someone else before he arrives. Start preparing immediately – food, music, wedding dress, guests – all the makings of a genuine wedding feast. Inform the Jews in the village that your daughter is getting married tomorrow evening at the kretchma immediately after sunset. And don't forget to invite the local judge to assure the legality of the wedding. Let's hope this works."

The tavernkeeper bit his lip. He didn't understand.

"How is this supposed to save us?" he asked the old man. "The poretz will show up with his thuggish friends and immediately realize the wedding is a sham. And how can there be a wedding without a groom?"

Reb Yossel placed his hand on the tavernkeeper's arm. "Do as I advise. There will be a wedding and there will be a groom."

When the tavernkeeper returned home, he told Sarah'le they had to begin preparing immediately for a wedding that was to take place the following day. "You will be the bride. That's the plan."

The next evening, Reb Yossel stood at the entrance of the freshly festooned kretchma, helping usher the guests to their tables on which they'd find plentiful food and drink. As soon as the sun set, a canopy was constructed and Sarah'le appeared in her bridal finery.

The frantic tavernkeeper pressed Reb Yossel. "I don't understand. We're ready for the ceremony to begin, and we need to hurry. Surely we can't have a wedding without a groom. Where is he?"

"What do you mean where?" Reb Yossel replied. "He's right here." He took hold of the tavernkeeper's shoulders. "Me. I'll be the groom for your daughter."

"You?"

The tavernkeeper blinked in disbelief. And yet, he knew he had no choice.

The music played as Sarah'le walked toward the wedding canopy to stand next to her betrothed. Reb Yossel pronounced the wedding vow, broke the glass under his foot, and a roar of *Mazel Tov* erupted across the room. But above the cheers, one could hear the roar of galloping horses.

Moments later, the poretz and his entourage burst into the kretchma intent on kidnapping Sarah'le. When he saw that a wedding had just taken place, he froze.

The tavernkeeper greeted the poretz with a deferential bow.

"Thank you for coming to my daughter's wedding celebration. Alas, I fear you've arrived a bit too late to observe the ceremony."

The poretz paid the tavernkeeper no attention as he scanned the room, noting the wedding canopy, the seated guests and the local judge among them. Without a word, he signaled to his retinue and hurried out to his carriage.

The next day, Reb Yossel sent for his new father-in-law, the tavernkeeper. After congratulating each other on the success of their ploy, Reb Yossel asked the tavernkeeper to secure a horse and wagon for a trip to Rovna, where Reb Yossel would divorce his new wife. The plan would then be complete.

But when the tavernkeeper told Sarah'le that they'd soon be leaving for Rovna, she demurred. She didn't wish to be divorced from Reb Yossel. She was happy to be married to a man of genuine decency and generosity – and a Torah scholar, as well.

Sarah'le's declaration caused a stir up in heaven, and a decree was issued: Because of her righteousness, she'd be rewarded with a son who would enlighten the world with his wisdom.

When a child was born a year later, they gave him the name Leib, but all called him Leib Sarah's in honor of his virtuous mother. And so he was called ever more.

Empathy

Please speak about this to my uncle," the man pleaded to the Yid Hakodesh. "He's one of your devoted Chassidim and will listen to you. Goodness knows he's wealthy enough. My business is in ruins, my poverty excruciating."

"I'll talk to him. I'll do what I can," the rebbe assured him.

"A few hundred rubles. Enough to get me back on my feet. That's all I'm asking for."

Soon afterward, the Yid Hakodesh had occasion to bring up the subject with Reb Leibish who'd come to seek his rebbe's blessings. The Yid asked that he perform the mitzvah of charity and help out his struggling nephew.

Reb Leibish responded in a fury.

"Rebbe, please don't speak to me about that reckless deadbeat. More than once I've lent him money. The man has no understanding of a ruble. What he is an expert in is turning money into mud, golden business opportunities into ashes. Believe me, he's done this more than once."

"Please," the rebbe said. "The man is impoverished. He doesn't have with what to feed his family."

"Better this way," Reb Leibish interrupted, forgetting to whom he was speaking. "Let him be hungry. Maybe hunger will be a good teacher for him."

The Yid recoiled, appalled by the heartless words. "If this is how you talk about your own flesh and blood, I think you might need the same teacher," he told his Chassid.

Reb Leibish didn't fully comprehend the meaning of the Yid's pronouncement, but he could read the anger on his rebbe's face. Realizing his impudence, he started to stammer an apology, but the Yid Hakodesh asked him to leave at once. He'd heard enough.

Over the following weeks, the rebbe's disturbing words haunted Reb Leibish. In an attempt to distract himself from his discomfort, he tried to lose himself in his business affairs. But events would not comply with his desires. Every day seemed to bring fresh bad news.

One day a major client switched to a competitor. The next, a fire erupted in his warehouse, destroying half his inventory. Not long afterward, thieves broke into his home and stole all of his possessions. And so it went, one calamity following another. Once a rich man, comfortable all his life, Reb Leibish now felt the indignity of famine. He now understood the helplessness of not being able to provide a piece of bread for one's family. "Father, please, I am so hungry," his children wailed night and day. For the first time, he experienced the agony of being unable to relieve his children's cries.

Reb Leibish went to see the Yid Hakodesh. He had no doubt that all his troubles could be traced to the harsh indifference he'd displayed toward his nephew.

"Rebbe, I recognize that I have sinned," he moaned. "I was callous. But why do I deserve a punishment this harsh?"

"They say, 'The sated never believe the complaints of the hungry,'" the Yid replied, his voice gentle. "I'm afraid, Leibish, you proved the saying true. What has happened to you isn't a matter of punishment. You dismissed the hunger of your nephew as a small matter – 'a lesson,' you called it. Yet you were the one who needed the lesson."

"But to this degree?" Reb Leibish cried. "Yes, I admit, I should have been more sympathetic, more sensitive to his grim circumstances. But what has happened to me is unnecessary."

The Yid's eyes met his Chassid's. "Alas, it was necessary. Until you experienced for yourself what it means to be desperate for a morsel of food, your nephew's hunger was an abstraction. You can't empathize with an abstraction."

Reb Leibish shook his head. The Yid Hakodesh could tell from Reb Leibish's hesitant half nod he was still unconvinced. And so the Yid Hakodesh offered to tell Reb Leibish a little story.

The armies of Frederick the Great, the King of Prussia, had laid siege to the city of Leipzig, a siege that lasted for months. Yet, the king knew that the blockade had not completely sealed the city – its citizens were able to continue their resistance by smuggling in sustenance. How were they doing this? Where were these undetected routes? The king decided to find out himself.

This mission required, of course, that the king dress in disguise. He put on peasant garb and sneaked into the city. What he didn't know was that Leipzig had its own spies, who quickly learned of Frederick's ruse; word went out that the king was circulating among them dressed as a peasant.

The king, for his part, soon became aware that he was the object of a manhunt. Desperate to find shelter, he entered the hut of a Jewish blacksmith, and asked the man to hide him until his army gained control of the city. He assured the man that he'd be rewarded handsomely for this protection.

Indeed, the Prussian army eventually prevailed, conquering Leipzig and rescuing their king. Frederick, true to his word, summoned the blacksmith and presented him with a substantial reward.

"Your Highness," the blacksmith said as he prepared to leave the palace, "I do have one question I want to ask you, a question that's been gnawing at me. How did it feel when you were hidden in my home, knowing that any second you could be captured and executed?"

The king stared at the blacksmith, then turned to his assistants at his side. "Such insolence! Take this Jew and hang him. Now."

So the king's men brought the blacksmith to the galleys. They prepared the rope and placed the noose around his neck. The hangman took his position and began pulling the rope when the king, standing nearby, shouted, "Halt! Release him." A wry grin on his face, the king approached the terrified man.

"Well? Did I answer your question? You wanted to know what it felt like to be a moment away from death. Words wouldn't suffice. But with a rope around your neck, perhaps you can appreciate what it felt like."

The Yid Hakodesh allowed a smile on his face and tilted his head toward Reb Zalman. "So? Do you understand the point of this story, Reb Zalman? True compassion has to be felt, not imagined."

Reb Leibish's financial condition eventually improved, but, more important, so had his moral character.

A Test of Character

Reb Menachem Mendel of Rimanov was one of the great Chassidic masters of his day. But this is not his story. This is, rather, the story of his father Reb Yosef, and why he was rewarded with a son like Reb Menachem Mendel of Rimanov.

Reb Yosef ran a kretchma not far from the shtetl of Fristik, in what is now Poland. He and his wife were childless but content, living out their simple life in peace and quiet.

One day, the poretz, the nobleman of the region, visited Reb Yosef with some news. He'd decided to move far away and, therefore, wished to sell all of his belongings.

"I've always been fond of you," the poretz told Reb Yosef, "always respected your integrity. That's why I want to present you with an exceptional offer. I am giving you the opportunity to buy all of my possessions at a cost of only one tenth their value. There's just one caveat: I intend to move very soon. So if you want to buy the estate's holdings, you'll have to come up with the money in the next few days."

"What should we do?" Reb Yosef asked his wife later that night. The poretz's offer was an extraordinary, once-in-a-lifetime opportunity. Buying these goods for only a tenth of their worth meant they'd be able to sell them at a huge profit. But Reb Yosef also knew they didn't have sufficient funds to make the purchase. Still, Reb Yosef's wife was determined to find a way.

"We'll sell our gold and silver pieces, all our furniture, everything we have," she told her husband. "And if that's not enough? Well, then, we'll borrow the rest." And so they hurriedly sold all that they had. As they were still shy of the sum needed to complete the purchase, Reb Yosef borrowed the remainder. And when he'd garnered enough money, he set off to the poretz's home to conclude the deal.

As he was walking along the road, he heard cries coming from the distance. Feeling compelled to follow the sounds, he soon found himself in front of a small hut. As he approached the entrance, the wailing grew louder. When he walked inside, he was met with a tragic scene: On the floor lay a dead man covered in a thin sheet, surrounded by his widow and seven bawling children, so lost in their grief they barely noticed the stranger in their midst. Reb Yosef quickly surmised that this was a family reduced to abject poverty without even enough resources to give the deceased a proper burial.

Reb Yosef knew at once that he had to help them. He withdrew from his pocket all the money he'd brought with him, and with which he had planned to purchase the poretz's goods, and handed it to the widow. After conveying a few words of solace, he returned home.

Chassidim believe that Reb Yosef's generosity created a stir in heaven. Surely he ought to be rewarded for his act of charity, the angels argued. Did he not deserve to be compensated not only for the money he gave to the poor family, but also for the profit he had forfeited? The Heavenly Court agreed – but went further, suggesting that Reb Yosef should be bequeathed a reward of his own choosing. And so it was about to be officially decreed...

When Satan stepped in.

"One moment," he pleaded. "To be sure, Reb Yosef demonstrated great compassion for the suffering of the widow and her children. For this, there's no denying he ought to be rewarded. But let us not get carried away here. After all, what we witnessed might have been a one-time event. Perhaps, only in this particular instance, Reb Yosef was overcome with sympathy. How do we know that generosity is an integral part of his character?"

"And what do you suggest, Satan?" the court asked.

"That he undergoes a test. Let me present him with a challenge to determine if he is someone sincerely committed to charity."

"An excellent idea!" said a voice in the room.

The prophet Elijah walked to the front of the tribunal. "Yes, I agree," he continued. "Before we bestow a reward, we should first put the man through an ordeal, see if he legitimately deserves this recompense. But Satan shouldn't be the one to determine what his test ought to be. Allow me to devise it."

The court agreed to Elijah's request. A reward would be granted only if Reb Yosef passed the test devised by the prophet.

Reb Yosef returned to an empty home. All his belongings had been sold. Moreover, he was without means to pay off his considerable debts and no longer was able to maintain his tavern. And so, he bid his wife good-bye and walked to a nearby town to see if might procure some source of income.

After days of finding no work, however, Reb Yosef went to the town's *beis medrash*, where he took a seat on one of the hard benches in the back of the room, opened up a book of Jewish law, and began studying.

Hours went by, and Reb Yosef's hunger intensified. Still, he refused to ask any of the congregants for something to eat, believing they would not allow a visitor to starve. Surely, someone would soon invite him for a meal. But no one did.

More hours passed and still he was ignored. Not a single congregant acknowledged this stranger in the back of their *beis medrash*. Reb Yosef ached from hunger. Exhausted, he closed his book and placed his head on the table, hoping to catch a bit of sleep. But just as he closed his eyes, he felt someone poking him.

Reb Yosef lifted his head and faced an old man.

"Sholem Aleichem," the man said with a smile, stretching out his hand in greeting.

"Aleichem Sholem," Reb Yosef replied.

"And from where does a Jew hail?" asked the old man, in a welcoming voice. "Tell me, how are you doing?"

Without knowing why, Reb Yosef answered at length, recounting the recent events of his life: how he had been about to purchase his poretz's belongings but instead gave away all that he had to a grieving family. And this was how he came to find himself, he explained, on this bench, in a distant city, hungry and destitute.

The old man nodded. "That was quite a mitzvah you performed, giving away all your money. But now? Sad, isn't it? You sit here impoverished, hopeless."

The old man leaned a bit closer to Reb Yosef. "But you're fortunate after all. Because I want to make a deal with you. I'm old, as you can see. But I'm also very rich. So here's my proposal: Sell me your good deed and I'll pay you all the money you lost. Better still, I'll also include all the profit you stood to gain with your purchase of the poretz's estate. Your lucky day, eh? What do you say?"

"What! Are you serious?" Reb Yosef replied. "Sell my mitzvah? God forbid I should do such a thing. There's no way I—"

"Okay, okay," the old man interrupted. "I understand. You don't wish to relinquish your mitzvah. Fair enough. So let's do this. I'll buy half your mitzvah…and for the same price. A wonderful deal, if I say so myself. You get to keep half the mitzvah and all the money besides. So what do you say?"

"I say what I said before. I don't bargain with my mitzvah."

The old man said nothing for a moment before responding. "All right then. Seeing you're adamant about this, I'll tell you what I'll do. I'll buy only one-tenth of your mitzvah. Not bad – you get to keep nine-tenths. And you know what? I'll double the offer: I'll give you twice the money you had in your pocket, plus twice the future profit you stood to reap. Now this is quite a bargain, no?"

Reb Yosef shook his head.

"You aren't listening to me, are you? Not for the wealth of the entire world would I sell my mitzvah. Please, take your money and go buy your mitzvahs elsewhere, but please leave me alone."

The old man nodded. It was clear this starving man was resolute. His deed was too dear to him; nothing could entice him to trade it away.

The old man leaned closer and embraced Reb Yosef.

"Listen to me," he said. "Do you know who I am?"

"No. Who are you?"

"I am the prophet Elijah. I came here to learn if you regretted giving away your entire fortune as an act of charity. So I tested you. A test you have passed. And so, you will be awarded a gift of your own choosing: a long, healthy life; success in business that will make you rich beyond your wildest imagination; or a son who will grow up to be a tzaddik."

"A son," Reb Yosef replied without hesitation. "A son."

When the child was born, Reb Yosef named him Menachem, which means comfort, the son who grew up to become the holy Reb Menachem Mendel, the great Rebbe of Rimanov.

The Rebbe Brokers a Deal

Reb Levi Yitzchak of Berditchev is celebrated among Chassidim as a great champion of his people; many stories are about his arguments with God on their behalf, pleading their cases even if they were sinners. Reb Levi Yitzchak of Berditchev had only one rule: when the sin was religious in nature, between a person and God, the Rebbe would intercede and make the case for God's forgiveness, but when the sin was between two individuals, if one had mistreated the other, the Berditchever Rebbe would always come to the defense of the victim. He used all his powers of persuasion to see that justice was done: cajoling, admonishing, cautioning, and sometimes even threatening – and carrying out his threats.

One night, two men appeared before the Berditchiver and asked him to serve as the judge in an arbitration. The plaintiff was a pale, emaciated man who continually pulled on his scrawny beard. The defendant was a well-dressed, and evidently well-fed, businessman.

The plaintiff immediately launched into his case, speaking in a thin, reedy voice. "Rebbe, I am a middleman, a broker. Well, that's to say, now I'm a broker. You understand, I don't run a flourishing business…to put it mildly. In fact, I barely make a living. But this is what I am able to do.

"So, let me get to what brings me here," the man said, swaying from side to side.

"I go to the marketplace to see if I could broker some exchange of goods. The merchants ignore me: They don't know me, they already have people they deal with. They won't even talk to me. I walk around the entire marketplace. I go from stall to stall ... nothing. I'm not earning a penny. So, the other day, I decide to try my luck at a smaller market nearby. There, I see a Jew with a wagon of rye seeds he's brought to sell. I strike up a conversation with him and he tells me he's been standing there for hours, yet has not managed a single sale. Not even one interested customer. He tells me he's concerned because he really needs money to purchase flour.

"So I leave the fellow and return to the main marketplace, where, as luck would have it, I come upon a man selling bags of flour. He too hasn't had a customer all day and needs to make a sale because he wants to buy rye.

"Perfect, no? I need only to bring these two merchants together. So I tell each about the other and seek to arrange the transaction. But when I suggest the exchange, both look at me with suspicion. Neither knows who I am or if I'm trustworthy. I have no reputation as a broker and can't provide any references. And, truth be told, I don't know how one goes about arranging such a deal. So what do I do? I go to an established broker for help. To this man here ... this thief."

With this, the plaintiff pointed to the man standing next to him, who proceeded to roll his eyes and shake his head. The plaintiff turned again to the rebbe.

"I explain to him that I found two merchants who need each other's goods. 'I'll tell you what,' I say to him. 'If you help me conclude the deal, we'll split the brokerage fee fifty-fifty.' This broker – the man beside me here – agrees to the proposal. So we proceed to the respective merchants, the deal is concluded, and each of the merchants pays his share of the brokerage fee. Ah, but when I ask this man for my share, he throws me a couple of rubles and keeps the rest. And that's why I am bringing this lawsuit. To receive my fair share."

The Berditchever Rebbe stroked his beard and nodded. "Very well. I see."

He turned to the defendant. "And what do you have to say about all this?"

"It's true what this fellow says," the businessman acknowledged, his tone contemptuous. "But, listen, this man is no broker. He knows nothing about how this business works. He should be happy with the few coins I did give him."

"Yes," said the rebbe, "but without him, you would never have known about these particular merchants."

"So I paid him for his minor effort," the broker interrupted. "I know what I'm doing and this is how it's done." He waved his hand in front of the rebbe as if to suggest that this was not something he would understand.

The Berditchever Rebbe was taken aback by the man's dismissive attitude. "Have a seat," he said to him. "In fact, I do know a little bit about your business. I'm something of a broker myself. Of course, I don't arrange the exchange of material goods between merchants. I facilitate a different sort of exchange – between the Creator and His people. Trades of a different sort…of spiritual goods, you might say. And you know, I once had a situation similar to yours."

The Berditchever paused to make sure he had the businessman's attention before continuing.

"I once brokered a deal between God and the Jews. I saw that in heaven one could get hold of a certain kind of merchandise – forgiveness, clemency, forbearance. These articles were of no value in heaven. After all, the angels, the souls of the righteous, what need do they have for absolution? But the People of Israel, alas, we desperately need these commodities. So I decided to do some brokering. I said to God: May I propose a trade? Take our sins – alas, we have amassed many – and do with them as You please. In exchange, give us Your mercy and forgiveness. And God agreed to the deal.

"The only problem was that when I went to my fellow Jews and told them of the barter I'd arranged, they balked. They didn't want to give up the pleasures that accompanied their sinful behavior. But what about the forgiveness they'd receive in return? Not good enough, they said to me. Forgiveness alone wasn't worth giving up their enjoyments. So I said, 'Suppose I can get more. Suppose that if you surrender your sins, not only will you be forgiven, you'll also be bestowed with fine children, health and sustenance.' I thought that I'd be able to procure these items – after all, they too are of no use in heaven. Finally, the people accepted the proposition. For *this* package of benefits, they'd relinquish their sins.

"So I proposed to God the new terms of the exchange: the people will give up sinning and, in return, receive children, health and sustenance in addition to forgiveness. Once more, God agreed to the deal."

At that, the rebbe took hold of the businessman's lapel.

"And do you know what I obtained as payment for arranging this transaction?"

The broker shook his head. "God said to me, 'As your brokerage fee, I'm giving you power over these three extra benefits – I will comply when you decide who begets children and who remains healthy and financially secure.'

"I'm saying to you now, give this man the money he deserves. If you do, all is well. But if you don't, I warn you, your well-being will be in danger."

"Hold on a minute," the man exclaimed. "Do you mistake me for this pathetic little man here next to me? Sorry, but I'm not frightened by a Chassidic rebbe's delusional threats. I'll tell you what. You keep your broker fees and I'll keep mine."

And with that, the man marched out of the rebbe's room.

A few days later, the rich broker became ill. Days later, his sickness worsened, but the local doctor could not diagnose the disease. Sparing no expense, the businessman visited the most esteemed doctors and professors of medicine in the region. The physicians wrote their prescriptions, but none proved effective. His condition deteriorated.

When the luckless plaintiff heard about his antagonist's illness, he visited the man's home and told his wife all that had transpired between them at the arbitration. He recounted how the rebbe had warned the broker of what would transpire should he not pay his debt.

The bewildered woman stared at her visitor.

"So what now? Are you here for the money?"

"No," the visitor replied. "I only wanted to tell you what I believe caused your husband's sickness. At this point, this is no longer a matter between your husband and me. This is between your husband and the rebbe."

"Take me there," the woman implored. "Let me speak with him right away."

When the woman entered the rebbe's room, she immediately cried out, "Please, Rebbe, my husband is gravely ill. He's a father of young children. A young man himself. Have mercy."

The Berditchever Rebbe shook his head. "Business is business. If he doesn't surrender his brokerage fee, I don't surrender mine."

"Take, take," the woman pleaded, opening her purse to the poor broker. "Take whatever you want."

The litigant looked to the rebbe, unsure whether to accept the money. Noting the rebbe's affirmative wink, he collected the sum he was owed.

The rebbe turned to the businessman's wife.

"All right, then. You've dealt with your brokerage fee, now I'll deal with mine. Go home. Go home to your husband who, I assure you, is now on the path to a speedy recovery."

The Temptation
of a Righteous Sin

Reb Moshe Leib Sassover, the Chassidic tzaddik, lived in a time when the poretz, the local Polish nobleman, enjoyed unlimited dominion over his province. It was not uncommon for the poretz to arrest his Jewish subjects when they were late paying the rent for the kretchmas, the inns they managed on his behalf. In such cases, not only was the innkeeper imprisoned, but so was his entire family, all locked in damp, cold cellars with hardly a morsel to eat. The Sassover Tzaddik made it his personal mission to travel from village to village, raising funds to ransom these hapless Jews from their terrible fate.

On one of these excursions, Reb Moshe Leib came upon a kretchma where he decided to spend the night. As was his custom, he engaged the Jewish manager in conversation, inquiring about the man's livelihood and his spiritual well-being.

"Business is fine," the man said. He explained that the poretz of his province was a decent fellow, with whom he enjoyed a cordial relationship. Indeed, there was little reason to complain.

And his religious life? Here, the man answered hesitantly. He tried to maintain the traditions he'd learned from his father and observed the important Jewish customs. He acknowledged, however, that, at the poretz's insistence, he kept his kretchma open on Shabbos. But other than this one exception—

Clearly, this Jew was unaware of the gravity of his transgression. The Sassover was deeply disturbed by the ease with which the innkeeper dismissed his violation of the holy Sabbath.

Here I am, traveling from village to village, the tzaddik thought to himself, far away from my home, my family, my time for Torah study, all because of the importance of ransoming incarcerated Jews. And now I meet another Jew who is also captive – not physically, but spiritually.

Reb Moshe Leib asked the man if he could remain in his kretchma for a while, perhaps a few weeks, if need be. The innkeeper immediately replied he'd be delighted to have the rebbe as a guest and provided him with his own room.

Every day, the Sassover discussed with his host the sanctity of the Sabbath. And each morning, when the Sassover walked into the nearby woods to pray, he included a prayer that the innkeeper open his heart to its observance. Eventually, the Sassover's words were heeded: The innkeeper agreed to close his kretchma on Shabbos. But when he went to inform the poretz of his decision, the nobleman was furious.

"Should you go through with this nonsense," the poretz warned, "you'll lose the right to manage the kretchma, and in the process, your livelihood. Is this what you want? All of a sudden you've decided to become an observant Jew? Tell me," the poretz continued. "What is the source of this foolishness?"

The innkeeper told the poretz about the saintly man staying with him the past week and how he helped him appreciate the importance of observing the Sabbath, even if it entailed financial sacrifice.

The poretz responded with a hearty laugh. "Saintly man? Please. Don't be naive. It's easy to be a saint when it doesn't cost you anything. Saintliness stops at the pocketbook. Believe me, if this saint of yours was faced with forfeiting *his* livelihood, he also wouldn't observe the laws of the Sabbath."

"Not so," the innkeeper insisted. "I assure you, Reb Moshe Leib Sassov would not transgress the Sabbath merely for the sake of money."

The poretz reached to tweak his nose. "I'll tell you what, Moshke," he said, nodding approvingly at his own resolve. "I'll make a deal with you. If I prove to you that even this holy man of yours would break the laws of the Sabbath for substantial monetary gain, will you agree to keep the kretchma open on Saturday? Because, trust me, he will."

Before the innkeeper could reply, the poretz added to his wager. "You know, Moshke, I'm so sure of this, I'll tell you what: If I'm wrong and this man doesn't yield to this temptation, not only will I allow you to continue running the kretchma and keep it closed on your Sabbath, I'll even forgive your rent for the next couple of years. That's how certain I am. When it comes to money, we're all the same. You'll see."

Seeking to familiarize himself with the object of his challenge, the poretz arranged for his confederates to track the Sassover's daily habits. When he learned that this Chassidic rebbe made it a practice to pray in the forest every morning, including the Sabbath, the poretz was ready to lay his trap.

The next Sabbath, the poretz mounted his horse and rode out toward the place in the woods where the Sassover prayed each day. He carried a bag laden with gold coins, which he carefully sprinkled along the Sassover's path. Then he hid behind a tree and waited.

A few minutes later, he saw Reb Moshe Leib trudging along the path, his eyes cast downward. The poretz held his breath. Suddenly, the Sassover stopped. He bent down, his eyes fixed on the glistening coins. The poretz could not restrain a broad smile. He'd been vindicated.

But then he saw Reb Leib straighten up and continue along his way, deeper into the forest. Disappointed, the poretz was ready to emerge from his observation post when he heard footsteps. The Sassover was returning! He was right, after all.

The poretz watched as the Sassover walked directly over to where the coins lay on the ground. The rebbe stood motionless for a moment, staring at the money. Then, lifting his head toward the heavens, he mouthed some words. He put his hand on his chin as if reaching a major decision, then walked briskly back into the forest.

The poretz continued to wait for some time, but it was clear the experiment was over. This time the Sassover Rebbe would not return.

The next day, the poretz visited the kretchma to speak with the rebbe.

"I see you are as pious as the tavernkeeper said you were. I was there, you know. I saw. Money wasn't enough to tempt you to violate your Sabbath. But tell me, why, after you first walked into the forest, did you return to the coins? I observed you linger there for a while before you continued on."

"It was a struggle," the Sassover replied. "When I first noticed the coins on the ground, I stopped to look. Handling money on the Sabbath is forbidden and the possibility of doing so didn't even dawn on me. But then, as I walked on, I thought to myself, Wait a minute, touching money on the Sabbath is not a biblical transgression, only a rabbinical prohibition. On the other hand, saving a Jew from death *is* a biblical command, which always trumps a rabbinical ruling.

"I thought of those poor Jews rotting away in their dungeons and how this money could be used to help rescue them. I asked myself, Moshe Leib, suppose it was your wife and children condemned to such a fate? Would you still be so strict with the law and not take the money to save them? And so, I decided to retrieve the coins. But standing there, I just couldn't do it. This was the Sabbath, after all. I went back and forth in my mind, unable to decide what to do. And so I beseeched the Lord Almighty, 'God, if you want to help me perform the mitzvah of redeeming those in captivity, why would You have me do this through violating the holy Day of Rest?' No, I concluded, surely the Lord will assist me through means other than transgressing the Torah. And so I hurried along the path and didn't give the matter a further thought."

The integrity of the Sassover Rebbe left a lasting impression on the poretz. Thenceforth, when faced with a difficult problem of his own, he would call on the Sassover Tzaddik for his wise counsel.

Elijah and the Clown

As was true of other Jewish villages in Eastern Europe, Zbarazh was noteworthy only because of the famed rebbe who lived there, Rabbi Meshullam Feibush. Zbarazh was otherwise a shtetl like all others, featuring the usual array of Talmudic scholars and ignoramuses, the pious and not-so pious, along with the usual medley of merchants, menial workers and mendicants.

And like small villages everywhere, Zbarazh boasted its own band of jokers. Chief among them was Motke, or Motke Letz as he was called, *letz* being the Hebrew word for a cutup, a clown. And that Motke certainly was. He even looked the part with his hefty belly that complemented a round face featuring a drooping but well-groomed moustache. As far as Motke was concerned, any conversation was an opportunity for comic display, an occasion to perform an uncanny impression of one of the town's well-known characters, or at least to interject a joke, and so be it if it skated at the edge of decency. "Every village must have its jester," Motke declared and he was proud to assume the role.

You might think of Pesach the water carrier as Motke Letz's opposite. Pesach was a simple Jew – you might even say, simpleminded. You'd never catch *him* bantering, for in truth, he was incapable of witty repartee. Subtlety flew by him like a gust of wind, all sarcasm wasted. Not that it mattered, for Pesach had no time for idle chatter. The poor man was always at work. On most days he'd haul water from the stream for his rich customers, but he'd graciously accept any job he was offered. He served as the assistant to the assistant of the synagogue, heated the rocks at the bathhouse and even dug graves when the gravediggers had already gone home.

One year, during the intermediate days of Passover, Motke Letz noticed Pesach the water carrier trudging along the road, a full bucket in each hand. What an opportunity for a little fun! Motke Letz rushed over to Pesach, grabbed the buckets from his hands and placed them on the ground.

"Today, Reb Pesach? Today you deliver water? Don't you know this is your special day?"

"Special?"

"Of course! Don't you know what today is?" Motke Letz suppressed an urge to slap his thigh in glee and said as earnestly as he could, "We are celebrating the middle days of the holiday of Pesach. Your name is Pesach. So this is your special holiday. Today, you are the most esteemed person in our entire town."

Pesach seemed not to comprehend.

"You don't understand? Let me illustrate." Motke Letz ran his hand over his chin as if deep in thought. "Take my name. Motke, short for Mordecai. I was given this name because I was born on Purim and Mordecai is the protagonist of that joyful holiday. That's why I'm playful, always the comic. No doubt your name is Pesach because you were born during the festival of Pesach. You should be proud to be connected to such an important festival. No, Pesach, this is not a day for you to toil."

The water carrier pulled at his straggly beard and scratched his head.

"You are right," he said. "I'm named after the holiday Pesach. I shouldn't be carrying water today. I should be celebrating. I never realized this before. Thank you, Reb Motke, for pointing this out to me."

"It's my pleasure," said Motke, a wide grin creasing his ample face.

Pesach hurried to deliver the water to his next – and now last – customer of the day, then dashed home to his small hut on the outskirts of town. He related his great discovery to his wife, who was astonished to see him home in the middle of the day and in such good spirits.

"I am not just anyone!" he exclaimed. "I am someone with a holiday name. I shouldn't be working on this, my special day."

Thenceforth, every year when Passover arrived, Pesach the water carrier was a man transformed. All year long, Pesach saved his measly kopecks in preparation for the festival. When the day arrived, he would stand proudly at the head of his holiday table, set with a freshly starched white tablecloth and sparkling cutlery. A bottle of sweet wine stood proudly at the table's center. Surely, the neighbors could smell the sumptuous meat and fish cooking in the kitchen. Pesach the water carrier presided over the Seder like true royalty, free of all concerns and worries. With his broken Hebrew, the remnant of his few years of schooling, he tried to recite every word of the Haggadah, and even composed commentaries on the passages.

Pesach's Seder was also an annual event for Motke Letz.

Each year he'd rush through his own meal and hurry to the hut of Pesach the water carrier, where he'd plant his ear to the door. What a mess this water carrier made of the tradition! How he demolished the Hebrew language! Motke Letz could hardly wait for the next morning, when he would regale his friends in the synagogue with the mangled recitation and ludicrous interpretations he'd overheard the previous night.

And so it went, Passover after Passover.

But then, one year, two weeks before the holiday, calamity struck Pesach the water carrier. He'd gone to retrieve the *knippel*, the little bag in which he kept his year-long holiday savings concealed among a pile of bundles in the closet. It was gone. A thief had discovered Pesach's hiding place and made off with all his money.

Pesach's wife wailed bitterly when he informed her of the theft. "Woe is us! This is our entire year's savings. We have nothing now."

Pesach tried to console his wife. "Please stop crying," he pleaded. "In truth, the money was never ours. We had no intention to spend it on ourselves. The money was dedicated to the holiday of Pesach. If the Almighty does not want us to have a resplendent festival this year, so be it."

But, in truth, Pesach's heart was no less broken than his wife's. At the Seder he recited kiddush on the cheap raisin wine he bought with the few kopecks he managed to scrounge together. There would be no meat this year; a small piece of carp would have to do. There would be no fruits; a single potato was all he could afford. Unable to control his sorrow, Pesach raised his eyes to the heavens.

"Father in heaven, You know how I saved all year, one kopeck, then another, to be able to celebrate the festival in grand style. After all, this is the special holiday that shares my name. But, I don't know why You ordained that a thief would steal my savings and now my table is empty. Creator of the Universe, this is your decree, and I must accept it. But why do I deserve this?"

With a broken voice, his tears flowing, Pesach began reciting the Haggadah, bemoaning his fate in heartfelt groans.

Motke Letz was listening closely. He was ready once again to harvest a new crop of malapropisms from the lips of the barely literate water carrier. But this year he heard something else. This year he heard cries of anguish. Motke Letz felt a pain in his heart.

He knew that Pesach the water carrier had too much pride for charity and would never accept a donation of food and wine, even for the holiday.

But he suddenly had an idea.

He rushed home and hurried to his bookshelf, where he kept the box containing the *esrog*, the ritual citron he'd used for the past Succos festival. The shrunken, now bronzed, fruit was still wrapped in its protective golden flax. Motke attached the flax to his own blond moustache and beard and even had enough left over with which to form flowing sidecurls. He gathered together meat, fish, carrots and eggs, fresh horseradish, extra matzos, a bottle of fine wine, even cake. All of this he put in a large bag, and hurried to the home of Pesach the water carrier.

As Motke approached the entrance to Pesach's humble shack, he could hear him reciting *Shfokh Khamaskha*, the passage that welcomes the Prophet Elijah to the Seder table. Pesach opened the door for Elijah, and stood agog. On his doorstep was a man with a long golden beard and flowing gold sidecurls. Surely, this must be Elijah the Prophet!

Motke Letz wasted no time. He ran into the house, placed the large bag on the table and dashed out just as quickly, all without a word.

"Wait! Don't run away!" Pesach shouted, chasing after the man. "Please, Reb Elijah! Let me at least thank you!"

But Motke Letz had already escaped into the night.

Each man had an interesting story to tell at services the next morning. Pesach the water carrier recounted his miracle to the small crowd that had gathered around him, explaining how Elijah had transformed his Seder from a meal of scraps into a feast, replete with delicious food and wine. At the other side of the synagogue, Motke Letz entertained his comrades with his preceding night's prank.

"You should have seen him," he told his eager audience. "'Don't run away, Elijah! Wait, Elijah! Let me thank you, Elijah!' The water carrier was convinced I was Elijah, as sure as the sun rises in the morning and sets in the night."

The merriment reached the ears of Reb Feivel, who soon asked to speak with Motke Letz. Motke explained to the rebbe the cause of the laughter. "What foolishness!" he told the rebbe. "The water carrier is convinced Elijah the Prophet visited his Seder. People will believe anything."

"And you, Motke? Are you so sure Elijah didn't visit him?"

Motke was bewildered by the question. "What does the rebbe mean? Of course, I'm sure. I'm the one who brought him the food and drink."

"It's true you were the one who went to his hut last night," the rebbe said. "But how do you know you were alone, that you weren't accompanied by Elijah?"

"Elijah with me?"

"As you know, according to tradition, Elijah the Prophet comes to the aid of the needy on special occasions. He appears in all sorts of disguises. He might be an ordinary worker, a simple beggar, a man, a woman, a Jew or a non-Jew. Sometimes he can even appear as a thought. Elijah can be the unexpected idea that leads an ordinary person to do the extraordinary. Last night, for example, you were inspired to do this wonderful mitzvah of charity for Pesach the water carrier. Perhaps you, too, Motke Letz, were honored with a visit from Elijah the Prophet."

Motke's tightened lips relaxed into a broad smile. Elijah his companion! This was no laughing matter.

Notes

The following notes comprise selected points of interest and brief descriptions of the various Chassidic rebbes that appear in this book. The reader who wishes to learn more about these and other stories, or about Chassidism in general, is encouraged to peruse the many books, articles and online resources currently available on the subject of Chassidic folklore.

THE BLIND ANGEL

Reb Moshe Leib (Erblich) of Sassov (1745–1807) was born in Brody and spent his youth studying Talmud before becoming a student of the Chassidic master Reb Schmelke of Nikolsburg. He was the author of several works on Talmud and Scriptures and was famed as well for his musical talents.

The Sassover is the protagonist in numerous Chassidic stories, many of which focus on his love for his fellow Jews and his attempts to help them escape their travails. (When asked how he was able to involve himself with so much suffering, he answered that if the pain was only that of others, he wouldn't manage, but inasmuch as their suffering was also his own, he felt compelled to ameliorate it.) The Yiddish writer I. L. Peretz's well-known tale "If Not Higher," about a "rebbe of Nemirov" who, instead of attending early morning penitential prayers (*slikhot*), puts on peasant garb and goes into the forest to cut firewood for a sickly widow, is based on a popular Chassidic legend about Reb Moshe Leib of Sassov.

— The name Tsurif means "artisan" in Hebrew.

TRADING FOR PARADISE

Rabbi Abraham Yehoshua Heschel (1748–1825), the Rebbe of Apt (Polish Opatów), was a scion of famous rabbis on both his father's and mother's sides. Already renowned as a Talmudic scholar in his youth, he later became a disciple of Rabbi Elimelech of Lizhensk and Rabbi Yekhiel Michel of Zlotchov. After moving from shtetl to shtetl, he settled in Mezhbuzh, the home of the Ba'al Shem Tov and the cradle of Chassidism, and is buried there next to the Ba'al Shem Tov. In Mezhbuzh, the Apter devoted himself completely to the study and dissemination of Chassidism and attracted thousands of followers, including many future Chassidic leaders. Chassidim often refer to the Apter Rebbe by the title of his collected teachings, the *Ohev Yisroel* ("lover of the Jewish people"). His namesake, the twentieth-century Jewish theologian Abraham Joshua Heschel, is a descendant of the Apter Rebbe.

CHARITY REDEEMS FROM DEATH

Similar tales are told about other Chassidic rebbes. For example, Reb Chaim Halberstam of Tzanz accompanied the funeral of a wealthy man who was dismissive of Jewish law in general but nevertheless had provided money for a groom to purchase a talis and *shtreimel* (fur hat) for his wedding. The Tzanzer Rebbe approached the casket and drove away the demons who'd surrounded it. In addition to having the power to promise someone a place in Paradise, the tzaddik can also advocate on one's behalf in the heavenly tribunal.

— Rebbe Pinchas of Koretz (1726–1790) was one of the Ba'al Shem Tov's closest companions; the Ba'al Shem Tov even entrusted him with the education of his grandson, R. Baruch of Mezhbuzh. A descendant of illustrious Talmudic scholars, he was born in Shklov, White Russia (now Belarus). In addition to his traditional Torah studies, the Koretzer mastered Jewish philosophy and Hebrew grammar as well as science and mathematics. In 1790, he set out on a journey to the Land of Israel with the intention of settling in Tzfat, but fell ill and only made it to the Ukrainian shtetl of Shepetovka, where he died. He was known for his humility, which he explained this way: "If someone wishes to honor me, that means he is more humble than I. Which means he is better and saintlier than I. Which means that I should honor him. But then, why is he honoring me?"

— The "Turkish talis" actually came from Tunisia. Tunisia was esteemed for its fine wool, but especially prized by Chassidim because these talisim were assured not to have *shatnez*, the biblically prohibited mixture of flax (linen) and wool. Apparently, they were called "Turkish" because Tunisia was under the rule of the Turkish Ottoman Empire.

— In his delightful book, *In Praise of Yiddish*, Maurice Samuel notes the irony of the tradition of calling out "*tzeddakah tatzil m'movis*" ("charity redeems from death") at a funeral: "a rather tactless reflection, one would think, on the man just buried."

THE PEDDLER OF TZFAT

Isaac ben Solomon Luria Ashkenazi (1534–1572), commonly known as the Holy Ari (*ari* is the Hebrew word for lion), is considered the father of contemporary Kabbalah. Over the years, his approach to Jewish mysticism, referred to as Lurianic Kabbalah, was adopted and integrated into Chassidism.

The Ari was born to a Sephardi mother and an Ashkenazi father (this is one explanation for his name Ashkenazi). Already in his early twenties, he began devoting himself to the study of the recently printed Zohar, the major work of Kabbalah. For seven years, he secluded himself in meditation on the banks of the Nile, only visiting his family on the Sabbath. He eventually moved to Tzfat, home to the leading Kabbalists of the time, including Rabbis Moses Cordevero and Joseph Caro. Although the Ari lived in Tzfat less than three years, he refined his mystical system there and gained the discipleship of important students, including Chaim Vital, who transcribed and promulgated the Ari's teachings.

— The Ba'al Shem Tov adopted and spread the teachings of Lurianic Kabbalah, with a focus on the recognition of divine omnipresence in the mundane, and the insistence that *d'veykus*, the mystical cleaving to God, is accessible to all, not only the learned. Throughout the generations, various Chassidic groups built upon the Lurianic concepts, accentuating different Kabbalistic doctrines and practices. A well-known Chassidic saying distinguishes between Kabbalah and Chassidism this way: The teachings of Kabbalah raise you to the heavens; the teachings of Chassidism bring the heavens to you.

THE SINS OF THE OLD

The "forces of evil" trace back to Kabbalistic sources and have a prominent place in Chassidic theology. Also referred to as the *sitra achra* (literally, "the other side"), this cosmic negativity is manifested in various personifications, e.g., Satan, evil spirits, dybbuks and the *yetzer horah*, the evil inclination. The yetzer horah in particular has an ancient pedigree in Jewish metaphysics, and is generally understood not as a demonic force, but as a psychological predilection towards the perversion of our basic human needs. The Talmud suggests that without the yetzer horah there would be no reproduction and thus no human life. However, the yetzer horah pushes us to go beyond legitimate sexual desire to licentiousness. Similarly, it encourages us to go beyond the appropriate enjoyment of eating to gluttony, or, as in this story, from the desire for reasonable relaxation to wasting entire days in sloth. Balancing the yetzer horah is the *yetzer tov*, the inclination to do the good. According to Chassidic thought, human beings have the freedom to choose between these competing motivations.

— Rabbi Shlomo HaCohen Rabinowicz, the Rebbe of Radomsk (1801–1866), was among the most esteemed rebbes in Poland and began a dynasty that attracted thousands of Chassidim. He was the author of a classic Chassidic work, *Tiferes Shlomo*, and renowned for his mellifluous voice.

A LITIGATION AGAINST GOD

Chassidim regularly address God informally and directly. In Chassidic stories, God is often chided, albeit in a loving, personal manner, for the harshness of the exile and the suffering of His people.

Indeed, arguing with God has a long pedigree in Judaism, tracing back to the biblical figures of Abraham, Moses, Elijah, Job and Jonah, and such disputes are recounted as well in Talmudic literature. This tradition is manifested in later "secular" Jewish literature as well, as illustrated by the well-known complaints to God expressed by Sholem Aleichem's

Tevye the Milkman and Elie Wiesel's play *The Trial of God* where God is the accused defendant. As the twentieth-century writer Joseph Roth remarked, "Of course the Jews can argue with their God and do. They are an old people and they know each other very well."

— In another version of this story, the two judges who preside alongside Rabbi Elimelech of Lizhensk are Rabbi Israel of Koshenitz and the Seer of Lublin.

THE BESHT ARRANGES A MARRIAGE

Jews have traditionally used a *shadkhan* (matchmaker) to arrange the marriages of their children. In addition to collecting a fee, the *shadkhan* was believed to be spiritually rewarded for having performed the mitzvah of facilitating a marriage. In Chassidic tales, the rebbe often serves as matchmaker, in many cases, for a poor girl or worthy young student.

— The Ba'al Shem Tov (literally, "master of the good name"), Rabbi Yisroel ben Eliezer (c. 1700–1760), the founder of Chassidism, has been the focus of intense recent scholarship as historians seek to separate the facts about his life from the myriad legends that have attached to him over the centuries. The evidence suggests that he was born in Okop, a small village in the Ukraine on the Polish-Russian border (Podolia) to elderly parents who died when he was still a young child. After working as a teaching assistant, at the age of thirty-six, he revealed himself to be a healer and holy man. His wondrous, often mysterious, ways are the subject of numerous Chassidic tales and anecdotes, many of which were recounted in the early Chassidic book *Shivkhei HaBesht* (In Praise of the Besht), printed in Hebrew in 1814. Chassidim are fond of saying, "Anyone who believes all the miraculous stories attributed to the Ba'al Shem Tov is a fool, but anyone who doesn't believe they *could* be true is a bigger fool" – or some say, a heretic.

THE MAGGID DEFEATS THE HEAVENLY PROSECUTOR

Rabbi Yisroel Hofstein, known as the Maggid of Kozhenitz (1740–1814), was among the influential early Chassidic leaders in Poland. His father was a poor but pious bookbinder and he and his wife were childless for many years. Yisroel, the future maggid, was born after his mother received a blessing from the Ba'al Shem Tov. The Kozhenitzer came to be renowned as a wonder worker himself and, sharing the name Israel with the founder of Chassidism, was sometimes called the "second Ba'al Shem Tov." When a wealthy Chassid once boasted about his piety, noting how he consumed only bread and water, the Kozhenitzer reprimanded the man, saying, "Don't do this, for if the rich eat only bread and drink only water, what are the poor to subsist on – stones?"

MIRACLES BEGIN AT HOME

The *melave malka* (literally, "escorting of the [Sabbath] queen") is the fourth and final meal of the Sabbath, and occurs on Saturday night. Along with the third meal, the *shalosh seudos*, it is a widely practiced ritual in Chassidim's communal Sabbath observance. The eating of a meal at the conclusion of the Sabbath is referenced in the Talmud (BT Shabbat 119b). Medieval commentators and Kabbalists deem this fourth meal the banquet of King David who, according to the Talmud (BT Shabbat 30a), was told he would die on the day of rest, and so held a festive meal at the completion of the Sabbath each week. Unlike the *shalosh seudos*, the *melave malka* is not obligatory, but Chassidim believe that in prolonging the Sabbath, this meal has meritorious mystical value.

    — The Yiddish word *dreidel* comes from the Germanic *dreyen* ("to turn"). The Hebrew word for dreidel is *sevivon*, which also comes from the root word "to turn." The dreidel is thought to be a Jewish variant of the teetotum, a gambling toy found in European cultures.

THE INTEGRITY OF DANCE

From the movement's inception, dance has played a significant role in Chassidism. Chassidic teachings assign to dance a vital, mystical component with the power to affect the heavenly world. This is especially so when a tzaddik dances. The theurgic feature of dancing-as-worship has its roots in Kabbalistic teachings.

    The ecstatic dancing, the *rikud*, of the Chassidim was sharply criticized – and mocked – in the movement's early years as disrespectful and indecorous. While most Chassidic sects eschew dancing during services, several groups do incorporate dancing into prayer and still more groups dance as part of the Shabbos services; all Chassidim dance on holidays and celebrations. (Breslov Chassidim dance after each morning and evening service, on weekdays as well as on Sabbaths and holidays. The Rebbe of Breslov declared, "One must dance each and every day – whether in thought or in action.")

The most common form of dance is, as described in this story, the circle dance, in which each participant holds on to the shoulders of the person in front of him. The singing and dancing can go on for hours. At weddings, more elaborate steps are invoked and the dancing is accompanied by traditional Klezmer musicians.

Women, too, dance at weddings, albeit on their side of the *mekhitzah* (the partition between men and women). A distinctive Chassidic wedding dance is the *mitzvah tantz:* male members of the two families are invited to dance in turn with the bride, the dancer holding one end of a sash while the bride holds the other. Numerous examples of these *mitzvah tantzes* in contemporary Chassidic weddings are available on YouTube.

THE ORPHAN AND HIS PRAYER BOOK

This tale is among the most well-known in the entire corpus of the Chassidic story: a child (or an illiterate adult) succeeds in reaching the gates of heaven because of the purity of his intent. In perhaps the most popular version of this theme, a young shepherd boy attends services on Yom Kippur, and, unable to read the Hebrew siddur, plays his flute instead. The boy's father and fellow congregants are appalled by this violation of the festival – the flute is *muktzah*, forbidden to be handled on holy days – but the Ba'al Shem Tov asserts that the child's heartfelt playing reached higher planes in heaven than all the other prayers offered that day.

— In Chassidic tales, these *tamim* (loosely translated as "simple Jews") are often depicted as heroes, able to bring about divine solutions to communal difficulties when the more learned and otherwise pious cannot.

STUDY IS NOT ENOUGH

Chassidim, like other observant Jews, take the injunction to study Torah as a cardinal obligation. But unlike the misnagdim, their adversaries, Chassidim consider mindful attachment to God (*d'veykus*) to be of even higher importance. For misnagdim, the study of Torah is an end in itself; for Chassidim, study is a sublime means to the true end, namely, closeness to God. Furthermore, misnagdim and Chassidim tend to emphasize different aspects of Torah study, the former focusing on theoretical analysis of concepts, the latter on the practical implications of Jewish law. Chassidic texts recognize the intellectual pleasure of Torah study, which seems, in principle, to undermine the religious obligation to learn *lishmah*, for its own sake. Reb Meshullam Feibush of Zbarazh writes: "It is true that it is impossible not to obtain pleasure from the study of Torah, for it is sweeter than honey. This delight is permitted to us, but we must not study for that sake." The misnagdim often argued that this "demotion" of Torah study resulted in deficient knowledge of Talmud among Chassidim and their rebbes. In fact, many Chassidic rebbes were known to be outstanding Torah scholars.

A TALE OF VENGEANCE

The basest of all sins in Judaism is, arguably, conversion to a different religion. In the Eastern European Chassidic milieu this usually meant conversion to Christianity. As one might expect, the apostate brings immense shame to his or her family, is despised as an outcast by the community, but as in this story, is inevitably welcomed back after repenting. In some Chassidic stories, the convert ends up living a life of degeneracy, while in others he attains prominence in Christian society The latter was particularly worrisome to the Chassidic community as he was sometimes able – and eager – to inflict harm on his former coreligionists. (For example, a convert by the name of Joseph Tarler became a censor in Lemberg and prohibited the printing of books by Rabbi Zvi Elimelech, the *Bnei Yissoscher*, noted above. Throughout Jewish history, several notorious converts caused far more serious harm to the community.) In most Chassidic stories, the Jew who converts to Christianity is also guilty of other transgressions such as thievery or adultery. The (somewhat) more sympathetic, though not exculpable, motivation for conversion depicted in this story is anomalous.

THE BESHT DISCOVERS HOW TO CELEBRATE THE SABBATH

The Ba'al Shem Tov asserted: "Fear of God without joy is not fear at all, but melancholia."

The concept of joy is a major focus of Chassidic teaching. For Chassidim, joy, *simkha*, is considered the sine qua non of a true religious life; moreover, a genuine appreciation of one's nearness to God, will, ipso facto, lead one to joy. Consequently, Chassidism manifests a distaste for asceticism, even when used as a means of repentance. Chassidic teaching distinguishes between sadness, stemming from regret over a particular wrongdoing – the sadness of a broken heart (The Kotzker Rebbe says: "Nothing is as whole as a broken heart") – and despair, *atzvut*, which can be traced to taking the wrong aspects of one's self too seriously. (Reb Heschel of Rimanov taught: "Every person is enjoined to redeem himself from diaspora. And the essence of one's personal diaspora is sadness and worry.")

Chassidism is also careful to distinguish between joy that stems from legitimate sources and joy that is mere frivolity. Joy is a vital component in the performance of a mitzvah, but Chassidism also insists that one also be joyous at work and in social interactions. This "daily joy" affirms both the external world and a connection to the deeper world hidden from view.

THE FIFTH QUESTION

Rabbi Yekhiel Michel Rabinowitz of Zlotchov (c. 1721–1786), known as the Maggid of Zlotchov, was a student of the Ba'al Shem Tov and, following the Besht's death, a disciple of the Maggid of Mezerich. The Zlotchover was a celebrated lecturer and largely responsible for the introduction of Chassidism to Galicia, Poland. He founded a multi-branched dynasty and had numerous prestigious students.

KHUNA'S MESSIAH

Simcha Bunim Bonhart of Peshischa (Przysucha, 1765–1827) was a key leader of an influential strand of Chassidism in Poland. Not wanting to take up a rabbinical position, he supported himself by working as a pharmacist and later became an agent for Temerl Berekson (Bergson), a wealthy businesswoman who supported the emerging Chassidic movement. The Peshischa was introduced to the world of Chassidism by his father-in-law and became a student of the leading Chassidic rebbes of his day, the Maggid of Kozhenitz, the Seer of Lublin and Rabbi Yaakov Yitzchak Rabinowicz, the Yid Hakodesh, whom he succeeded and whose "rationalist" approach to Chassidism he furthered. R. Simcha Bunim was known as the "rebbe of rebbes," and his influential disciples included the rebbes of Kotzk, Ger and Alexander. He advised his disciples to write two verses and place them in two different pockets: "For my sake the world was created" (a verse from the Sages) and "I am dust and ashes" (a verse from the Torah). The Peshischa taught that there are times when we need to remind ourselves of one perspective and times when we need to remind ourselves of the other.

LIE AFTER LIE

In this story, the transgression that leads to the woman's murderous act is not greed, as in the rebbe's tale, but the shame of having produced a child from an illicit sexual relationship. Adultery, in particular, is deeply condemned in Chassidic stories and is often presented as a cause of distress to the community at large. In some Chassidic legends, the rebbe himself is propositioned to commit a sinful liaison, usually while on one of his journeys, but, of course, successfully withstands the temptation.

— This story is typical in its description of how the rebbe is able to detect that an infidelity has transpired and help the sinner to atone. The fact that the rebbe delivers his message to his intended audience by means of a story rather than a direct rebuke is characteristic of the Chassidic approach to repentance.

THOU SHALT NOT STEAL

Rabbi Baruch Tam-Frankel (sometimes spelled Te'omim-Fränkel) (1760–1828), the author of a well-respected Talmudic commentary, though not a Chassid, was the father-in-law of Rabbi Chaim Halberstam, the Rebbe of Tzanz, one of the major Chassidic leaders of his generation.

— In introducing this tale, my father said, "This story is taken from the book of Chassidic stories *Sipurei Chassidim* by Reb Shlomo Yosef Zevin. And let us hope that I haven't committed thievery by retelling his story about thievery."

BEIRISH THE BATLAN

The Maggid, Dov Baer of Mezeritch (1704–1772) was, aside from the Ba'al Shem Tov, the most influential figure in Chassidism. In fact, many historians see him as an equal of the Besht rather than a student, though Chassidim themselves consider him a disciple and successor. He was a master organizer and, undoubtedly, his administrative skills were largely responsible for the early promulgation of Chassidism. Chassidic lore recounts that after the Maggid's parents' house burned down, along with the papers documenting the family's illustrious lineage, the then five-year-old Dov Baer comforted his mother by promising to start a new dynasty. In his youth, Reb Dov Baer studied with the renowned Talmudist Jacob Joshua Falk and became a *maggid* (literally, "preacher") in various small towns before settling in Mezeritch. He later became an ardent follower of the Ba'al Shem Tov and assumed the mantle of leadership after the founder's death, establishing Mezeritch as the new center of Chassidism. As in all Chassidic courts, adherents included the learned as well as the well-meaning but naïve. As a result of the Maggid and his students' efforts, in but one generation Chassidim claimed tens of thousands of followers. The Maggid left no writings of his own but his devoted followers quoted him copiously in their own works.

A MOTHER'S LULLABY

Music and song have always been integral features of Chassidic life and thought. Each Chassidic sect has its own distinctive melodies, which have been passed down through the generations. Because Chassidim did not set their music to paper (unlike many of their stories), the melodies were transmitted orally, through communal services, family rituals and celebrations. Today, Chassidic music is widely available in contemporary media and on the Internet. Over the years, Chassidic music has remained a major source for popular Jewish music for non-Chassidism as well. The well-known tune *"Hava Nagila,"* for example, was originally a *niggun* (wordless melody) sung in the Chassidic court of the Sadigora/ Rizhin sect; in the early 1900s, a group of Sadigora Chassidim brought the melody with them when they immigrated to Jerusalem.

— Chassidim believe that music, and in particular the niggun, is invested with a spiritual power that facilitates the attainment of *d'veykus,* communion with the divine. Chassidim believe that even secular songs contain holy sparks that have the potential to become sacred. Toward this end, the rebbe in this story, Rabbi Yitzchak Isaac Taub of Khalev (1744–1828), was famous for refashioning tunes he heard from soldiers and shepherds. His song, *Szol a Kokosh Mah* ("The Rooster Is Crowing"), is still sung among Khalever Chassidim in the original Hungarian.

IT TAKES A THIEF TO CATCH A THIEF

Chassidic tales, as do other religious traditions, make use of stories, anecdotes and parables to present spiritual and moral messages. But it's worth noting that Chassidic stories, as does this story, also make use of these literary devices to highlight psychological insights in the service of practical human affairs.

THE REBBE'S MIND AND THE MASKIL'S HEART

An *agunah* (literally, "anchored" or "chained") is a woman whose husband has disappeared and not returned, or who has gone missing during wartime. It also refers to a woman whose husband cannot or will not grant her a divorce. The *agunah* is thus considered legally married, and therefore forbidden to remarry, until she receives a writ of divorce or testimony confirming her husband's death. The issue has serious implications for Jewish law because were the husband to resurface after the woman has remarried and given birth, the child of the new union could be deemed illegitimate. The problem of *agunot* has been an issue throughout Jewish history, as Jews were often kidnapped, murdered or otherwise disappeared. The fate of *agunot* – and their pleas for assistance – are a central concern in many Chassidic tales. The challenge is often resolved when the rebbe, though his extraordinary (or extrasensory) perception, helps the unfortunate woman find her lost husband.

— Rabbi Yekheskel Shraga Halberstam (1813–1898), known as the Shinover Rov, was the eldest son of the Divrei Chaim, Rabbi Chaim Halberstam of Tzanz, with whom he sometimes differed vehemently on matters of Jewish law. (The Shinover suffered much personal tragedy, having been widowed five times.) He was highly esteemed by other rebbes for his immense learning. On his visit to Tzfat in the Land of Israel, The Shinover founded the Tzanzer shul, which is still active today.

— The Haskalah, an ideological movement that developed concurrently with Chassidism, advocated for the social and cultural integration of Jews into wider European society. Its adherents, known as Maskilim, were archrivals of the flourishing Chassidic movement, especially in Eastern Europe; as part of their sustained campaign, they composed literary works satirizing Chassidism and Chassidic rebbes, and on some occasions even enlisted the state authorities to aid their cause. As illustrated in this story, Chassidim pushed back against the Haskalah, which they considered a significant threat to traditional Judaism.

A LAPSE OF MEMORY

This story is well known among Chassidim, having been recorded in early texts and retold for many generations. In one of its various versions, the wealthy patron, the former priest, lives in Rome; in another telling, Reb Yaakov must appeal twice to the priest before he agrees to meet the Besht; in still another, he merely has to beckon with his finger.

— The notion of *kefitzas haderekh*, the miraculous shortening of a journey, mentioned in this story, is already posited in the Talmud and post-Talmudic literature as a magical power belonging to biblical figures and great rabbis. Chassidism ascribes this capacity to several of their Chassidic masters, especially the Ba'al Shem Tov. In Chassidic tales, the tzaddik calls on this supernatural ability to expedite an important mission. Typically, as noted in our story, the wagon driver faces backwards as the horses speed off to their destination, shortening the distance by several hours or even an entire day.

THE PIOUS THIEF

Chassidus posits a concept known as *yerida l'tzorich aliya* – descent that facilitates ascent. According to this notion, sometimes, before a miracle is experienced or in order for someone to attain a higher spiritual plane, that person must first experience the depths of sin. The lower the descent, the higher the potential ascent. There are several explanations of this phenomenon, including the recognition of regression as a feature of personal growth, and a Kabbalistic idea that the act of creation encourages the intermingling of the "higher and the lower." Chassidic literature elaborates at length on this psychological and metaphysical process.

A CAUTIONARY NOTE

Thousands of Jews worked as tavernkeepers, *arendas*, during the eighteenth and nineteenth centuries in Eastern Europe, leasing taverns from the local nobility. These taverns were often located in isolated regions, with the Jewish innkeeper and his family living on the premises. Jews were often more educated than the local Polish peasants, and were therefore hired by the ruling poretz, the Polish nobleman (the *szlachta* in Ukrainian), to supervise his estate.

Not surprisingly, many Chassidic stories feature Jewish arendas and their, often horrific, struggles. In addition to owning most of the town's real estate, the poretz had absolute rule over the peasants on his land. Arendas were expected to extract profits from their peasant clientele to pay for the often exorbitant lifestyles of their noblemen. Inasmuch as these exploitative noblemen were generally absent, peasants would turn their venom on the Jews. As this story recounts, when the tavern owners would be unable to pay the excessive rents demanded of them, the noblemen would throw the Jews and their families into their private dungeons.

THE BLESSING OF A DRUNK

The rebbe in this story, as told by my father, is anonymous. However, I took the liberty of identifying him as the Rebbe of Dinov and placing some of the events in the nearby town of Krosno. The Dinover Rebbe, Rebbe Dovid Spira (c. 1804–1874), was the author of the book *Tzemach Dovid*. He was the son of the famed Chassidic rebbe Zvi Elimelech Spira (1783–1841), most often referred to as the Bnei Yissoscher, the title of one his many books. The Bnei Yissoscher was an adherent of his uncle Rabbi Elimelech of Lizhensk and Rabbi Yaakov Yitzchak of Lublin (the Seer of Lublin), who told Reb Zvi Elimelech that he was a direct descendant of the Israelite tribe of Yissoscher. Reb Zvi Elimelech was also instrumental in bringing Chassidism to Hungary. My father, a descendant of Rabbi Zvi Elimelech, published a well-received annotated anthology of his works (*Toras Bnei Yissoscher*), and told me countless stories about him, his children and grandchildren, all famed Chassidic rebbes (and founders of flourishing dynasties such as Munkacs and Bluzhov). Some of those stories were about the Dinover Rebbe, my father's great-great-grandfather.

— The potency of an ordinary person's blessing is an established tradition in Judaism, as captured in the saying *Al tehi birkat hedyot kalla b'eynecha* – the blessing of a layman should not be taken lightly. In many classic Chassidic stories, the prayers of a simple person have significant cosmic results. Even the sinner may have that potential, as demonstrated in this story.

A GOOD DEED THWARTED

Rebbe Meyer of Premishlan (c. 1780–1850) was sometimes called "the poor man's rebbe," as he devoted so much of his energies to those in need. He himself was poor all his life. Nonetheless, his dearest friend was the Rebbe of Rizhyn, who was known for his luxurious court. Rebbe Meyer wrote no books in his lifetime, although his teachings were collected and published by his Chassidim after his death.

— Many Chassidic tales, as illustrated here, portray the efforts of the tzaddik to collect money from rich patrons to provide for the needs of the poor. Also exemplified in this story is the theme of the rebbe acting on behalf of God, so to speak. The underlying assumption is that the successful performance of a mitzvah, particularly by a Chassidic master, has deeper cosmic meaning, and so, too, its failure must be attributable to deeper cosmic causes.

THE LIGHT OF THE MENORAH

Rabbi Schneur Zalman of Liadi (1745–1812) was born in the Vitebsk region of Belarus and was a disciple of the Maggid, Reb Dov Baer of Mezeritch. He founded the branch of Chassidim known as Chabad (the Hebrew acronym for the Kabbalistic attributes of **Ch**ochma ("wisdom"), **B**ina ("understanding"), and **Da**'at ("knowledge"). Members of this Chassidic sect are called Lubavitchers after the town in which their rebbe later resided and are perhaps the best known of contemporary Chassidic groups. Reb Schneur Zalman was the author of many well-known works, including the *Shulchan Aruch HaRav*, a code of Jewish law, and the *Tanya*, a work of metaphysics that seeks to present Chassidism on a rational basis. In 1798 he was arrested on suspicion of treason; the anniversary of his release is still celebrated by members of Chabad.

WHY ROTHSCHILD BECAME ROTHSCHILD

Meyer Amshel Rothschild (1744–1812) was born in Frankfurt-am-Main, studied as a young man in Fürth, Germany, then apprenticed in Hanover before returning to Frankfurt where he established his banking enterprise. Therefore, it is highly improbable that this story is indeed about him. A similar, more likely account, concerns the wealthy Berekson (Bergson) family, Polish Chassidism's preeminent patrons. The family progenitor, Samuel Zbitkower, was called "the Rothschild of Warsaw," and in some versions of this story, the devoted disciple is his son Dov Ber Berek. Unlike the Rothschilds, however, the family did not continue to expand its wealth in successive generations. The renowned French philosopher Henri Bergson was a great-grandson of Berekson.

THE ONCE AND FUTURE BRIDE

Though atypical of Chassidic tales, this story is included in the canon because it was told by the Rebbe of Rizhin. Rabbi Yisroel Friedmann of Rizhin (1797–1850), the great-grandson of the Maggid of Mezeritch, was already a charismatic leader by the age of fifteen, when he assumed the position of rebbe and soon attracted a huge following. Greatly respected by the other Chassidic rebbes and Jewish leaders of his generation, "the holy one from Rizhin" as the rebbe was called, is one of the more intriguing rebbes in the Chassidic pantheon and the subject of many contemporary scholarly studies. He lived lavishly in the style of Polish nobility, maintaining a staff of servants, an orchestra of musicians, and a splendid horse-drawn coach. (The Rizhiner claimed he did so not for his own personal pleasure, but to raise the status of Chassidism. Indeed, he fasted often, slept only three hours a night and is said to have placed discomforting peas inside his elegant shoes.) Tsar Nicholas I of Russia had the rebbe imprisoned for nearly two years on an unsubstantiated murder charge. After his release, the rebbe fled to Austria, where he re-established his court in Sadigura, Bukovina, attracted thousands of Hasidim, and provided for the Hasidic community in Israel. Although he did not write any books, the Rizhiner's sayings were widely disseminated. It is particularly worth noting that the Rizhiner was instrumental in elevating the status of the story within Chassidism, promulgating the idea of storytelling as a form of prayer.

WHO ARE YOU TO JUDGE?

Charity is a requirement of all religions, particularly in the form of hospitality, whose importance is illustrated in this story. The Chassidic tzaddik Reb Uri of Strelisk, for example, exhorted his followers to try to have at least one guest at the table for every meal.

An early source for the imperative to welcome guests without interrogation is Genesis 18. Abraham greets three messengers, asking not for proof of their identities, but instead beseeches them: "Please do not go away from your servant. Let me get some water and wash your feet and rest under the tree."

— According to Chassidic legend, the father of the Ba'al Shem Tov, known for his welcoming home, was once tested by Elijah, who came impersonating a guest and proceeded to publicly violate the laws of Shabbos. He was, nonetheless, accepted and fully embraced by his host. As a result of his hospitality, the host was blessed with a son who became the Ba'al Shem Tov.

— Reb Chaim Halberstam of Tzanz (Polish: Nowy Sącz) (1793–1876), also known as the Divrei Chaim, after his major work on Jewish law, was legendary for championing the poor; he gave all he had to the needy and made sure to go to sleep each night penniless. The Tzanzer Rebbe was a disciple of leading rebbes of his time, especially Reb Naftuli Zvi of Rupszitz and, in addition, was acclaimed as one of the foremost Talmudists, legal decisors and Kabbalists of his generation. During his forty-six years as the rabbi of Tzanz, the city became a center of Chassidism, attracting tens of thousands of followers and disciples. He had seven sons and seven daughters, and his offspring founded major Chassidic dynasties such as Klausenberg and Bobov. The author of this story collection is a direct descendant of the Tzanze Rebbe.

— The Kabbalah divides this world into either *sitra d'kedushah* (the side of holiness) or *sitra achra* ("the other side," that is, the side of impurity) – every thought, speech, action or creation has its source either in one or the other.

HOW REB LEIB SARAH'S GOT HIS NAME

Rabbi Leib Sarah's (Aryeh Leib the son of Sarah) was born in Rovna in 1730 and died in Yaltishkov in 1791. He was a disciple of the Ba'al Shem Tov and later of the Maggid of Mezeritch. Reb Leib Sarah's was considered a *tzaddik nistar*, a hidden tzaddik, whose righteousness was largely unknown. The Ba'al Shem Tov sent him on missions to various Jewish communities in need of help and to collect funds for other hidden tzaddikim. Thus, Reb Leib Sarah's spent much of his life wandering throughout Poland to assist Jews in need. Unlike other early Chassidic masters, he chose not to become a rebbe, to lead a dynasty or produce written works. He is, therefore, remembered primarily through his depictions in Chassidic legends.

— In another version of this tale, when the pious daughter Sarah'le learns that the poretz's son wishes to marry her, she is the one who proposes marriage to the elderly teacher Reb Yossel, the tutor of her brothers. Later, after they marry and escape the village, Reb Yossel informs his young wife that because she chose a life with him over the far easier life as a young nobleman's wife, she'd be blessed with a son who'd become a great tzaddik.

EMPATHY

Yaakov Yitzchak Rabinowicz (1766–1813), known as the Yid Hakodesh, (literally, "the Holy Jew") was the founder of the Peshischa branch of Chassidism, which focused on Torah study and rationalism in contrast to the miracle-centered approach of some other Chassidic sects. Towards that end, the Yid saw the role of the Chassidic rebbe as a facilitator rather than an intermediary. He was among the leading disciples of the Seer of Lublin before his wrenching split with his mentor. (This dispute is dramatically depicted in Martin Buber's historical novel, *Gog Und Magog*, published in English as *For the Sake of Heaven*.) The Yid was succeeded by R. Simcha Bunim, who continued and further developed his legacy.

A TEST OF CHARACTER

Rabbi Menachem Mendel of Rimanov (1745–1815) was one of the main disciples of Rebbe Elimelech, and the teacher of significant rebbes of the succeeding generation, including Naftuli Zvi of Rupszitz and Rabbi Tzvi Elimelech Spira of Dinov. The Rimanover became an adversary of some leading Chassidic rebbes when he joined those who favored Napoleon in his war against Russia. His writings and sermons were published posthumously.

— According to Chassidic tradition, the parents of Reb Menachem Mendel were promised a son (some say by the Besht himself), on the stipulation that they consent to be wanderers, and that the father would die soon after conception, his wife a few years later. It was said of the Rimanover Tzaddik that his father's countenance would appear to him every year on the anniversary of his father's death.

THE REBBE BROKERS A DEAL

Reb Levi Yitzchak ben Sara Sasha of Berditchev (1740–1809) is among the most legendary of all Chassidic rebbes. He is celebrated as a beloved leader of his community, and an unwavering advocate of the Jewish people, always ready to plead their case at the Heavenly tribunal. Martin Buber devotes a substantial portion of his Chassidic tales to these efforts of the Berditchever. The Berditchever was one of the main disciples of the Maggid of Mezerich, and of Reb Schmelke of Nikolsburg. He is the author of a Chassidic classic work, *Kedushas Levi*, a commentary on various books of Jewish law, arranged according to the weekly Torah portion.

— A plaintive melody recounting the rebbe's bargain noted in this story continues to be sung in both Yiddish and Hebrew. The rebbe's role as a "broker" between God and the Jews also inspired the writing of a lyrical Yiddish text, *Din Torah mit Guht* about a lawsuit with God. Many Americans were introduced to this tune when an English version, "Chassidic Chant of Isaac Levi," was sung by the renowned Paul Robeson at his Carnegie Hall concert in 1958.

THE TEMPTATION OF A RIGHTEOUS SIN

There are many anecdotes about Chassidic masters successfully fending off the temptation to sin. Often the temptation involves an illicit sexual liaison, but rarely does it involve money, as in this story. This tale also differs from the genre in that the deflected transgression depicted here is motivated by the desire to do a good deed, i.e., gather funds to pay the ransoms of those who've been unfairly imprisoned. Although the injunction of *pekuakh nefesh* (the requirement to save a life), suggests that retrieving this money on the Sabbath would not only have been permitted but perhaps mandatory, in this tale, the tzaddik senses that there is a superior way to attain his aims.

ELIJAH AND THE CLOWN

Chassidic stories about the prophet Elijah derive from a rich repository of Jewish literature that includes Talmud, Kabbalah and folktales. In these accounts, Elijah appears in various guises with various aims. Instances of *gilui Eliyahu*, an encounter with Elijah, appear often in Chassidic tales about the Ba'al Shem Tov, but also in accounts of other Chassidic masters (some of whom averred they had the ability to call upon Elijah at will). While it is sometimes the piety of the Chassidic tzaddik that merits these exchanges, ordinary individuals, too, claimed unusual interactions with Elijah, as exemplified in this story.

— The traditions of preparing a goblet of wine for Elijah at the Seder (the so-called "Elijah's Cup"), and of opening the door for his entrance, are relatively recent; neither is mentioned in the Talmud or in medieval rabbinic sources. The first known written reference to these customs dates to the late fifteenth century; woodcuts and drawings from the period depict the *Moshiach*, the Messiah, on a donkey, preceded by Elijah. A variety of theories have been offered connecting Elijah with the Seder, particularly regarding his role as the savior of Jewish communities in peril, but these explanations seem to be retroactively "read into" established practice.

— Reb Meshullam Feibush Heller of Zbarazh (c. 1742–1794), a student of the Maggid of Mezeritch and Rebbe Yekhiel of Zlotchov, was one of the formative figures in the earliest years of the Chassidic movement. He is the author of *Derekh Emet* (The Way of Truth), a short book that delineates the Chassidic approach to Judaism.

Note: Earlier versions of the following stories appeared in the novel *A Seat at the Table*, by Joshua Halberstam (Sourcebooks, 2009): *The Blind Angel, Blessing of a Drunk, The Fifth Question* and *The Boy and his Prayer Book.*

Acknowledgments

A Chassidic rebbe once noted, "While it's true that one must be clever to tell a story well, one must be even more clever to hear a story well." While I can't vouch for my own cleverness in retelling these stories, I am thankful for the cleverness of so many who heard or read these tales. And I'm especially grateful they shared their cleverness with me, offering constructive criticisms (from polite shakes of the head to emphatic "No, no, this doesn't work") along with continuous encouragement. Some of these clever folks are good friends, but others are anonymous members of audiences to whom I read a few of these tales.

Eli Mosesson was an early Yiddish reader of some of these stories and offered helpful suggestions. Chaim Victor Steinberger did so as well, and his trove of Chassidic knowledge along with his friendship was a constant, much relied upon resource. Thanks, too, to Dr. Amy Kratka of the Jewish Studies Program at City College of New York, who taught some of these stories in her classes and invited me to discuss them with her students.

Translation is a unique challenge and I lucked out by having Barbara Harshav invite me to join a monthly gathering of expert translators...a crew of extraordinary people who translate from French, Spanish, Chinese, Russian, Polish and beyond. Barbara (Bobbi) is the accomplished matriarch of this fun, supportive group and my thanks to her and the others is abiding.

I'd written an article about Maimonides that noted in the author description that I was engaged in translating Chassidic stories. Matthew Miller of The Toby Press asked me to send him a few of these tales and though not aware of any of my previous books, he liked these stories well enough to invite me to have them published by his press. I'm so glad I accepted the invitation. Carol Mann, my always dependable, capable, literary agent, helped see the arrangement to its conclusion – my appreciation, again, Carol.

What a delight it has been working with Matthew and his excellent staff, and with Sheryl Abbey who helped conceptualize the structure of the book. I was so fortunate to have Sara Sherbill, a master of the trade, serve as editor for this collection. Her input improved the entire manuscript, including titles, notes and, of course, the stories themselves. Sarah, thank you, thank you.

My gratitude, as well, to the National Endowment for the Arts for their 2011–2012 grant for these translations. I imagine how surprised – and delighted – my father would've been to learn that the translation of these Chassidic tales he'd retold, stories he'd heard in his small *cheder* and shul in Galicia, Poland, was the recipient of this generous award.

These Chassidic tales are my father's a"h legacy, especially to our family. My mother, may she be well, is a veritable storehouse of Chassidic life in "the old country" and helped me understand the nuances of words and descriptions. My sisters, Rivy and Miriam, provided the necessary cautionary responses as only siblings can. My children, Ariana and Amitai, among the cleverest of listeners, had to endure my discourses on these tales and listen repeatedly to the same punchlines. I appreciate your indulgence. And *achron achron chaviv*, last but most. How blessed one is to have one's beloved, life-long partner also be one's best friend, best critic and wise counsel. Yocheved, this book would not have been without your constant encouragement and assistance…like just about everything else that is good in my life.

The fonts used in this book are from the Arno family